Break and Run

Break and Run

Bobby Hodge

AuthorHouse™
1663 Liberty Drive
Bloomington, IN 47403
www.authorhouse.com
Phone: 1-800-839-8640

© 2012 by Bobby Hodge. All rights reserved.

No part of this book may be reproduced, stored in a retrieval system, or transmitted by any means without the written permission of the author.

Published by AuthorHouse   04/20/2012

ISBN: 978-1-4685-9622-9 (sc)
ISBN: 978-1-4685-9621-2 (hc)
ISBN: 978-1-4685-9623-6 (e)

Library of Congress Control Number: 2012907223

Any people depicted in stock imagery provided by Thinkstock are models, and such images are being used for illustrative purposes only.
Certain stock imagery © Thinkstock.

This book is printed on acid-free paper.

Because of the dynamic nature of the Internet, any web addresses or links contained in this book may have changed since publication and may no longer be valid. The views expressed in this work are solely those of the author and do not necessarily reflect the views of the publisher, and the publisher hereby disclaims any responsibility for them.

Contents

Acknowledgements..vii

"Candy Sticking"..1

"Bad Habits"..8

"Playing with lives"..14

"The Making of a Criminal".................................49

"The heat is on/ Heat waves"................................71

"Routine change of Learning".............................83

"Rainy days of sunshine, again"..........................97

"Flashing life, Memories of better times".........116

"Auburndale"..127

"Sam and Me"..140

"Jesse's Escape"...162

"Elcie"...172

"Betrayed by love"...178

"What is reality"..185

"Life turn around"...194

Acknowledgements

I have prayed and thanked God for the appreciation, the inspiration, the encouragement and the never tiring help that has been given and shown to me in the compilation of this book. For you are the most important vessels.

To Charity Gary, I say to you first of all, I love you! Thank you for setting up the format that eventually formulated these pages. In the world of flowers, you are truly a "Rose". Thank you.

Ms. Sheila Kennedy, oh my God, where would I be without you? How did you find the time? Where did you get the untiring energy? Well I guess those are just a few of your good qualities! Thank you and I love you. May God always show you his uniqueness, through his blessings.

And to you Shenita Hodge, I want to thank you so much for your never-ending and continued encouragement. "Have you been writing?" "Did you write last night?" "Well, since I'm your last customer for awhile, maybe you can write a little"!! These were your favorite words. You made sure that procrastination was the last thing on my list and now I realize that "you" were the vessel that God chose to keep me inspired. I love you Shenita! I could go on for a while, but I'll just say to you whose names I didn't mention, and you know who you are, Thank you very much for just believing in me, for you have caused the sunshine in my life to really brighten my spirit! I love you all,

"Candy Sticking"

At 10:35 a.m., it was quite obvious that it was going to be a very hot day. The humidity was already beginning its sticky wetness. The heat had absolutely no significant meaning to Jesse and me. As we cruised down the freeway in the air conditioned Oldsmobile, we talked excitingly about the job we'd just pulled off.

Jesse and I had gotten an early start that morning after planning the robbery the night before. Jesse and I always dressed very immaculate, wearing very expensive clothes. We were constantly elected the best-dressed students during our school years.

When we entered the finance company earlier that morning, the little short fat man looked up from behind the desk where he was sitting with a glowing smile on his face. That smile almost disappeared at the sight of the two black men who were approaching him.

"Good morning," he said, trying to sound cheerful. "I'm sorry gentlemen, but we won't be open for business for about twenty minutes."

I looked around the office, making sure there were no employees in yet. The office had long blue drapes hanging from the ceiling to the matching carpet on the floor, covering the windows completely. I looked at the filing cabinets against the wall and for an instant I thought of all the people on record in that cabinet, bringing their money in to this little fat cracker and walking out, hating for the thousandth time that they ever borrowed it because of the extremely high interest rates they'd have to pay back.

I was quite sure they were all mostly poor black people, but this morning, my brother and I had planned to collect some personal interest and sue them since the first ship sailed over.

"Twenty minutes huh, well that gives us more time than we'd expected, but since we hadn't included any coffee breaks in our plans we'll just take the money and leave," Jesse stated, his voice becoming more serious with each word.

The little bald headed man was rising from his soft comfortable reclining chair now. "I'm sorry sir, but I don't quite understand," he said, trying to sound convincing.

Already his voice was beginning to tremble. That lump of fear was bulging in his throat.

"Well, you better try and understand motherfucker, before I put some lesson from this teacher in your fat ass," Jesse said firmly as he leaned forward.

Grabbing the man by his collar and pulling him over the desk, he put the big dangerous looking .38 Magnum to the fat man's head. He left no doubt in the man's mind that he was as serious as a heart attack.

"Please mister, don't—don't hurt me, please," the man fearfully stated.

The little man had turned red and he felt his forehead getting hot. His heart was beating so fast and loud, he was sure the large black man could hear it. I looked at the fat blob I saw when we walked in, now acting like a sixteen-year-old bitch about to get raped. The sight was enough to make me want to burst out with laughter. Instead, I continued to look around, keeping close watch on the door at all times for employees. The fat man looked at me briefly, as if he wanted to ask for help, but my right hand remained underneath my coat since I'd entered. Now he assumed that I had a gun also, probably bigger than this one.

The fat man led Jesse toward, what seemed to me, an office with a plaque above the door that read "Proprietor". I looked at my watch noting that this job should take less than five minutes, but I was still ready to get the fuck out of this place. Even the thought of being caught gave me an itchy feeling.

I had only been inside of a jail once in my life, for shoplifting at fifteen. Even though my mother was there to bail me out within three hours, the little time I was there flooded my mind with the thoughts of how miserable it was to be confined like an animal. I swore to God that I'd never steal again, but now I was twenty-two years old. Every time I think of how scared I was when those detectives were taking me down to headquarters, I get the urge to want to prove to myself that I was more than that. Jesse had always told me not to let one mistake get me down if I didn't want to be a forty-five year old wino, sitting around on corners begging for wine money with no place to stay. I'd always admired and listened to my older brother because somehow, it just seemed like Jesse attracted money where I couldn't make a penny.

Jesse had already been to a reformatory when I was sixteen for burglary and did two years in the state penitentiary when he was twenty-one for strong-arm robbery. Jesse had plenty of heart; taking chances was just a way of life for him.

"Please mister, don't shoot me," the man cried.

I heard the man cry out from the office as I heard a scuffle against the wall.

"Honkie, where's the rest of the money?" Jesse asked, hitting the man up side his head with the butt of the gun again.

"I swear mister, that's all the money there is, I swear," the man said.

He was crying and begging for his life. He could see the hatred in Jesse's eyes that could only mean death for him, if he didn't believe him.

"Lay down on your stomach, quick before I decide to blow your goddamn head off cracker!" Jesse said.

These words were sweet music to the fat man's ears as he moved to the floor in the corner, where Jesse was pointing with the gun. At last, the man thought he just might get out of this alive. Jesse pulled a roll of tape out of his pocket and put his foot on the man's head as he repeatedly wrapped the tape around his wrists. After Jesse finished with the man, he took the black bag containing the money and rushed out to where I was waiting. We walked down the street to the car, talking about how the air pollution takes the freshness out of a beautiful day. We got in the car; l slid under the wheel, started the car, and pulled into the traffic as if nothing happened.

"How much do you think we got man?" I asked.

"Looks like a lump, but not as much as I expected," Jesse said with disappointment.

"Fuck man, you can't be too choosy about free money," I told him. "Shit, we don't even have to worry about a tax deduction." I was laughing with satisfaction expressed all over my face. Jesse smiled, looking out the window.

"The bigger the lump, the less you have to lick," he said with warning in his voice.

We both were silent after this, as we listened to the Mongo Santamaria tape, filling the car with beautiful music. I turned into the duplex apartments where Jesse and I lived. We had chosen the apartment because of the very quiet neighborhood, mostly being young newlyweds and no kids or pets, even though we both loved kids. Our lifestyle was another dimension of the generation gap. There was a large swimming pool surrounded by the apartments and neatly trimmed hedges. I loved the landscaping of the complete neighborhood, but it was nothing unusual for this section of the city because all white neighborhoods consumed the city taxpayer's dollars.

There was only one other black couple living in the apartments we lived in, Marvin and Carol. I had met them during a party one night at the pool. Marvin was tall and slender with a large Afro and a very light complexion. He talked fast, but very plain and clear. He was an x-ray technician and Carol was a secretary for some company. And what a secretary she was. She had smiled at me that night, which I instantly thought was more than just a friendly smile. Carol was short, about five feet four inches, very neatly shaped from her head down. She had beautiful dark brown eyes that were very quick. She'd taken an overall view of me; it seemed, without moving her eyes. I thought of how nice it must be to squeeze the large tits I was looking at. Yes, a fine little lady, I thought.

Jesse was opening the door to the apartment when he noticed a letter sticking underneath the door. He pushed the door open as he bent and picked it up with the initial *J* on it.

"What's that man?" I asked closing the door.

"It's a letter. From who, I don't know yet;" Jesse said. "I'll bet it doesn't have as much information inside as this black bag," Jesse stated, smiling at the bag as he headed toward his bedroom with it.

"You got that shit right!" I said, following Jesse.

I walked to the king size bed and opened the bag, dumping the money and checks on the bed. He and I started counting the money. We put all the checks back into the bag. We'd get rid of all that shit later.

"It wasn't such a bad lick after all, shit," I said, looking at the two stacks of money on the bed.

"I got twenty three hundred here," I said, still holding a roll of twenties in my hand.

Jesse continued to count as he shook his head in agreement with me. The phone rang on the night table at the head of the bed. Jesse let it ring four times before leaning back to take the receiver out of its cradle.

"Hello," he said.

"Jesse, are you home?" The female voice shrieked in excitement.

"Nah bitch! This is a recording. Wait two hours and call back," he stated with annoyance in his words as he roughly guided the receiver back to its resting place.

"Bitches always disturb a motherfucker when he's busy," Jesse stated angrily, as he started back counting the money with a frown on his face. I never looked up or spoke, but continued the silent lip movement. We had fifty-seven hundred dollars total. Twenty-eight hundred and fifty dollars wasn't bad for less than five minutes, I thought as we walked into the living room, ruffling the cash with my right thumb. I sat back in the soft comfortable recliner and wondered how Jesse knew about the money being in the finance company. I thought finance companies and loan companies wrote checks for their clients, never keeping any cash in those places. Again I thought of how Jesse always found some hole in the wall with money in it. It seemed to me, my brother was born to be a stickup man.

I looked around the living room making sure everything was in its proper place. Jesse and I kept the apartment very neat and clean at all times. We had the gold colored shag carpet shampooed earlier that week. The living room had a sliding glass door that led onto the patio and the long gold drapes were partially drawn, letting the sunshine inside. Jesse came into the living room, walking over to the five feet tall stereo cabinet, switching the set on and putting on some albums.

"What is it little brother?" he said to me, moving toward the sofa with the beat of the music.

"Man, we'll have this room full of money one day and it won't be long, dig?" Jesse stated.

He sat on the long curving gold sofa, kicking his feet up on the marble stone coffee table in front of him. For an instant, I imagined the room overflowing with hundred dollar bills. I could go to some island and live a king's life. Jesse sounded so very sure of himself. How could everything be so drawn out for him? I thought.

"You know, it's funny how a nigga can fall so deeply in love with a dead honkie on a green square like this man," I said.

We both burst out with laughter behind my remark.

"Not only niggas that's got that green power jones," Jesse canted," white folks too."

"Say man, I think I'll slide downtown and take off that suit I was telling you about. Want to ride with me?" I asked.

"No Peil. I think I'll lay low until you get back," Jesse replied.

Jesse also liked buying clothes and new things, but he thought I actually spent too much money, but he never said anything to me. He didn't want to seem too much a big bro, but in so many small ways, he'd shown he didn't approve of letting go of money so easily.

"Think I'll take a shower before I go," I said. Heat and funk starts people asking about your love life."

I was laughing as I got up and started toward his bedroom. I opened the closet and stood looking among my expensive wardrobe, trying to decide on attire that gave more meaning to this sun shiny day. I started to take out a burgundy two-piece suit, but instead decided on a pair of lime green silk pants with a matching double knit sweater. I laid them out on the large bed and went to the dresser. I began to look through the variety of silk underwear for a set to match the outfit I'd chosen to wear.

After I finished my shower, I went back into my room to dress, humming the whole time I moved around. I walked before the full-length mirror, turning as I checked out the outfit. Satisfied, I smiled, looking into my own eyes.

"Jazzy motherfucker indeed," I said, with admiration of myself.

I was quite handsome. I had a very smooth dark complexion and was often complimented by ladies about my sexy dark brown eyes. I stood five feet ten and half inches, and a very neat physique I was very proud of. My chest was wide and I thought my build really made my clothes fit me neatly. I walked back to the closet, taking out a pair of black boots and reached up, taking a hatbox off the shelf. It contained a white gangster brim, which had cost me fifty dollars.

After I finished dressing, I started back into the living room, taking a last glance in the mirror before leaving the room. Jesse was lying down on the full-length sofa. He looked at me as I entered the room and before I could ask for his approval, as each of us always did, Jesse spoke.

"Dig you!" Jesse replied. "Ain't no flaws in your looks here man."

"If a sucker do find a flaw in my game, I'm gonna play it off so tough they'll swear to God it was only a decoy to attract their attention," I answered, going into a Bill Cosby act and strutted toward the door as we both laughed.

Later on, Jesse told me that he thought of how beautiful it was to have a brother like me. He remembered the first day I had gone to school and went running in every room, trying to find him. Jesse really loved me. Now his mind went back to the job we'd pulled this morning again. The feeling of disappointment invaded his thoughts. Leroy had assured him that there would be ten grand or more, being it was that time of the month for payment collections.

Leroy had once worked for the company and was responsible for taking the moneybag to the safety deposit at the bank. They let him go after finding out that he was having an affair with one of the employees. Leroy thought that revealing the easy rip-off method to Jesse was one sure way of relieving his conscience of being fired. Jesse agreed with him because Leroy never spoke about a piece of the take. Jesse liked Leroy even though he thought he might have sold himself too cheap. He knew that Leroy would work the rest of his life and still die broke, but he was good people.

Jesse was tall, six feet one, medium build and had a light complexion. There were no identical features between us except our eyes. Many people told us we'd both walked like our father. Jesse always had his choice of ladies. Everyone dug his quiet easygoing style. A lot of players and hustlers had told him he should be pimping and playing the bitches. For Jesse, the requirement of patience was too long and the money was too slow. He was a stickup man and he enjoyed it. He couldn't rely on someone else to support his lifestyle. He knew how to make too much money to remain street people. Jesse was unaware of the stereo having played the last album and had turned itself off as he drifted off into a deep world of sleep. He completely forgot about the letter.

"Bad Habits"

It had been two weeks since the robbery. Jesse and I were laying back, planning, and enjoying life.

"Hey Peil, I got a thing that might be sweeter than honey," Jesse spoke softly as he sipped a glass of apple juice.

"Oh yeah?" Run it," I replied, looking up from a *Jet* magazine. "My cash is getting funny anyway," I told Jesse.

"I got cash if you need some." He said.

"It's just that this thing might really pay off good. I don't need any, but I don't wanna get in that position you know?" Jesse replied. I laid the magazine face down on the coffee table to keep from losing my page.

"You know that Tego Night Club? Dig this. They got a private gambling room in the basement. Very few people know about it, and only them "richies" go down there," Jesse said. Then he hesitated and took another drink of apple juice.

"What kind of games do they play? Poker, craps, or what?" I asked.

"I'm not sure, but it's probably poker, whitey's specialty. I wouldn't be surprised if they rolled a few craps too. Now Peil, if it's a private club for only the richest crackers in this city, then you can imagine the money they have down there," Jesse said.

I was sitting back in the recliner, staring into the color T.V. set, but never realizing it was there. My mind was somewhere in a basement filled with money.

"How you know they don't pay off in checks?" I asked without moving my eyes from the T.V. set. "Simply because it would expose too much of the gambling room," Jesse answered, drinking the rest of the liquid from the glass. I cursed myself under my breath for not thinking of that.

"The only problem we'll have is getting down there," I said, waiting to see if Jesse had the solution for that.

"Well, like there's still quite a bit of checking and planning to be made cause we can't afford any mistakes," he said. Jesse got up and started for the kitchen. "But they only have two bouncers and they're both in the club and not in the gambling room, we can beat them easily," Jesse said.

Jesse went to the sink and washed the glass he'd just used and put it in a tray, which contained the remainder of the matching set. He started back into the living room and was about to say something when the doorbell ranged. He swiftly turned and walked towards the door as I reached for my magazine and began to read. Jesse looked through the peephole and smiled to himself. He opened the door and stood looking in Cynthia's face.

"Hey baby! What brings you over here?" Jesse asked, still smiling at her.

"You did," she replied, looking into his dark brown eyes.

"Well, ain't you gonna hug me baby, or did you just want to look at me and leave?" Jesse asked.

Cynthia blushed as she walked inside and saw me." I didn't think you even wanted to see my face, let alone let me touch you," Jesse replied.

Cynthia slowly eased her arms around Jesse's waist and before Jesse spoke, she turned towards me.

"Hi Peil, long time no see," Cynthia said.

"What it is Cint," I said looking up from my magazine smiling. "You know how I have to keep moving," I said. "Maybe if I can get as lucky as Jesse, I can lay back too," I said . . .

I looked at her, giving her my brotherly smile.

"Oh but Jesse's very unsatisfied with me. Ain't that right?" she asked, directing her question to Jesse and tugging at his shirt.

"Shit baby, a man would have to be insane not to want you!" Jesse said, pulling her into his arms and kissing her on her neck.

You got that shit right, I thought as I glanced at them out of the corner of my eye. Cynthia was a beautiful woman, her eyes held a slight glitter that was very noticeable. She wore her hair in two ponytails on the side that gave her the resemblance of a little girl. I admired her neatly shaped body, but I admired her in general even though she was my brother's lady. I knew that Cynthia held her position with Jesse only by constantly keeping herself in her place and at Jesse's demands. I'd seen Jesse abuse lots of women when they aroused his anger, and some of them he really dug.

"Jesse, I haven't seen you for nearly a month and you didn't even bother to come by. Now you pretend you're so glad to see me," Cynthia said with much concern in her voice.

"Sweetheart, you know how busy I've been. It's a fucked up world out there and I lose a lot of sleep trying to figure out ways to survive," Jesse said.

Jesse was looking deep into her eyes as he led her towards the sofa.

"But it's quite obvious that you're not very concerned about me. You didn't hurry to come over," Jesse said. Then he slumped down diagonally on the sofa, glancing for the expression on Cynthia's face.

"I called you! You hung up in my face. You told me to call back in two hours and as stupid as it may sound, Jesse, I called back!" Cynthia explained.

I could hear the desire to want to be near him in her voice. I also remembered the phone call. It was the morning we'd robbed the finance company.

"Man, I can't cut all this sweet shit. In a few minutes ya'll be freaking all over the place and I don't wanna be around," I told them.

We all laughed as I got up and started for my room.

"I was quite disturbed that morning sweetheart. I had the whole world on my mind cause my money was out," Jesse lied.

His face was so honest Cynthia couldn't detect the slightest trace of falsehood.

"Honey, you know you can always ask me for money and that morning was no exception," Cynthia explained.

She eased over near him on the sofa and took Jesse's hand in hers. Jesse looked at her without a trace of a smile and said, "Is today an exception?"

"No day is an exception. Jesse, don't cut me out of your life when things get rough for you. You make me feel like half a woman," she said.

"Well, I don't wanna make you feel like that baby. I need a woman and a half to keep me satisfied," Jesse said.

He was smiling and pulling her toward him. Cynthia frowned at his words, but she tried desperately not to let it show. She laid her head on his chest as his hands slowly slid down her back.

"What I tell ya?" I said, walking back into the room.

Jesse and Cynthia started laughing.

"She's trying to freeze up on me man. Say I wouldn't come get it, so she got the impression I didn't want it," Jesse said, still laughing.

"Hey, maybe that's right," Cynthia said, sitting up and looking at Jesse curiously.

"You'll see. Just wait until I leave," I teased as I headed for the door.

"What did you mean by that remark mister?" Cynthia asked.

"What could I possibly mean baby?" Jesse asked. "Did you say that?" Jesse asked.

Cynthia looked at him with her childish stare. She really loved this man. They had been going together for more than a year. Jesse was the best thing that ever happened to her, even though he'd never told her he loved her. She accepted this as only a man's way of doing things. They'd had some wonderful times together. She loved him but still didn't understand him at all. Since she'd met Jesse she didn't understand anything if it meant not being with him.

"No baby! I didn't say it but you could've been trying to give me a hint," she replied, still sitting rigid on the sofa.

"Don't fool yourself Cint. Don't try stroking me cause you know I don't play that hint game shit. If I got something to say, I don't know but one way to say it," Jesse said.

He pulled her back into his arms and tightly embraced her as their lips softly touched. Cynthia's arms encircled his waist and she felt a tantalizing feeling going through her body. They kissed hard and long and with hunger for each other. When their lips finally parted, Cynthia slowly opened her eyes to find Jesse staring at her. She started to speak but before she could get the words out, Jesse was kissing her lips again and stroking her lovely thighs.

"Oh baby. I missed you so much. I don't ever want to be away from you anymore! Tell me you won't leave me Jesse," Cynthia whispered, squeezing him to her.

"I'm not going to leave you baby. You know I won't leave ya," Jesse said.

They were now deeply infatuated and fondling each other's vital needs.

"Take me baby and make love to me. Okay?" Cynthia said.

Her voice was a mere whisper and Jesse continued to fuel the flame now burning inside her. Finally, Jesse slipped out of her arms and stood up, pulling Cynthia to her feet. He kissed her forehead and wrapped his arms around her small-framed body and started towards his bedroom.

"Are you sure you want me to make love to you?" Jesse teased as he opened the bedroom door.

"Baby, can't nobody, and I do mean nobody, make love to me but you and it's been too long since I had you," she said.

Cynthia was slipping the white strapless sandals off her feet, almost unconsciously. She began to unbutton Jesse's shirt. Jesse's bedroom was blue with long navy blue silk drapes, matching the thick carpet on the floor and the blue velvet king size bedspread. A small color T.V. set was sitting in a built-in cabinet underneath it. Very few books were neatly placed inside it. The large mirror in the Spanish style dresser was spotless and the room smelled like honeysuckle on a summer morning.

Cynthia slid the shirt off Jesse's wide shoulders and began to rub, massaging her hands over his chest. Jesse enjoyed her in his arms, kissing her and gently lowering her onto the bed, his full weight resting upon her body. He began to unbutton her blouse, still kissing her until she began massaging his back and moaning.

"Jesse," she whispered between moans.

"Yeah baby," he answered.

"Not in our clothes," she said.

Jesse could hardly hear her, but her words made him smile and release her. He rolled off her and removed her blouse, then started unhooking the snaps on her bra. The large breasts flung forward, freeing themselves from confinement. Cynthia slid off the bed and began to remove her skirt. Then slowly, slipping her thumbs into the elastic of her panties, she wiggled her body as she pushed them on down her smooth thighs.

Jesse sat on the bed watching her undress and admiring her lovely golden body. Cynthia neatly placed her clothes on the dresser and moved slowly towards Jesse on the bed as he stood up. She began unbuckling his pants and pushing them down his legs, then his underwear. When he stepped out of them, she picked them up and placed them neatly over hers.

"What's wrong baby?" she asked as she turned the covers back on the bed.

"Nothing's wrong sweetheart. I'm just overwhelmed by your beauty. Now what's wrong with that?" Jesse asked.

He was walking slowly towards her and just admiring her in the shadows of his mind.

"You're so quiet," she replied.

"This is no time for talking my love," Jesse said, embracing her with one arm as he fondled her breast with his other hand.

They began to cuddle and melt into one another as they faded into a night of pure ecstasy.

"Playing with lives"

I drove away from the apartment trying to decide what to do with my time. I started once to go by the pool hall for a couple of games, but immediately disbanded the thought. The movies weren't the way I wanted to spend my day. I had driven several blocks when I saw the young lady standing on a corner waiting for a bus.

The skintight slacks captured my attention immediately and I pulled over. Pushing the power button with my finger, the right window slid down. She continued to look down the street for the bus as if I had passed her by. I leaned over in the seat.

"Say sweetheart, can I give you a ride?" I asked very calmly.

"No thanks!" she replied without looking around.

"Say Queen, I just wanna save you thirty-five cents. What do you think I am, a rapist or something?" I asked her. My determination was building up inside me now.

"Look mister, I don't mine spending thirty-five cents, so if it's ok with you, I'll take the bus," she replied.

She was looking at me for the first time and her voice revealed her disturbance. I opened my door and stepped out of the car with the keys in my hand. I walked around the car to where she was standing.

"Miss Lady, never have I felt so insulted by a lady thinking I'm something other than a gentleman. Baby, ain't nothing spooky about me. Your sexual features didn't attract my attention or inspire me to stop, but the mere fact that you're my sister gave me the impression that our understanding could be a little blacker than this," I told her.

My voice was attracting the attention of some people standing only a few feet away, as I continued to throw my hands about.

"But since you think that I'm some kind of maniac here, you take the car and I'll take the bus," I said. l grabbed her hand, forcing the keys into it. She started to pull away in total puzzlement then she looked into my face.

"Mister, I don't want your car and I never called you a maniac or anything. I just prefer catching the bus," the woman said.

She was trying to give my keys back but I kept walking away from her and still talking. She was beginning to feel silly with these people looking at my performance in amazement.

"Can you drive?" I asked.

"Yes, but I . . ." the woman said.

"Then just leave the car downtown anywhere. I'll ride the bus until I find it or if you want to, call me at home and tell me where you left it. That's cool too. I trust you. Here's the phone number . . ." I told her.

"Hey if it means that much to you, ok. You can give me a ride, my God!" she said.

She walked over to the car, opened the door, and got in. l looked at the people standing near me and winked my eye. l walked around the car and slid under the wheel, concealing the big smile I'd just given the people.

"Are you sure you don't mind?" I asked questioningly.

"Yes! I'm sure. Now will you please go?" she snarled back.

"I will, as soon as you up the keys," I said to her.

She couldn't help but flash a smile after it occurred to her that she was clenching the keys tightly in her hand. She thrust the keys toward me and tried her best to look disappointed, but there was something about my mysterious self that she liked. But what was it? I started the car and pulled away from the curb.

"You know, you don't even know me and already you hate me. I can't understand it baby. What did I ever do to you besides save you some money?" I said glancing at her.

"Well, you did a good job of embarrassing me back there in front of those people," she said. She looked at me and held her stare as if waiting for an apology.

"You embarrassed me too, but I still don't hate you. In fact, I really like you when you roll your eyes like that," I stated, never taking my eyes off the street.

"How could I embarrass you? And besides, what if I'm married, what do you think my husband would say about this?" she asked.

"I don't know of his ways sweetheart, maybe the brother would say that his baby had made other plans. He is a brother ain't he?" I asked.

"What do you think?" she asked. My question had come as somewhat a shock to her.

"Well, you acting like a little white girl or something, being surrounded by the Black Panthers and all of that shit puzzled me," I told her.

I looked into her eyes. We stared at each other a long moment. She was silent as she broke the stare. I thought as I drove along, I was sorry I'd even went through the trouble of stopping, even though she was one fine stupid acting b . . . . . I was becoming disgusted fast. Only the sound of music could be heard as we rode in silence.

"What's your name?" she asked. Her words were almost a whisper.

"Peil," I replied.

"Peil, I never meant to make you mad at me." She hesitated before continuing. "I'm sorry, but it's just that I'm not used to becoming so personal with strangers," she said. Still she never bothered to look in my direction.

"You don't have to apologize to me sweetheart. I'm everyday people. There's nothing strange about me," I said to her. I tilted my head to the side, cutting my eyes at her and flashing a smile. For the first time, she smiled back.

"How do you know where I want to go? I mean, you haven't asked me anything," she said. She seemed relaxed now.

"Well, I figured I was going right 'cause you ain't screamed for the police yet," I said to her. I laughed and before she realized it, she was laughing too.

"Oh come on now. If I was afraid of you or anything like that I wouldn't have gotten in the car with you now would I?" the woman said. She couldn't take her eyes off me now.

"Well, maybe you feel like I do about some things," I said.

"And how's that?" she asked.

"That all of life is just another chance you have to take," I said. I stopped for a red light and looked at her for a moment without speaking, but my mind was beginning to roam. Before I said anything, she spoke.

"Yeah, life is a chance and everybody takes them whether they realize it or not. I try to be aware of the chances I do take because they could be detrimental to me or maybe somebody else," she said. I started talking. "You know, life is a funny thing. As far as chances are concerned, you have to weigh the odds and decide whether it's worth it or not. Once you come to a conclusion you have to plan your strategy to a 'T' and make sure that you got your thang together or you just might wind up taking a dive!" I said to her.

"Wow, you sound like you wanna tip the whole world off," she said, teasing.

She didn't have the slightest idea that my mind was inside the bank across the street. I was visualizing myself holding an M-16 on the people while Jesse made the manager open the vault and fill the bags with crisp new wrinkle-free hundred dollar bills that had nobody's fingerprints on them except the printer's. I was aware of the fact that she was watching me, so I simply tilted my head and said in a grave voice, "Well, not the whole world."

I smiled. The light changed and I was about to pull off when I saw Michael approaching the car on the right side. He was saying something with a big grin on his face as he reached for the door.

"My man, what it is?" Michael shouted.

"It's you baby!" I replied as the young lady slid to the center of the seat to let him in.

"Man, I don't know when the last time I saw you and Jesse. How's life been?" Michael asked.

"Hey, it's been nice Mike. You know, a few ups and downs, but we're not complaining. What about yourself?" I asked.

With that smile, I knew so well, he said, "Man, you know life is sweet for us people who choose to love like we do. Everyday's payday, and the ladies love me anyway. You dig it Peil?" Michael asked. I was laughing because I knew how Michael was coming out of his mouth. We had known each other from childhood and went to the same school. He had always been crazy. The nigga was actually funny. He was the kind of dude who always had an answer and whether you agreed or not, it made sense yet sounded stupid. I remembered the days when we used to play pool and Michael would buy a pop and sip on it for an hour, it seemed. Then he'd ask someone to hold it for him while he put a quarter in the jukebox. When the music started to play he'd dance across the floor, clapping his hands and imitating James Brown. When the guy realized he was still holding the pop, he'd say, "Hey Michael, here's your pop, man."

Then Michael would start looking crazy and staring at the dude and say, "Man, who the fuck you think I am? You don't slobber in no fuckin' pop and then try to give it to me. Nigga, don't you ever do no bullshit like that again."

He'd turn around, knowing he had captured everyone's attention and say, "You mean he tried that shit on ya'll too? The nigga must be one of them old con playing niggas thinking he done found him a pool hall full of suckers."

Sometimes the dude would speak out in a violent tone, defending himself, "Nigga, ain't nobody trying to take your goddamn money. You probably ain't got none anyway."

Then Michael would really go into his shit. "Man, ain't nobody said nothing about money but you. Now I don't know about the rest of these niggas in here, but if you think you that slick,

I'll play you in some pool, roll you some dice or either we can skin a little and I don't even gamble. You ain't gonna come in here and make no fool out of everybody," Mike would say.

Eight out of ten times Mike tricked them right into gambling with him and gambling was his whole life.

"Puchi, you never told me you and Peil had a thing going on girl," Michael said.

"Oh, we don't have anything going on Mike. I only met him ten minutes ago," she said with a complementary smile.

"Don't stroke me Puchi cause you know I wouldn't tell your man even if I knew him. If you ever have to choose between him and Peil, baby my man here is a sure bet!" Michael said.

I knew exactly what Mike was doing, so he sweetened the pot a little. "Maybe she don't want you to know that she knows people like me Mike," I said.

Puchi stared at the sly smile on my face as she blushed in total surprise.

"Hey don't do that. Tell him the truth, you didn't even know my name until Mike called it," Puchi said.

I couldn't help but admire the innocent tone in her voice, but Mike quickly changed the subject. He and I went into small talk that obviously excluded Puchi, and her interest was not in our conversation. Her mind was puzzled as to why I had lied with not the slightest trace of guilt on my face. She felt embarrassed, insulted, yet there was a strange feeling of appreciation. We had ridden several blocks before the conversation targeted questions directed at her.

"How long has Sandra been gone Puchi?" Michael asked.

"For about three months. She'll be coming back soon though. She changed her mind about staying through the winter," she replied.

"I told the girl she can't find another man like me. God just wouldn't make any more cause the world couldn't stand it," Michael said.

"Ya'll go back for quite some time don't cha?" I cut in.

"Mike use to go with a friend of mine but I think my man here found a greener pasture," Puchi stated.

She was looking at Mike with those 'I knew about you' eyes accompanied by a charming smile.

"No baby, you know I dug that girl, but she was half-stepping and trying to holdout on me. She knew where I was coming from," Michael said. Mike moved around in the seat relaxing his body and said, "But Puchi, 'flower child' was a bad sister wasn't she?"

Sticking his hand out to get some play, Michael laughed out. "Say drop me on the next corner Peil, and hey man, what's happening with you tonight? Can we get together?" Michael asked. "I might have something you can use," Michael stated. "That's cool Mike, what about Felt Hat around eleven?" I asked him. "That's on time with me, and tell Jesse to take care man," Michael said. He gave a brief stare of honesty as he slid out the door. "And Puchi, you be cool baby. Hey girl, you know there are only two good men and I'm getting out," Mike said to her. Mike was back to his old self just that quick. "Man you something else, gone," Puchi said. She was laughing as he closed the door giving them the right on.

"Can I ask you a question please?" Puchi said.

"Yeah shoot," I said to her,

"Why did you give Mike the impression that we go together? I mean we are total strangers, I don't understand," she asked. "How do you tell a stranger? I never met one Puchi." "Now there's people everyday that I never saw before, but they're no different from the people I've known all my life, so I guess what you consider strange is the same things that come natural to me," I told her. I continued talking never looking in her direction.

"It's not everyday I see in a woman, the things that I see in you. And the personality that I see in you is the kind that I want to accompany me through my journey of life. It takes a lot of things to truly combine a man and a woman together as one," I said. "Someone who's willing to always share and forever care about the other person. To compete against the world and never let obstacles of any given situation, rearrange the basement of their understanding," I said to her.

"Maybe I told Mike that because I'd be pleased to tell anybody that you're my woman," I said. I was looking Puchi in the eyes. I noticed that she was blushing. Puchi broke the stare when she spoke, "Yeah, I really dig what you're saying, but how do you know that my personality is not contradictory to my ways and actions when you don't know anything about me?" Puchi asked. "I mean, people have to do more than just believe in those things, they have to live up to those morals as well," Puchi said.

"Puchi, everybody lives up to the morals that they really believe in. If they are fantasy, then they're not believing, they're hoping and sometimes it becomes such a psychological satisfaction that most people are just content with themselves," I said.

I continued, "But you Puchi, I don't psyche myself out behind something I'm not satisfied with because I know what I like, I know what I want, and most of all, I know what I need. And in you, all these things that I don't see, I'd like to create if given the chance to," I explained to her.

Puchi couldn't just disregard the things I was saying because the way I spoke with such confidence in my masculine tone seemed to have hypnotized her momentarily. She could hardly believe that the man, who seemed like a street hoodlum and gangster type only minutes ago, was now so sweet, humble, and understanding. I no longer seemed like a man who forced my way through the doors that I want to enter, but more like a flower that blooms only in the springtime and captures the hearts of millions. She was beginning to appreciate my presence more and more because my style was so different from any guy's she'd ever met before. She stole another glance at me from the corner of her eye without turning her head then Clifford creped into her mind it seemed.

She said she'd met Clifford at a party that Sandra had given. Until then she had really made up her mind to be a free lady for a long time because she'd had some terrible experiences with men. Clifford kept watching her with a look of interest on his face and he was no doubt a very handsome guy. He was tall and his wide shoulders gave her the impression that he must've been a great football player. She felt her body getting warm and her blood rushing through her veins when he approached her staring into her eyes. His voice really threw her off guard. She had never expected it to be so soft, so tender. She had imagined it would be more like Mean Joe Greene's or some big time Hell Raiser's.

They had been going together a year now and the excitement had begun to slowly vanish from their relationship. The first six months they were together was everything she'd ever wanted in an affair. She had even entertained the thought of marrying Clifford, but lately she wasn't sure that she could go through with the idea because things had changed so much. Puchi was so involved with her thoughts that she forgot where she was going.

"Hey, I'm going to that bank across the street over there. I almost forgot," she said with a smile.

I looked over at her. "Are you going to deposit some money or rob the place?" I asked.

"Neither one. I work here," she answered with an air of concern for my remark. "I've been working here for five and half years now," Puchi said.

I could hear the pride ringing in her voice and immediately associated her amongst the more prominent citizens.

"You must have it made. I mean, you've been there long enough to call some shots by now right?" I asked her.

My tone gave her the feeling of an authoritative figure.

"Well, I don't know about the shots and all that but I'm head cashier, which don't impress me that much," Puchi said.

She tried to defend the liberation of her position by placing herself in an average working lady's class. I stopped the car directly in front of a side door entering the bank. The space was reserved for *The Manager* and written in bold yellow letters. I turned the key and the engine died into total silence.

"Now you see that sweetheart?" All the way across town and I never even tried to feel your big ole' pretty legs. Plus I saved you some money, and you met an old friend. Now what can you do with that?" I asked.

I was staring at her with a faint smile on my lips. Before she realized what she was saying she spoke.

"Peil can I call you sometime?" she asked seriously.

"Better than that, you can come over baby," was my reply.

"Well, I'd hate for your 'ladies' to get upset just because I stopped by," Puchi said. She gave me an I-know-men kind of look accompanied with a matching smile.

"There are no ladies who could produce any kind of claim on me sweetheart. But to be real about the whole thing, personally baby, I don't give a damn who gets upset if you want to see me, not even your husband," I said to her.

We held each other's eyes for a long moment then I continued, "But never would I show any disrespect for him in any way. Nor do I want to come between you and him if it's against your will," I said. She was about to speak when I continued. "But I will if I have to."

My face suddenly twisted into a heart-warming smile as I slid my hand across the velvet-covered seat shyly covering her hand with mine.

"Wow. You have yourself a nice day playboy and I'll call you soon, okay?" Puchi said to me. I opened the glove compartment taking out an address book with a pen attached to the pad. I opened it and began to write. Puchi was getting out of the car as she looked over at me.

"Hey, I really appreciate the ride, but my mother always told me not to ride with strange men," she said jokingly as she got completely out of the car.

"Some rules were made to be broken sweetheart," I came back.

I started the car and pulled away not concerning myself with whether I ever saw her again or not. I decided to just drive with no particular place in mind. Days like this really had the kind of meaning that you just couldn't justify or specify for any given situation because it was the kind of day where anything goes. I was meditating on the performance of the day's plight so deeply that I almost didn't see the guy crossing the street in the pedestrian zone. After coming to a complete stop, I noticed the man had a moneybag underneath his arm and heading straight towards the bank across the street. As soon as the bag registered, Jesse popped into my mind. Automatically I began searching the streets for police and alleyways for possible escapes. I knew that if Jesse had been in the car with me it would be time to go to work. I even entertained the thoughts of trying to take the lick off myself, but the man was too close to the bank, and besides, the biggest job I'd ever done alone was petty shoplifting.

I proceeded on down the street and had driven for approximately fifteen minutes before I realized I was in Audrey's neighborhood. Audrey and I had been pretty close once upon a time but her refusal to submit to me, body, and soul created conflicts that eventually ended our relationship. We met in the First National Bank one day when I was cashing a check and I couldn't produce any I.D. verifying that the check was mine. She knew that the check was hot, but she just smiled and said, "Make sure you take your wife to dinner tonight."

The words decreased the rush of blood speeding through my heart and I replied, "Well, since I'm not married, why don't I take you to dinner?"

"That's a bet! Call me at this number around eight," Aubrey stated.

Upon my arrival her first words were, "Nigga you better leave them goddamn checks alone! What if you had gone to one of those cracker's window and she wanted to start some shit? What would you have done?" she yelled.

"I would have politely reached across and caught her in the collar like so and kissed her perfect lips," I said to her.

My demonstration was the beginning of the real thing. She politely pushed me away as I tried to kiss her.

"Man, you're a helluva nigga. First you get me to help you rob a bank then you come to my house and try to seduce me. I beg of you mister, please don't try to blow my mind okay?" she said in a quizzical tone of voice, melting into a charming childlike smile.

We had lots of good times together and it had all seemed so unrealistic to the both of us. We constantly expressed our disbelief in each other's actions, but we dug each other very much because our entire relationship was woven with respect and admiration. Somehow our experience with each other was the least expected. Audrey had been working in the First National Bank as the head teller for two years when she met me. She always talked about her job to me, her duties, the amount of money she played with from day to day, and her credibility with the bank manager. I had become so fascinated by her "Gig Gossip" that I would start the conversation every time with questions. Then my questions began to sound so serious that she could see me actually contemplating her every word. The day before our dream world fell apart, I had come over to take her to a movie but circumstances took its course.

"Hey baby, let's get fucked up before we leave. Then I might just settle for a good love making compared to the movie," Audrey said, putting her arms around my waist.

"Is the smoke any good?" I asked.

"I'm sure both of us together can get you off," Audrey said.

"Shit, sexy lady, when you serve it on that side you know I'll get off just being near you, and sometimes even in my pants," I said, laughing and squeezing her body to mine.

"It's supposed to be Columbian. Let's check it out," she said.

Neither one of us were pot smokers. Audrey couldn't fit it into her job and I didn't like getting too far away from reality. As the aromatic scent of weed began to fill the living room, we became conscious of only the objects surrounding us and the hallucinating effects was slowly reforming our entire beings into oneness.

"Hey, when are we leaving for the movie?" Audrey questioned.

Lying back on the giant beanbag, I smiled and began a lecture.

"Sexy lady, every time you enter my mind I truly enjoy the thoughts, and when I compare your sweetness with manmade movies, my decision is just as clean as a Windex commercial," I said to her.

She went to applaud my poetic thoughts but I continued before she could get her hands together.

"So you see sweetheart, I'm really consoled in happiness just being here with you. And the most fascinating part of the whole trip is just realizing that you're the star of my show!" I said.

We both burst into laughter until it became a burning passion that could only be subdued through the arts of making love. I began talking about a plan I knew would work.

"Hey sexy lady, how would you get out of that bank with money if you ever decided to take some?" I asked.

"Shit baby, I ain't about to try no stupid shit like that. I would never get my black ass out of jail," Audrey said.

"I didn't ask you to do anything like that. I just wanted you to hypothesize the idea," I answered.

"I don't know. I never thought about it," Audrey replied.

The weed had taken its toll on her now. After a long silence, I started talking. "I know how you could get that money out of there sexy lady," I said.

"How?" she asked in a fantasizing tone of voice. "Not that I'm interested o.k.?" she said.

"Okay, dig this," I said. I rolled up on my elbow facing Audrey. "All you have to do is put the money in a bag and have someone walk in. Give them the bag then wait three minutes and scream you've been robbed," I said to her.

There was excitement in my voice and I had certainly captured Audrey's ear. She didn't know what to say.

Audrey couldn't believe that I was really trying to get her to do something that had never even crossed her mind. She had been on her job too long to ever entertain such foolishness.

After all, we really didn't have any kind of committed relationship. We didn't see each other on a regular basis, and she was certain that she was not the only woman in my life, yet I'm asking her to literally help me to rob a bank.

And for some strange reason that she's yet to understand, she must admit the idea had a certain kind of nervous energy that truly excited her.

"One day I'll walk into the bank, come to your window and you give me about fifteen or twenty grand. I turn around and walk out of the bank, you give me three minutes and then you scream robbery to throw the heat off you. Do you follow me?" I asked her.

Something in Audrey's head was telling her that she was being persuaded to rob a bank, but still something was making her like the idea more and more. Maybe it was the weed.

"Yeah, I follow you, but . . ." she said.

"There ain't no but's baby. Listen Audrey, there's no heat if they want to know why you waited so long to scream. Tell 'em the robber told you that a man was standing inside the bank with a shotgun under his coat and if you screamed, within three minutes somebody would get hurt. So you were scared, what the hell did they expect?" I said to her.

Her eyes questioned me for the assurance of my clever idea and it wasn't hard for me to figure out where her head was so I began to add the sweetness of temptation that very few personalities like Audrey's would refuse.

Three in the morning found us locked in an embrace and smoking another joint of the Columbian weed. Audrey had agreed to carry out my plan only through my gentle words because after that smoke, I had literally fucked up everything.

It had been almost a year since Audrey and I had carried out the bank plan. Audrey had become so nervous and jittery after constant questions from the F.B.I., she begged me to just stay away from her. After she assured me that she wanted no part of the money. She didn't have to beg too hard.

It was a rainy Wednesday morning when I walked into the bank shortly after a grumpy looking man walked over to the self-service counter sitting in the middle of the floor. He began filling out, what seemed like, some sort of deposit slip. The man never looked up from his interest in whatever he was doing. He wore a raincoat and hat that covered most of his face. I walked straight over to Audrey's window and passed her a scribbled written note. When Audrey looked up at the man, she nearly fainted. Her first thought was how could she be robbed twice in one day, but slowly she began to realize that this taller, afro, "Gold tee" wearing man with thick glasses, was me. She was so nervous that she almost dropped the note that read: *There's a man in this bank with a shotgun under his coat. So if you alarm anyone someone will be hurt, you first.*

There was something about the words in the note that gave her a very frightening chill. All of a sudden, this seemed much more serious than what we had planned. She was thinking, *oh God, why did I ever agree to something like this?*

All kinds of thoughts were running through her mind now. Her blood was at an explosive boiling point. She even thought of screaming. This was too unreal. Instead, she calmly gathered her composure and began to lift the crisp bills from the money drawer and placed them into my hand without even glancing at me. I casually slid the bills inside my shirt underneath my coat and, making sure I didn't attract any attention, I calmly but briskly walked out of the bank. Audrey swiftly turned toward the cashier in the next booth with bulging eyes filled with water.

She was very hysterical as she screeched out the words in a low, but excited voice, "That man just robbed me."

Passing the girl the note, she fell to her knees sobbing and shaking. The blond headed teller pushed the panic button without even reading the note. At that time all hell broke loose.

Loan officers, investment counselors, and unfortunately bank security was the last to arrive in the lobby. They immediately approached and apprehended the grumpy looking man in the raincoat, only to find out that he was making a deposit and cashing his check.

The bank security police, with his gun drawn, made the man lie down on the floor with his hands behind his head as he cautiously walked over and began to search him. After reading the note, all the while the man was yelling, "What's going on? I ain't did nothing!"

The security police quickly put the handcuffs on the man. By now, the streets were filled with the sound of sirens and the bank was filled with police officers and detectives. For Audrey, it was the beginning of a long grueling nightmarish day.

Once l had exited the bank, I walked a few steps to the corner before I started running down the street where I'd parked, leaving the keys in the ignition. I didn't want to be fumbling with any keys. I started the camaro, pulling out into traffic, making a U-turn. As I drove, I began pulling off the wig, the glasses, the gold tee, and the fake gold teeth I had in my mouth. I put everything in a bag and later dropped it in the river. I was certain I'd planned a good job. I had visualized and set everything up just right.

* * *

It all started one day as I was casing the bank. I saw a man coming out of the bank and walked over to a 55 Chevy, got in it and pulled away. I followed him for several blocks before the guy stopped at a service station and l pulled in behind him. I got out of the car and walked over to the guy and began complimenting him about the car.

"Man, is this a '55 or '56?" I asked as if I didn't know.

"A '55," he replied.

"I bet this thing will fly won't it?" I asked, walking around looking and admiring the interior. I really liked the car.

"It runs pretty good, but I still have a lot of work I want to do to it when I get the money," the man said.

"Yeah, I know how that is when you start restoring old cars," I said. "Oh man, my name is Peil," I introduced myself, stretching forward my hand.

"Charles Brown," was the man's reply, grabbing my hand with a good firm grip.

We talked for a few minutes after the man had finished pumping the gas. "Hey man, let me pay for this gas before these crackers think I'm trying to beat them," said the man. We shook hands again.

"Say man, how can I get in touch with you? Cause I know a guy with two of these cars and you all might be able to help each other with parts and shit," I said.

I did know a man who owned two 55's but I also knew that he wouldn't sell a damn thing. Besides I've been around old cars all my life. That's all my daddy ever had, old raggedly cars, he had to be a mechanic.

"Hey that would be outta sight," Charles replied, getting a pen out of his shirt pocket. He wore a blue denim uniform. I thought he might be a mechanic, but he didn't have any company name or anything on his shirt.

I went in my pocket, pulling out a card, "Put it right here and I'll give you a call," I said.

As Charles was passing me the card back, I said, "Hey, it's nice to meet you Charles. I'll be in touch."

We bided each other farewell and I walked back to my car. Even though I was very fond of old cars, Charles's car was the least of my interest at the moment. I was thinking and planning how I could get the money out of that bank with no trouble. My mind was thinking fast. I needed involved help. Charles and I had been talking for about three weeks before I made my move.

* * *

A few days later I called Charles and asked him if the guy had called him. It was a lie but a good reason for me to start a conversation. After we talked a few minutes, I said, "Hey Charles, I'd like to get with you man for some conversation, cause if you'd really like to fix up that '55, you might want to hear what I have to say."

"Hey, that sounds like a winna man. Ain't nothing wrong with listening," Charles said, sounding kind of quizzical, but interested.

"Say man, you know where Applebee's is over on Chancelors?" I asked.

"Yeah I know where that is," Charles replied.

"Why don't we meet there tomorrow at 7:00 p.m. It's on me ok? You ain't greedy are you man?" I asked as we both started laughing.

"Nah, I ain't greedy, but I will be hungry as hell when I get there tomorrow," Charles said.

We had a big laugh and hung up. I was a pretty good judge of character from my street knowledge and hustling, cause hustling the streets and playing at the ladies was the story of my life. I could sense that Charles would be perfect for my plan, as long as I explained it properly and with self-assuring confidence.

After the phone call to Charles, I got dressed and went over to Audrey's house. On the way over, I stopped and picked up a dozen roses and a bottle of champagne. When I rang the doorbell and Audrey appeared in the door, she was so astounded that her feminine gestures of appreciation could not be mistaken. We later drifted off into a very romantic and endearing afternoon filled with hugs and kisses and lovemaking. But to me, all of these were mere tools for the work I was planning.

I got up the next morning and went for a long jog. I could always think better when I ran and since I had no plans for that day, other than meeting Charles, most of the day was dedicated to thinking how I would drop my plan on Charles. After the run I went to the health spa where I was a lifetime member. I spent quite a bit of time there, but after using the steam room, the sauna and swimming a few laps in the pool, I went back home. I ate a couple of apples and just relaxed the rest of the day.

Waking up to the sound of the telephone, I raised up from the Lazy boy recliner, reaching over to the phone.

"Good afternoon," I said in a sleepy sounding voice.

"You sound sleep." It was Audrey.

"Girl, you knocked me out last night. I'm trying to get my strength back," I said to her.

We laughed.

"Only you would answer the phone and say something like that," she said in a laughing voice.

"I just wanted to hear your voice and tell you how much I enjoyed and appreciated last night. You really impressed me!" she said. Her voice was as sweet and serene as she was.

"You ain't trying to propose to me on sly are you?" I joked.

"Ah nigga, don't get cute now. I don't need those kinds of problems," Audrey said.

Our conversation was quite warming.

"Are you coming over tonight?" she asked.

"I have a few things to do a little later. I don't wanna make any promises. Besides, I don't want you to get bored with me, cause my grandmother told me that seldom visits make long friendships," I said My words were humorous and somewhat serious. Audrey didn't quite know the meaning, but she didn't want to give away her feelings with the wrong response.

"Well, just don't take your other lady any roses. Ok?" she said.

"That's why I'm hoping you put them in some water cause I might have to use them again. You know how much those things cost?" I teased her. I was laughing, she was coy.

We were both laughing now.

"You're so crazy," was her laughing reply. "But I will at least hear from you tomorrow, right?" she asked.

"I'll meet you for lunch. How about that?" I replied.

"Sounds great! So I'll talk to you tomorrow!" she said.

She was about to hang up when I said, "Hey, just pat that thang for me, ok?"

There was another clamor of laughter. "Bye fool!" she said then hung up.

Those were beautiful times for me and Audrey. I could never say that I didn't have great feelings for her cause she was something else.

* * *

It was 5:30p.m. I took a shower and got dressed. I wore an Italian silk blue casual suit and a pair of black Italian lizard shoes, a black brim Stetson hat. I was very fond of hats. I was pretty sharp. I pulled up to the Applebee's restaurant at 6:55p.m. Charles was already there sitting in his car. I thought that was a good sign. He seemed to be a man of promptness.

"What's up my friend? How was your day?" I asked as I walked over meeting Charles, who was now walking toward me.

"Hard work man. I worked up a good appetite," Charles said.

We laughed as we shook hands and headed for the restaurant entrance. A very pleasing young white girl greeted us and led us to a seat in the middle of the room. I asked if we could have the table near the window.

"Sure," she said, flashing a friendly smile. "Your waitress will be with you. Thank you," said the greeter.

"Man, this place employs some fine looking women, don't you think?" I said, looking at the young lady's butt as she walked away.

"No shit man," Charles said.

"Them white girls done started getting asses like sisters, haven't they? They're catching on," I said.

We continued with small talk until a beautiful black haired Puerto Rican looking white girl walked to our table.

"Good afternoon gentlemen. My name is Lisa and I'll be your waitress for the evening," she said.

"See man, I knew this was the section for us," I said, admiring the beautiful woman.

She was eating it up.

"You must ride a bicycle to work everyday?" I asked.

"No. Why do you say that?" she asked.

"Cause I don't see how you got those big beautiful legs driving a car," I replied.

We were all smiling.

"Ah, you sure know how to flatter a girl don't you? What will you gentlemen have to drink?" she asked.

"I'll have a Lowenbrau," Charles replied.

"Well, since I'm only drinking water, you can bring it with my food," I said.

"I'll give you a few minutes to look over the menu while I get your drinks. Are you sure you're only having water?" the waitress asked, directing her question toward me.

"Well, if I was having dinner with you, I'd be drinking wine. But since you're on duty I'll hold out until you get off," I said to her.

Lisa blushed with a big smile. "You're something else," she said.

"I'm serious too," I said.

Lisa walked off. Charles and I engaged in small talk until she returned with the drinks.

"Are you ready to order now?" she asked, sitting a big glass of ice water in front of me and a Lowenbrau and glass in front of Charles.

"I'll take the Blackened chicken salad with blue cheese dressing," I said, still looking over the menu as if I wasn't sure.

Then all of a sudden I closed it up and gave Lisa a big smile. Charles was still looking over the menu like he was puzzled before he finally spoke.

"I think I'll have Chinese stir fried chicken and rice. Ok? And can I get a side order of sautéed mushrooms?" he asked.

"If that's what you want, you can," Lisa said in a joking manner.

"So you can get anything you want up in here, huh?" I asked in a flirtatious voice.

"Let's stick to the menu for now, ok?" she laughed, patting me on the shoulder and leaving.

Charles was anxious to know what this meeting was all about, but I talked about everything but the meeting. However, Charles wasn't going to push the issue.

Finally, the food came and we both complemented the looks of the food before tasting it. We continued our conversation as we savored the dishes. Finally I asked, "Do you do business at that bank I saw you at the other week?"

"Oh yeah, I have a savings and checking account there," Charles answered.

"How do you feel about making money if you don't have to work for it man?" I asked, looking directly into Charles's eyes.

Charles stopped chewing and looked back at me.

"Oh, I'd love it man, but there ain't no such job," Charles replied.

He had an air of concern in his voice now. I stared out the window for a long moment before I spoke.

"First of all, I have two requests Charles, ok?" I said.

"Sure thing man. What's happening?" Charles asked.

"Number one, I ask that everything between me and you are strictly between me and you, deal?" I asked. l was extending my hand across the table.

"That's a bet Peil," Charles said, grabbing my hand, confirming our agreement.

"Number two, I don't want you to say a word nor make any decisions until you've heard my plan. Deal?" I asked.

Again Charles agreed.

"I'm very serious about what I do man, so I'm going to be very frank with you, ok?"

"Ok," Charles said, looking more puzzled than before.

"I have a plan, and all I need of you is your presence. Nothing else," I said. l hesitated as Charles stared at me blindly. "You will have absolutely nothing to do with me and my plan at all, you dig?" "All I need is your presence and everything else has already been taken care of," I said.

Suddenly Charles lost his appetite and l could sense it.

"Just listen to me Charles. Man, this shit is so sweet. I started to get my momma to help me, but she got high blood pressure," I teased.

We started laughing, but Charles still had that air of concern.

"Here's the plan. I have a lady in the bank that's going to give me $40,000.00 okay? All I have to do is to figure out how to get out of the bank with the money. Here's where your presence is the key," I said.

Lisa walked back to the table. "Is everything alright?" she asked.

"Oh yeah sweetheart, everything's fine," l replied.

"Are you sure I can't get you anything else? No dessert or anything?" the waitress asked.

Charles seemed to come out of a trance and said, "Oh, could I get another Lowenbrau please?"

"Sure can!" Lisa replied.

"Can I get your phone number?" l asked. "I'm finished with the menu. From now on, it's me and you."

"That has a rhyming ring to it, don't it?" Lisa said, hitting me on the head with a menu she was carrying and walking away again.

"The only thing you have to do Charles is be in the bank. When I give you the details you'll see my plan is foolproof. I have figured out everything. I have masterminded this thing. Are you with me so far?" I asked holding his stare.

"Yeah, but I'd like to know how I fit into this plan cause I—" Charles said. I interrupted. "Don't think about it yet, ok? Listen to me. Let's get out of here and I'll give you the details, ok?"

"That's a bet," Charles replied, turning up the glass, drinking the last of the beer.

As we spoke of leaving, Lisa walked up with the check. "I hope you guys enjoyed your meal as much as I enjoyed serving you. You will come back, right?" she asked.

Lisa's voice was filled with hospitality, even though I knew that it was tip time and these girls were good at their job.

"Well, since you wanna be stingy with your digits, I guess I'll have to come back here to see you, right?" I asked.

"Well, when you come back, maybe we'll work on it. Ok?" Lisa said with a quiet grin, while taking the check back with a $10.00 tip.

"Keep the food warm ok?" I said as we were leaving.

"I think she digs you man cause she really giving it up," Charles said.

"She's counting money man, and so am I," I said.

We laughed.

"Listen, why don't you leave your car here for a few and let's take a ride," I suggested.

We got into the camaro and pulled into the street headed for the freeway. George Benson was playing on the cassette, but I turned it down low so that it did not disturb our conversation.

"Now, as I was saying, this plan will be executed on a rainy day; the harder the rain the better. After tonight we won't be seen together in public at all. I want you to wear a raincoat with a rain hat on your head. You'll walk into the bank, walk to the counter in the middle of the floor. Take out your checkbook and if you have a check, you'll either sign it or write a check. Anything that will keep you at the center counter until I exit the bank. Don't look up or pay anyone any attention. I'm going to walk up to my lady, give her a note that will read, *'There's a man in here with a machine gun under his coat. If you attempt to alert anyone within three minutes someone will be hurt, you first!'* She'll give me the money and I'll stuff it in my shirt under my coat and leave. Once I exit the door, you will unbutton your raincoat and walk to a teller, not the one I did, but any teller and cash your check. Once she sees you don't have a gun, she's going to go into her thing and alarm the bank that she's been robbed and you're just as surprised as anyone else. Now here's the good part for you. They'll probably apprehend you, but you scream bloody murder, you ain't done nothing. You don't know anything about no bank robbery. You do business here and once they take you down, you can hit them with the biggest lawsuit they ever had! Mo money! I promise you that when I walk in that bank, you won't know me. Whatcha' think?" I explained. I had been talking for fifteen minutes and Charles never said a word.

"Wow man, that's incredible. Let me think about it and I'll get back with you tomorrow. How about that?" Charles said

"Sounds great Charles," I said.

I was sure Charles would go along with me. "Now we'll get together and go over details to the T," I said. And everything else was sweet like sugar cane!! Everything went just fine.

* * *

The F.B.I. Detectives started asking Audrey all kinds of questions about the description of the robber, and she was very willing to cooperate with them after she had calmed down and stop shaking so much.

"How tall was he? How much did he weigh? Did he have any identifying marks, etc?" the detectives asked. She answered everything to the best of her recollection. Even the six feet two inches tall was correct, however, I was wearing a size thirteen big tall-heeled shoe with a whole roll of toilet tissue in the bottom, making me about three inches taller than I actually was.

Even though Audrey was in complete control of her emotions, she couldn't help the nervousness of the moment. Now she was wondering if this was such a good idea and why had she gone along with me. Could this cost her job? Could she possibly end up in jail? The thoughts were too intriguing. She had to change her train of thoughts before these detectives could read her body language. Suddenly the door opens and two more detectives walked into the room with Charles in handcuffs. Upon seeing this, Audrey's nervousness began a whole new tingling throughout her body.

"Is this the man the note referred to?" the tall red headed detective asked, looking slyly toward Audrey.

"Well, I don't know. I don't know who the note was referring to," she said. She was looking stunned and puzzled. "When I read the note, I looked out into the lobby and there was a man with a long coat on and really, I just froze. I thought he could've been the man," she said.

"Man, I told you I don't know nothing about no robbery. I was just signing my check. I save my money here," Charles said in a frightened voice, but also in a voice of strong and serious conviction.

"Did this man seem to be a part of the robbery scheme?" he asked Audrey.

"I don't know. He never seemed to know from what I could tell, but I was scared," Audrey said.

And even beyond her control, tears began to roll down her cheeks, but her facial expression never changed. The telephone rang and the assistant bank president answered it and immediately handed the receiver to the red headed detective.

"Well, I don't really know at this time. I think more interrogation would be appropriate," were his words then. "There were no weapons on him," the detective said.

Then he hung up. He turned to the other detective and said, "Get him down to the station and wait for me." His words were sharp and crisp.

"Man, you can't be serious about this!" Charles screamed, with panic in his voice.

"We're not charging you yet. We just want to ask you some questions," the red headed man said.

As they were leaving the room, Charles screamed, "I want a lawyer man. This shit ain't right."

"Hopefully, that won't be necessary," the detective said.

By now, both Audrey and Charles were thinking maybe this was not such a good plan after all. I was the only one not getting the heat. As they were leaving the room, the detective turned to Audrey and asked, "Why didn't you put a dye bomb in the bag?" His eyes were questioning.

"He didn't want the money in a bag. He said to give it to him in his hand and he stuck it inside his shirt," Audrey said.

He momentarily held her stare and said, "If you think of anything, anything at all, call me at this number." He handed her a card.

"Yes sir," was her reply and they left the bank.

Mr. Edwards appeared to be more dysfunctional than Audrey was, and his words were so relieving when he said, "Audrey, I know how you must feel after this, so why don't you take the rest of the day off and just relax yourself."

They embraced each other as she began to cry. The entire bank was in a panic uproar as Audrey exited the side door. She was so nervous she could hardly put the key in the door lock. For the first time, for reasons she couldn't explain, she began to hate me in a smothering, but loving kind of way. She wanted to hold me in her arms gently and then squeeze the life from me. She wanted to kiss my lips, but at the same time she wanted to bite, scratch, and gouge my eyes out. She hardly remembered the directions she took home and before she realized anything, she was pulling up in her driveway. She rushed inside her apartment, going straight to the bar and getting a bottle of Remi Martini VSOP, which I had left over to her house on a previous occasion. Taking a glass from the cabinet, she poured it almost full and turned it up, drinking about half of the contents. She barely felt it burning down through her chest. She was so numb and immediately the alcohol began to take effect and her body was becoming so warm she started to reminisce about me making love to her. Why couldn't I be there now, holding and caressing her and kissing her lips, rubbing her body all over? Suddenly she started to calm down. It seemed that her thoughts were becoming much clearer.

Why had she gone along with my scheme? What if everything had went wrong? She could even see her picture on the front page in the newspaper. Oh God, how dumb could she be, was her only thought, filled with hostility. Maybe I was too fast for her, cause sometimes I could seem so ruthless and carefree. Maybe we weren't meant to be together. Maybe we were two people who never should have met, cause for the first time in our relationship, she began to analyze the differences in our lifestyles. She was a college-educated woman climbing the corporate ladder. I was a man of the streets, cultured in the games of cunning and scheming.

As she took another big gulp of the alcohol, she began taking off her clothes, walking blindly into the shower, trying to wash away this entire day.

* * *

Charles had been detained in police headquarters for more than three hours now. The detectives had crossed examined him in every imaginable way, but the only thing that stuck firmly in his mind was, I didn't have anything to do with any bank robbery and I want a lawyer.

"You people are making a big mistake and I'm going to sue this department and the bank," Charles said.

After the detectives had learned that Charles was making a $600.00 deposit and had maintained a bank balance of good standing, and also had a steady job for approximately five years, they realized they didn't have much of a case. So, at that point they began their scare tactics, telling Charles that they would drop the case if he forgot about the whole ordeal. But Charles had gotten control of his jittery nerves by now and the scare tactics didn't work. I had been so thorough in telling Charles how to handle any situation they might have created until he began realizing he was now in the driver's seat.

The chief detective came into the room and gave Charles a solemn apology and insisted that they give Charles a ride back to his car, which was still at the bank. Charles was very upset and he didn't hold back his feelings. Neither of the detectives said a word during the ride back. When they got back to the bank, Charles got out of the car and went into the bank, asking a teller to get the president. A fairly middle-aged woman directed him into the president's office.

"I'm very upset and disappointed about the way I was treated here this morning!" Charles shouted. "I was humiliated and embarrassed and slandered. After all these years of doing business with this bank, I don't think an apology will do," he said.

The president, Mr. Edwards, seemed very nervous and was quite reluctant to speak while Charles was talking.

"Mr. Brown, on the behalf of the bank, I'd like to sincerely apologize for the misunderstanding. You see, once this kind of thing happens everyone's a suspect at first," Mr. Edwards said.

Charles was somewhat surprised that this man knew his name, but he replied bitterly, "I don't give a damn about that man; I wasn't the only one in this bank. Why was I singled out?"

His anger was obvious. Before Mr. Edwards could speak, Charles spoke again.

"Fuck it man. I'm closing out my account as of this moment and you'll be hearing from my attorney!" he shouted.

"Mr. Brown I'm sure we can work this out. Please give us the opportunity," he pleaded.

"No we can't work this out. So why don't you get me some assistance with my business!" Charles shouted.

"Ok Mr. Brown, I'll get someone to help you. Once you calm down, can we meet here in my office or anywhere you want and work something out?" Mr. Edwards pleaded, while at the same time he called a cashier into the office to transact Charles's business.

"I'll have my attorney to set up a meeting with you," Charles answered.

"I assure you Mr. Brown, there's no need for an attorney," Mr. Edwards said.

Charles ignored his remarks and turned, walking out of the office behind the lady who'd just entered the room. The cashier, a very pleasant light brown haired woman, she asked Charles to have a seat very politely. She began to type out some forms. Finally she broke the silence by saying, "Mr. Brown, I'm so very sorry that this bizarre incident happened. I can't imagine how you must feel because I've seen you come in here several times. I know that you're a nice person."

"Thank you," was Charles's only reply.

The lady retreated back into her silent mode and continued typing. Once Charles had signed the papers, he spoke to the lady.

"I appreciate what you said. I don't want to be rude to you, but I'm deeply hurt ma'am," he said to her.

As Charles stood up to leave, the lady said, "Mr. Brown, again I'm sorry and I do wish you the best of luck."

She had a warm smile on her face. Charles thanked her and walked out of the bank.

* * *

I was now on the expressway, discarding the wig, gold teeth and the shoes and coat. I made a right turn off the freeway onto another street that took me out of the city. I went to a lake I knew about and pulled out a pillowcase from underneath the seat, packing all of the garments into it. I picked up two large sized rocks and put them into the bag, tying the top of the pillowcase with one of the shoe strings and threw it out into the lake as far as I could. I stuffed all the money into my spare bag and put it behind the seat and threw a towel over it. I started the car and pulled away. I had finally calmed down from the adrenaline rush and now I was feeling great! I reached into the glove compartment and got out a Jackson 5 tape and stuck it in the tape player, fast-forwarding to the cut of "I Want to Be Your Sugar Daddy". Rolling down the freeway with $40,000 at your back was a feeling you can't explain. You just have to savor the moment, but I never forgot that it was time to put security on myself. I was making a right turn off the freeway, going east from the city. I headed to Macon, Georgia, where Margie lived.

I first met Margie during the summer of '69 in Fort Knox, Kentucky during a graduation ceremony.

Her brother Wilbert was stationed in my unit. We were both in the Army buts that's another story.

Margie was a very delightful person with a gratifying kind of humor. She showed a lot of admiration for her countrymen. We had no problem agreeing with one another.

As soon as I was back state side after a Germany tour, I immediately looked her up, cause we'd always keep in touch.

Earlier in the morning, I called Margie Hunter and invited her out to dinner. Margie was more than eager to accept. She was nine years older than me, but we had been sexual companions for more than five years. I knew that I could always depend on Margie for a few dollars and in most cases, a few hundred. Margie was a formal postal worker who had been retired by the post office for some sort of injury she'd received while working. She never volunteered to give me the details of the situation and I never asked. All I knew was that I was never denied anything I'd ever asked Margie for, so by that token, I let everything be everything.

Margie had always been an escape from whatever for me. Regardless of how long I was gone, she never asked where I'd been. When I asked for money, she never asked for what. She was always overjoyed to see me. I pulled up into Margie's driveway, parking closely behind a brand new Cadillac. I rang the doorbell and stood to the side of the door. Suddenly the door opened and there stood Margie in her robe.

"Come on in out of the rain stranger," she greeted me.

Margie was a very fine woman. She'd taken extra good care of herself over the years and the milk she'd been drinking had really done her body good.

"Hey baby," I greeted her, sliding my arms around her waist. "Where the man driving that fancy ride out there?" I asked her. "You know I can't compete with him."

I was kissing her on the neck and squeezing her gently.

"Honey, you know you don't have to compete with anyone. Besides, that's my gift to myself for all those years of hard work," Margie said.

"Oh really?" I asked.

I was somewhat surprised, because I didn't know Margie had bank like that.

"You mean you been sitting on that kind of cash and letting me ride the bus?" I asked laughing.

"Baby, I'll give you that car just as soon as we get married," she said We both burst into laughter.

"Your car is as sporty as mine, and you never did a hard day's work slickster. I know you," Margie said.

"Ah baby, I'm working all the time. That's why you haven't seen me. I have three jobs. Every time I get up, I'm going to work," I told her.

We were laughing and enjoying these moments.

"You should be ashamed of yourself, lying on a job like that," Margie said.

She was laughing and pulling me into her arms. She was glad to see me because I always made her feel special when I was around, which was not quite enough for her.

"I've been daydreaming about that thang. You been keeping it warm for me?" I teased.

I was caressing her breasts and kissing her passionately.

"Yes." she whispered, "I've been wanting to see you so bad. My body needs you."

Her words were becoming muffled with moans and groans. I started laying her down on the large white sofa and begin gyrating between her legs. She started undressing me and I was helping her. We started making love on the sofa and ended up on the floor. After what seemed like a world of ecstasy, we both lay nude on the floor laughing and caressing each other. We showered together and again made love while the water drenched our bodies.

After we were dressed and ready to go out, Margie asked, "Are you just taking me to dinner or can I look forward to a night like my day was?"

Her eyes were searching mine. I pulled her close to me, kissing her on the lips.

"Baby, if you make love to me like that, I might not ever leave you," I said. "Never go home."

I was smiling, but Margie knew I was just filling the moment with joy and lying at the same time.

"You want to take my car?" she asked.

"Why, of course. We ain't riding in no heap like mine with a Cadillac in the driveway," I replied.

"Oh stop it." She was smiling and passing me the keys.

"You back out and let me put this junk in your garage. I don't want to clutter up your neighborhood," I said.

We were laughing again. I felt much better now after concealing my car and my money. Now I could really enjoy the day. The Cadillac was a real dream car.

"You know, just before you got to the house, I was watching some program when the news came on. Somebody robbed a bank this morning and they don't even have a clue," Margie said. "In your city, did you hear about it?" she asked.

"Really? Black or white?" I asked.

"They say he was black, but you know how that goes. Could've been a white girl in that bank and she gave the money to her boyfriend and they put it on us," Margie said.

She started laughing. My heart skipped a beat when she unknowingly described the robbery.

"Damn, I sho' wish that had been me," I said jokingly.

Margie looked at him surprisingly. "I know you're joking. You wouldn't do anything like that would you?" she asked.

"Oh get real baby. I said I wish it were. I didn't say I did it," I said.

She started laughing the laugh of relief. We had dinner at Red Lobster's and drank a carafe of white Chablis. Later we went to the park where we walked, talked, and acted like children. We also went to a jewelry store where Margie left her ring to have it cleaned and I was just looking at the fabulous ice when Margie walked over to me and put her arm around my waist and said, "See anything you like?"

"In a jewelry store? Hell, I like everything I see in here, even the ugly old jewelry cashier lady," I said.

We were beaming with laughter when the lady suddenly asked, "Is there something else I can do for you Miss Hunter?"

Margie looked at me with a questioning look, smiled and said, "Let me answer that tomorrow, ok?"

Margie and I hugged each other as we laughed our way out of the door. We drove around the city for hours, just talking and fondling each other. Margie could never remember me being so joyful and humorous. I was an afternoon of total hysterical jokes. Finally, around 10:30pm, I asked Margie if she felt like dancing.

"Dancing?" she asked shyly. "I haven't been dancing in years. Clubbing yes, but dancing?"

She was obviously flattered because in her younger day she really did love to dance, but the invitation had not been extended in years.

"Why not?" I asked.

I pulled into a nightclub parking lot called Big Daddy's. The flashing lights on the sign read, "Lady's Night".

"You're not just using me for cover to check out the merchandise are you?" she asked, caressing my thigh.

"If I was shopping for merchandise, I wouldn't have brought any sand to the beach. You dig baby?" I asked her.

As we strolled into the club, arm in waist, l acted as though we were newlyweds. Margie couldn't help but act as though she was the bride of the year. We danced very close, romantically and fast as well. After what seemed like a fountain of white wine and kisses, I got up and walked over to the DJ's booth and when I came back to the table, I was singing along with Teddy Pendergrass, "Turn Out The Lights", followed by "Come On Over To My Place". Oh what an evening it was!

* * *

When l woke the next morning, to find myself in this big spacious king size bed alone, I had to gather my thoughts to remember what had really happened. As reality slowly came back to me, I just laid back with a big smile on my face. I'd gotten up and taken a shower and was getting dressed when I heard Margie coming in the front door.

"I thought you were in the kitchen," I said.

"Oh, I'm about to fix your breakfast now, but I had to run out for a minute," Margie said.

"Hey, don't be sneaking out on me like that. I could've missed you," I said.

I was caressing her from behind.

"Ah cut it out Peil. You must have been swimming in the Nile River cause you didn't even know that I wasn't in the house," she said.

We laughed as she started taking eggs out of the refrigerator and preparing breakfast.

"By the time you get dressed, I'll have your breakfast on the table, sweetmeat," Margie said.

She grabbed at me as I fled for the bedroom. As I came back into the kitchen where I smelt coffee and toast, I couldn't help but notice the black velvet box sitting in the plate with my eggs. Without saying a word, I picked up the box and opened it. It was the two-karat diamond I'd looked at the day before.

"Wow baby. I heard of the goose that laid the golden egg, but I didn't know about the chicken that lays diamonds," I said with a smile.

I was very excited and she could hear it in my voice.

"Are diamonds really forever?" I asked while hugging and kissing her.

"You tell me. I just want you to remember me Peil," was her reply. She was searching my face. I kissed her on the nose. "Every time I see a sparkle, I'll remember the glitter in your eyes, with eggs in your mouth," I said.

I was putting a big forkful of eggs in her mouth as we started laughing uncontrollably. Later we sat down and had a good breakfast in a lovingly romantic fashion.

"For that, I'll do the dishes," I said.

"Oh no," was her reply.

"But I insist," I said as I began to clear the table.

While I was scrubbing the skillet, the eggs were fried in. I started thinking how serious this relationship was getting. Later, as Margie entered the room, she was dressed in a beautiful turquoise velvet suit. I immediately complimented her loveliness and she blushed and said she had some things to do.

"Will you be here when I get back?" she asked.

I paused for a long moment before I answered, realizing that this was a good place to exit. "I have some things that I should've taken care of already, but you almost made me forget," he said.

"I'll be seeing you soon, right?" she asked.

"Diamonds are forever," he said, then smiled and flashed the beautiful nugget in her face.

"Boy, you're something," she said. As we both headed for the door we wondered if next time would be this good?

* * *

As I pulled the camaro out into the street, the day before started to replay itself all over in my mind. I wondered how Audrey was doing and if Charles had handled himself as I'd instructed. I knew that this would not be a good time to call either of them. My plan was to give them at least four weeks before any contact was made. I knew that it was not at all unusual for the detectives to watch any suspect or believed suspects for days, weeks, months, or years even though I was certain that they couldn't trace anything between us.

I could hardly stop looking at the glittering gem on my finger as I drove in the direction of my home. I thought it would be wise for me to just lounge around the house today and do some careful planning. My mind kept telling me that Florida would be a great vacation at this particular time, and I really wanted to get away. Once I got home, I parked the car in the back yard and immediately began to wash and wax it. A day like this was the making of a bright and shiny future. After some water and some soapsuds, I said to myself, "Miami, here I come!"

I later decided to postpone the Miami trip for a while. I didn't think it would be too cool to leave the city without knowing what was going on.

It had been approximately five weeks since that rainy Wednesday morning. I hadn't made any kind of contact with Audrey or Charles.

In fact, I was planning a way to bump into them without any visual contact or phone calls.

I knew that Audrey went to the beauty salon every Saturday morning. I knew where the salon was and about what time she went. That Saturday morning, I went jogging down the street on First Avenue and saw her car parked in a space just beyond the salon. I'd already written out the note on a white business card that belonged to someone else. As I approached the car, I ran by on the driver's side and quickly stuck the note in the driver's door window, without really even missing a step. (The note read: Jogging down your street) I knew that Audrey would ride down her street as soon as she got the note, and she did.

I was really glad to see her, cause I was tired as hell! She was looking simply marvelous in her weekend dress down clothes. I wanted to grab her and just melt away in hugs and kisses.

My adrenaline was at an all time high when she started walking towards me. I walked into the parking lot of an auto parts store.

"I can't believe you stuck this shit in my window, nigga!" was her first reply.

As I looked into her eyes, I knew at that very moment that our relationship had taken a turn for the worst.

Hey baby, you ain't glad to see me?" I asked. I was really reading her body language now, and it wasn't good. "Hell no," Audrey shouted. "I ain't glad to see you, and I don't think we should see each other anymore, this is it," she said. "Man you almost caused me my job. I nearly had a nervous breakdown and you don't give a fuck about nobody but your damn self.

Audrey was extremely upset with me, and refused to listen to anything I had to say. To be honest, I really didn't know how to change her at this moment; therefore I just stared her in the eyes and listened to her vent.

I could understand her frustrations, but why wouldn't she listen? Her unstable attitude started me to wonder, just how upset she really was. Had she gotten weak and told anybody anything? Had she shown any incriminating emotions around the bank? Questions like these, and her irritated state of mind started me examining my trust in her now.

"Audrey, can we meet somewhere tonight and talk baby; it's nothing like that, sweetheart. You know I'd never do anything to hurt you," I pleaded. "No, let's not wait until tonight, please Audrey, meet me in Flat Rock Park in two hours, ok?" I continued to plead.

Audrey looked away as if her heart really wanted to be there, but her mind it seemed, could only focus on the dark side of nervousness.

"I don't know Peil," she said, "maybe we should let it go, just call it off!" "No, no, no baby, we can't let it go just yet," I said. "Just meet me there o.k.?" I asked. "Do it!" I said slightly demanding her.

Before Audrey could reply, I was backing up and turned around breaking into a jogging run in the direction of my house. I gave her no escape for meeting with me, and something in the back of my mind assured me that she would show up.

The jog home was very refreshing. It was like I'd just started running. I barely even noticed the traffic as I ran cause my mind was now completely occupied. Once I got my car, and got to the park, I was really just ready to sit down and relax. I was exhausted from running. I found a nice comfortable spot underneath a tree. I spread out a blanket and laid back with a *JET* magazine I had in the car. I waited for Audrey to show up. About thirty minutes later, I saw her car slowly rolling down the narrow one way path park road. She pulled up beside my car and got out. I got up and started to meet her. "I thought for a minute that you weren't coming," I said, looking her straight in the eyes.

"I started not to, and I shouldn't have," she replied with a bit of hostility in her voice. "Baby you shouldn't feel like that. We're going to be alright," I was saying when she interrupted.

"Damn Peil, you just don't get it do you?" she asked. "Man I could've lost my job, and went to jail. I've been a nervous wreck ever since that day. I ain't heard shit from you, and you say we'll be alright?" asked Audrey. "No Peil," she continued, "we won't be alright cause we won't be seeing each other anymore after today, understand?" she asked. "I want you out of my system. I can't live like this Peil, so will you just leave me alone?" Audrey asked. "I mean it!" she yelled. I'd never seen her this upset before, and some how I just knew it was over.

"I don't want any of that money, and you don't have to worry about me ever saying a word to anyone about anything. I just want to forget about that day," Audrey said. She paused then continued, "and this relationship too, o.k.?" she said. At that very moment, she turned and got back into her car, started the engine and drove away, never looking at me again.

As I watched, Audrey drive away. I knew that I wouldn't be seeing her again unless we just happen to bump into each other which would hardly be likely, cause I had other plans in my head.

To be honest, I was feeling kind of bad, after all, I'd just lost probably the best woman I'd ever met, and it was all my fault.

Being a criminal was costing my heart too much grief. This was definitely not the ending I had planned.

After this little bitter meeting, I decided that trying to contact Charles might not be the best idea. After all, I knew that he was never charged and that he also had a lawsuit pending against the bank.

Suddenly the $40,000 crept into my mind and before I knew it, I had nodded into a peaceful sleep right there in the park. When I woke up, I knew it was time for Miami.

"The Making of a Criminal"

---•❈•---

Mommy said Jesse has been stealing every since he was a year old, and he's still doing it at forty-six. Mommy said she and my aunt took Jesse to H.L. Green's Department store to take some pictures. Once they had left the store, she noticed Jesse had a box of Ritz crackers in his arms.

She said to my aunt, "Ann, what did you buy that boy those Ritz crackers for? He don't need them."

Ann said, "I didn't buy him any crackers. I thought you did!"

Mommy got excited and told my aunt, "Let's go back and pay for them before this boy get us put in jail."

When she entered the store, she went straight to the cashier and began to apologize for Jesse's action.

"Miss, I'm so sorry. I didn't know my baby had picked up these crackers. How much are they? I'll pay you for them," said mommy.

The white cashier was bursting with laughter and replied, "No, you don't owe me for them. I was looking at him when he got them. It was so cute I just couldn't say anything. When he noticed you weren't looking, he got them and started for the door, but don't worry about them. He's a darling!" said the cashier.

Mommy said when they were away from the cashier, "Darling my ass Ann. This is a little thief!"

Maybe if she'd whipped his ass then, she would've saved herself many restless nights. Taking things appeared to just fascinate Jesse every since that time.

Bobby Hodge

* * *

At nine years old Jesse and I went to the fabric shop with my mommy's sister, Aunt Essie Mae. She used to make clothes for everybody in the neighborhood and she was a lot of fun, always cracking jokes about somebody. Aunt Essie Mae got some cloth and needles and went to the counter and paid for them. The white female cashier didn't have a pleasant look on her face to me. I thought all white folks were mean and nasty just from listening to my daddy talk about them.

As we walked out into the parking lot, on this beautiful sunny day, a spool of thread fell out from under Jesse's shirt. Aunt Essie saw it and all hell broke loose.

"Boy, what you got?" she screamed and before Jesse could say anything, Aunt Essie was tearing his ass up. "You gonna stop this shit if I have to beat all the black off of your ass, and I mean it!" she yelled.

What was so puzzling to me was that Jesse didn't seam surprised *or* hurt by the incident. He just stared at her.

"Now let's take it back into the store. And you're gonna tell this lady what you did, you hear me?" said my aunt.

Aunt Essie was furious and I knew it was time to be quiet. Aunt Essie grabbed Jesse by the back of his shirt and began to march him back into the store. I followed suit without a word. Once we entered the store, Aunt Essie's temperament and display captured all the attention inside the building!

"Now tell this lady what you did," she said

The lady was looking at Jesse as if she felt sorry for him. Her reply was unbelievable, even to Aunt Essie.

"Honey, I started to tell your mommy what you did, but I didn't want you to get a whipping. So don't you do that anymore, okay," said the cashier.

Aunt Essie was shocked to know that the lady saw him getting the stuff and didn't say anything. "You should've told me 'cause I ain't his mommy. I'll whip his butt cause he knows better," said Aunt Essie.

"Oh, don't fret 'bout that. It's only 'bout twenty cents. Besides, he's so cute," the lady said.

Well, we didn't get that scoop of ice cream Aunt Essie promised us and I was pissed off with Jesse too.

It was a long ride home with nobody talking, but Aunt Essie, and believe me; she didn't have anything nice to say. The sun had begun to really beam down on the ground when we got home. Aunt Essie was determined to make Jesse remember this day!

"Get the broom and start sweeping the yards," she said to Jesse in a voice that brought no argument.

Even though I was old enough to know that Jesse had stolen some things that had Aunt Essie so upset, I still didn't know exactly what was going on. Well, I got my marbles and started playing near the end of the porch when Jesse walked over to me. He looked like he had won the Heisman trophy as he pulled a pack of buttons out of his socks. Looking at me with pride in his eyes, he said, "I betcha they didn't find these!"

Although I was young, I knew then that Jesse was crazy! Jesse was the kind of big brother that you just couldn't help but be proud of. He was always doing unexpected and, sometimes, fascinating things.

For example, our mother used to fix our lunches for school every morning. There was always one ham biscuit, two preserve biscuits, and a nickel for milk or juice. It seemed like every morning Jesse would step into my classroom right before recess or first period and ask the teacher, "Mrs. Thomas, may I speak?"

It was so routine that most of the time Mrs. Thomas would already be shaking her head.

"Yes Jesse, you may," she would say.

I felt like a very special kid when Jesse would come over and give me a dime, sometimes fifteen cents. I never knew where he was getting the money from until years later. I found out that Jesse would steal cigarettes from daddy's pack and sell them to the bigger guys who thought they were macho. Sometimes he would just bully some of the younger guys and take their money. Jesse just always had a scheme for doing something and he didn't care what it was.

The only time I really hated Jesse was when we would be around the house all week and the tension just had a way of building up. When Friday and Saturday arrived, we knew mommy and daddy were going to be out all day and late at night. On Friday afternoons, Mommy would get ready to go meet Daddy because she knew if she didn't, we wouldn't see him until Saturday morning and by then he'd be broke! Mommy just knew what to do about shit.

Mommy would always give us chores to do before she left.

"Jesse," Mommy would say in her serious voice, "you get some wood cut and some water for this house. Doll, you and Peil sweep these yards and ya'll make sure you wash your feet and be in this house before dark!"

Doll was our sister, the second child, and well maybe the third. Doll was a twin and the other one died in childbirth. When Mommy gave out her words of command, Jesse would look at Doll and me and wink his eye.

"I'm gonna whip that ass when Mommy leaves," he would say.

We knew not to tell Mommy anything while she was leaving 'because she'd be gone too long. As soon as Mommy got in that old Plymouth and pulled off you couldn't hear anything but Jesse's mouth.

"Alright you sorry motherfuckers, I'm the boss now and ya'll got a lot of work to do. So let's get to it!" Jesse would say.

It didn't matter how diligent Doll and I worked, it was never good enough. He was whipping our asses anyway. Jesse had us mind-locked for a long time until one afternoon. He beat my ass so bad that he hit me in my stomach, like the cowboys would do, and I started throwing up! That was when I really started loving Doll. She jumped up with a broom handle and drew it up in the position to hit Jesse and yelled, "Stop hitting my brother!!"

She was in tears when Jesse turned to her with surprise all over his face. "Who you gonna hit with that stick?" he asked.

Doll yelled, "*You nigga!*"

Jesse was stunned at her bravery, but he still tried to maintain control as he tried to rush her to take the stick. He wasn't quite fast enough because Doll got in one good lick with that stick, right in Jesse's side before he grabbed her. Doll's undeniable will to break that cycle inspired me to jump up and help her. I jumped on Jesse's back and grabbed him around the neck while Doll grabbed his legs. It was like we knew from that moment on we had to win or this fool would have a field day on our ass. With my legs around his waist and my arms around his neck, Doll had gained control of that stick and we kicked Jesse's ass! Jesse had knots and bruises, scratches and bites all over him. Jesse had been kicking our ass for so long that that day marked the emancipation of slave and master. It was a glorious day!

After that, Jesse would always try to play us against one another, but that shit never really worked for him. He knew that Doll and I had bonded and we knew exactly who and what he was. As the years rolled by, Jesse's attitude never really changed about things. As a matter of fact, it seemed to grow.

Like the time when Ole' Red, a big red rooster, who was my Momma's alarm clock every morning. As soon as Ole' Red yelled out his cock-a-doodle-doo, Momma would call Jesse and he knew it was time for him to get up and start a fire. He hated that more than anything 'because, at this particular time, it was winter. The mornings were frosty cold and heat was something you had to make early in the morning. Jesse decided to come up with what he thought was a clever idea for not having to get up in the morning. After Momma and Daddy had gone on their potential jobs that day, Jesse decided to kill Ole' Red. He succeeded by hitting him in the head with a broom handle, but to Jesse's surprise, Ole' Red put up quite a fight. It was as though he knew he was in a fight for his life, because he charged at Jesse with everything he had. However, Jesse had the last lick. After Ole' Red flopped around the yard for a few minutes, he gave up on life. Jesse got Ole' Red and set him up in the hen house as though he was asleep.

The next morning Momma overslept by thirty or forty minutes. When she finally got up, she thought, oh, Ole' Red didn't crow this morning, and got up and fixed breakfast. Around eight o'clock she went out in the yard and noticed Ole' Red was still in his nest. She thought it was strange and that the rooster was sleeping too late. Immediately Momma knew something was wrong. It only took one more ass whipping from Jesse for me to tell Momma everything.

* * *

The first run-in Jesse had with the law was not the beginning of his incarceration; however, it all happened when he was fifteen years old. The first time he was picked up by the police was during a gambling raid. They put about six guys in the back seat of the police cruiser, but by the time they got to the county jail Jesse had laid down on the floor. When they got everybody out, somehow they missed Jesse on the floor. Now that was a good idea, but it still had its drawback. Once they closed the door, Jesse couldn't get out. It just so happened that a trustee that was outside cleaning the parking lot was close enough for Jesse to get his attention. The trustee walked over and opened the door and Jesse fled the area.

At fifteen years old, Jesse bought his first car. We never knew where he got the money, but he bought the car from our cousin. One night there was revival at the church and Jesse ran out of gas near the church, and knowing Jesse, there were too many cars there for him to not get him some gas. He got his gas can and cipher tube and headed for the church parking lot.

As he began to draw gas out of the car, to his surprise, the driver's door opened and out stepped a man that began cursing at the thief stealing his gas when he realized it was Jesse.

The man was our cousin, the one who sold Jesse the car.

Our cousin, Horace, made a disturbing joke out of the incident.

He said, "If I had known that I was gonna have to supply Jesse with gas and make a thief out of him, I never would've sold him the car."

Momma then quickly assured him that he hadn't started anything. It was quite clear Jesse was a natural born thief. During that same year, Jesse's real troubles began.

Jesse and a friend of his, Steve, broke into a cleaner's and stole everybody's clothes. They started selling three-piece suits and silk dresses for four and five dollars. Well, it didn't take long for the police to catch up with them, and that was Jesse's first arrest. Because of his age and no prior convictions, Jesse was sentenced to two years, with one to do, but he was released after six months on good behavior. Jesse was sent to Alto Juvenile Boy's Corrections and Momma was sure this would change his life; She was right, but in the wrong direction. When Jesse came home from Alto, we could tell that his bizarre way of thinking had intensified and he was somewhat slightly a different person. He seemed much more mature and more aggressive in his attitude.

At seventeen years old Jesse got a job at the S & S cafeteria as a waiter, in which he worked the breakfast shift. He got off around 9:30 a.m. for a two hour break, then came back to work at 11:30 a.m. until 2:30 p.m. and again at 4:00 p.m. until 8:00 p.m. Most of his hours off, during the day, were spent at the pool hall, and he became known as one of the best pool hustlers in the city. He could win two or three hundred dollars playing pool, then turn around and bet it all back on one very difficult shot. He was so good that eight out of ten times he would make the shot.

One memorable day in the pool hall, Jesse was playing this guy for fifty dollars per game and Jesse just seemed to be in a zone. Everything he did was right. He won six games straight and they raised the stakes and Jesse won three more for a hundred dollars per game. When he was playing the last game, the nine ball was pretty easy to play for Jesse from where the cue ball had stopped. Jesse got up off the ball and said to the guy, "For another hundred dollars, you can put the nine ball anywhere you want to."

The guy quickly grabbed the nine ball and froze it on the cushion and said in a braggard voice, "Motherfucker, you gonna pay me, and I don't want no shit!"

Jesse just looked at the guy with the calmest smile on his face and replied, "Are you sure that's where you want it? Are you sure?"

"Motherfucker, shoot the ball!" the guy yelled, a confidant look on his face that said, "Ain't no way!"

Jesse chalked his stick, walked around the table, got down on the ball, and like magic, he banked the ball across the table in the corner pocket. The guys looking on just went wild, but the guy playing just went to cussing and threw his stick on the table and walked off. Jesse didn't say a word. He just got some balls out of the pool table pockets and started shooting them off the table. By this time the guy was really talking a lot of shit about losing his money. After about ten minutes, Jesse walked over to him and said in a very calm voice, "Man, you told me I was going to pay you if I didn't make that shot, and you didn't want no shit."

The guy squared off as if he was ready to kick Jesse's ass. He yelled, "Get the fuck out of my face young motherfucker!"

Before he could completely finish his threatening sentence, Jesse hit him across the head with the pool stick. He continued to beat him down and was yelling at him at the same time.

"That's why you're gonna take my money motherfucker, 'cause I'm young? Bitch, I'll kill you!" Jesse said.

Another man sitting on the side witnessed the entire ordeal. He jumped up and ran his hand into his pocket, peeling off five twenty dollar bills and said to Jesse, "Hey man, here's your money. Don't hit him anymore. He was wrong, but here's your money."

Jesse took the money and ripped it up into pieces and threw them on the man he'd just beat, who was lying on the floor. As we walked out of the pool hall I asked Jesse, "Man, why did you tear up that money?"

Jesse replied, "After the stupid motherfucker made the shot so easy for me, I was gonna give him that money back anyway. I already got him for eight hundred dollars, but don't ever let a motherfucker think he took something from you."

So I replied, "That shot didn't seem so easy to me!"

Jesse looked at me and said, "A pool table is simply mathematics. Once you learn the angles and hit the ball right, you can put it in the pocket."

I used to sit in the pool hall and wait for Jesse to get his break because I truly enjoyed watching him play. He was very good, and he played cards and shot dice the same way!

* * *

Jesse had worked at S&S Cafeteria for more than two years when he came up with his so-called master plan. He was making most of his money in tips, and he had a lot of free time for his hustle game, but knowing Jesse, that was not enough. Somehow Jesse found out a little too much about the way the cafeteria handled their money. He knew exactly where they were making their night deposit, which was down in the basement in a safe.

Once Jesse found this out, he now felt that all he had to do was figure out how to get enough time to crack the safe. That's when he involved Steve. Once they figured out their plan, they began to watch every move that was being made from the office, and especially when they went toward the basement. From the stock room, Jesse discovered that you could go into the basement through an unlocked door, but not from upstairs.

* * *

It was a beautiful sunny Saturday morning when Jesse went to work. This was the day that they would put their plan into action. Jesse brought a change of clothes for the next working day. They chose to carry out their plan on a Saturday night because Sunday was always a very busy day at the cafeteria. All of the big time white folks had their breakfast there. The Saturday went as always until the last shift, in which Jesse always finished. He bid them good night and went out the door as usual. The plan was that Jesse was to go down the street, cut back into the alley, and come back to the back door, which Steve had left open. Steve normally made most of the stock room deliveries to the kitchen.

Once Jesse got inside, Steve locked him inside the stock room. Jesse hid in a box until

11:00 p.m. He was sure everyone was gone by that time. He had all night to crack that safe. It took him almost all night, but around 4:30a.m.—bingo, the door just eased open. There were cash, business license papers, insurance papers, and some kind of certificate, but Jesse only took cash money, $129,500.00. He made sure he put everything back as it was except the cash. Once the safe job was complete, Jesse changed his clothes so that he was freshly starched and wrinkle free. He put his other clothes in the bag with the money and stashed it in the stock room and got back in his hiding place to wait for Steve.

It was not unusual for Steve to come in a little early on Sunday mornings because he had to be ready for the crowd. On this particular Sunday he was even earlier than usual. Steve was nervous as he maneuvered his way to the stock room and the back door, but Jesse was waiting to ease out. Everything went just perfect. Jesse went out the back door, ran down the alley to the street, and walked two blocks over so if he was seen, he would be coming from the bus stop where he got off the bus everyday.

When Jesse walked into the cafeteria that morning he was all jolly and ready for work, but the safe job was not yet complete cause Steve had to get the money out of the stock room while making a garbage run. That would take place during their first break. He and Jesse never made direct contact except for a few head nods and smiles. Steve had done this for so long it was only routine for him, but this time he took the money out to the parking lot where he'd parked the old Ford. He quickly put the brown paper bag into the trunk and Steve dashed back inside without notice.

It had been about four or five days before shit started to hit the fan. Jesse went to work a little late for the second or third time, and this time he'd already made up his mind that it was time to leave that place and this was his first way out.

"Jesse, we're here at five o'clock so that you can start serving the customers at seven o'clock. What's the problem?" the short white man asked.

"You seem to be the one with the problem. And if you have one, then you still got it cause you can just give me my time!" Jesse replied quite angrily.

"Now you don't have to quit," said Mr. Williams.

He was beginning to sound apologetic because he didn't have a replacement.

"Nah man, you ain't going to talk to me any kind of way on a job like this. Just give me my time and you can have this job," Jesse said.

Jesse had been planning for this day! The next day, after the safe cracking, Jesse went to Bill Heard Chevrolet and asked the sales person if he could try out that 1964 Chevy parked out on the grass with a sign that said "Hot". That '64 Chevy was very "hot". Jesse took the car over into another state and went to a hardware store and had some duplicate keys made. Then Jesse took the car back to the dealer and told the salesman that the car was too fast for him and that he'd changed his mind.

So on the day that Jesse quit his job, he was anxious to get with Steve that night and split up the money. He had been gathering clothes together and doing things all day, him and Steve, but Steve never had a clue that Jesse had made other plans. After everything had been divided equally, Jesse was in a hurry to get going, but Steve still didn't know what was happening.

Around one-thirty that morning, Jesse very boldly walked onto the car lot, over to the Chevy, and stuck his key in the door. At the click of the door lock, Jesse was starting the car and driving off the lot. Since he was only two blocks from the state line, he crossed over in less than two minutes, which was already heading south. Two hours later Jesse was on the freeway heading to Miami!

* * *

As Jesse drove down the freeway to Miami he was thinking how he had shitted Steve on the take because he told Steve the safe only had twenty-nine thousand and he had kept a hundred grand for himself. After all, Steve didn't contribute much to the game plan and he was always scary as hell, so Jesse thought that $15,000.00 for his input was sufficient and Steve still had a job. Jesse was thinking of what he would do once he got to Miami, although he knew he had to be cool and not show any flash. He would just buy a new wardrobe because that free Chevy really deserved a new style of clothes. Jesse made sure that no one knew where he was going, especially Steve because he didn't want him to start tripping about the take.

Jesse traveled about 230 miles before he stopped to gas up again. He pulled into this service station that seemed to do quite a bit of business at this time of night. He needed some coffee to stimulate him and to stretch his legs. As he entered the store, a nice slim cutie pie was standing behind the counter. Jesse noticed that she was checking him out, but he was so much of the I-don't-give-a-fuck kind of fellow, he acted as if he didn't see her. As he walked over to the counter where he saw the coffee pots brewing, the cute young lady spoke up in a very pleasing kind of voice.

"If you'll give me a minute, I'll make a fresh pot of coffee. That one's been there for a good while," she said.

"That's very sweet of you," Jesse said in a smooth tone of voice.

He began to look at her as she walked from behind the counter. She was quite a beautiful woman, but immediately Jesse could tell that she had a very pleasing personality and some damn pretty eyes.

"Are you doing this just for me or everybody?" Jesse asked with a questionable smile.

"Well, everybody else can have what you don't drink," she replied and they shared a laugh.

"Well, if I could pour you in a cup no one else would have anything to drink because I'd take all of you with me," she said.

She leaned up on the coffee counter on one arm and said, "Now see there, you don't even know if I'm sweet or low. You're just bumping your gums."

"But you see lady, with a coffee drinker it wouldn't matter," Jesse said.

In no time flat they had embarked upon some kind of flare that Jesse could see was obviously going his way.

"I bet you have a pretty name too, don't you?" Jesse asked her with a flirtatious smile.

"Huh, I have just a plain old simple name and I really don't know why my parents named me Phyllis."

"Phyllis. That's a beautiful name. What's wrong with it?" Jesse asked.

"Well, actually it's Phyllistine Hill, but I just go by Phyllis for short," she replied.

"Do you work all night every night here?" Jesse asked.

"No. I work the morning shift three days and the nights two. I really don't like this night shift because everybody that comes in here is not nice like you," Phyllis said.

She smiled and they both realized they were staring at each other.

"So if I wanted to come take you to dinner one day, would that be on your work day?" he asked jokingly.

"Well, I don't know but if you let me know a day ahead of time I won't be working. How
'bout that?" she asked. Now Phyllis was flirting too.

"Anybody working in this damn place?" a voice said.

Their little banter was shattered by a voice over at the cash register. There was a guy leaning on the counter looking over at them. From his appearance and mannerism Jesse kind of figured he was a local guy. As Phyllis started back behind the counter she blurted out at the man, "Ah be cool Robert. You know you ain't gonna spend but a dollar."

"Nah, seventy-five cents, and I want my change too. You know ya'll be keeping folks change round here," the man said.

All the while the man was talking to Phyllis, he was looking at Jesse. Jesse knew exactly why the man was looking at him. He was very well dressed and the '64 Impala parked outside kind of gave the impression that they went together. As Jesse finished making his coffee, he walked over to a rack that had fresh slices of pound cake. He picked up one and walked to the back of the store to the milk & beverage area. He opened the door and got a quart of buttermilk and then went up to the counter.

"So where are you from anyway, talking about taking me to dinner," Phyllis asked.

Phyllis was talking to Jesse as she counted the man his money.

"I'm from Birmingham, Alabama." Jesse replied as they resumed their conversation.

"So I guess you're gonna drive all the way from Birmingham to take me to dinner, huh?" Phyllis asked. She looked with unbelieving eyes.

"If I have to," Jesse said without breaking a smile and looking her straight in the eyes. "How can I get in contact with you?" he asked.

She took a piece of paper from the cash register and wrote her name and number on it. "Don't have me giving you all this information for nothing," she said.

"Trust me," Jesse said.

As Jesse was leaving the store he knew he had made contact with something in his future and he was excited about it. As for Phyllis, she didn't have the slightest idea what she had just done, but she knew that she had a feeling that she never felt from a man before.

As Jesse pulled on to the highway he also was thinking of how effective he'd been with Phyllis. She was a magnificent woman and a very good prospect to have as an 'Ace' in the hole.

* * *

Jesse drove about 200 miles before he saw a sign that read "*Miami, 128 miles.*" He thought about getting a room for the night but the thoughts of Phyllis and the coffee had really energized him. By now he was sure he could make Miami in a couple of hours. After loosing himself in thought and what seemed an eternity of twitching around in the seat and turning the radio, Jesse was around by the sign that said "*See Miami.*" When he actually looked around he was about to enter a long stretch of water heading for the tall bridge and by him being from Alabama, he had never seen that much water. All he could see now was water and it was so high it seemed as if it was elevated on each side. "Dade County" a sign read. A few minutes later he saw a White Castle Restaurant and decided to stop there for breakfast. While Jesse ate the hot cakes and eggs, he read the Miami Herald, making a mental list of what he had to do this very first day in this fabulous city.

He had to find "Titus", his cousin who'd been in Miami since '57. Then he had personal business to take care of. First of all, he had to change his driver's license with another name. While Jesse was reading the paper he saw a picture of a man whose home had burned down and the paper stated that the man didn't save anything. He stopped chewing as he looked at the man and thought that there was a strange resemblance between him and the man in the newspaper. Jesse started thinking about the things that this guy could've lost, such as his driver's license, his identity on paper as a whole. He started contemplating what he could do to change his own identity.

"Can I have another glass of milk please?" Jesse asked the waitress.

The little lady that was standing near him with her order pad just nodded in agreement while she continued to tally up some people's order who was sitting across from him. Around the same time, a man walked through the door with his hat turned to the back of his head. He had the look of a streetwise person, which was exactly what Jesse needed in this city so that he wouldn't have a lot of problems finding his way around. However, Jesse went back to his food and the newspaper without giving this guy anymore thought. He finished his breakfast and laid a twenty-dollar bill on top of his check but he continued to sit there until the little lady came back over to him and asked him if everything was alright.

"Yes ma'am. Everything was just fine. Now if you could tell me how to get to Liberty City I'd appreciate it," Jesse said.

For the first time Jesse realized the little lady was of Cuban descent.

"I don't know this place," she replied with a warm smile, "but maybe this guy knows," she said referring to the guy with the hat turned backwards.

"I will ask for you if you like," she said.

"Thank you very much," Jesse said.

She walked over to the counter where the guy was sitting and asked him something. Then the guy looked over at Jesse and immediately got up and walked over to his table.

"What's happening man?" the guy asked in a husky-like voice.

"Nothing much," was Jesse's reply as he was extending his hand to the guy. "Jesse man, Jesse is my name."

"They call me Buster man," the guy said, taking a seat at the table. "So you trying to get across town to Liberty City, right?" asked the guy.

"Yeah man. My cousin lives in Liberty City. I just got in here. I'm from Alabama and I need to find out where he lives, but once I get to Liberty City I can find him," Jesse said.

"Well, I can tell you how to get over there man, but if you got a moment, let me grab this food. I'll show you how to get there because I'm going over there. I live on that side and I know a lot of people over there. I might even know your cousin," Buster said.

He started talking as though he'd known Jesse long before now.

"Yeah, that's cool man. I got plenty of time. Go ahead and eat," Jesse said.

He was indirectly trying to analyze this guy. So far he seemed to have his head on pretty straight.

"My cousin's name is Wallace Wilson. They call him Tit," Jesse said.

Buster's face lit up, "Tit from Alabama man. I know him. He works down at the laundry. Is his wife's name Ella?" he asked inquisitively.

"Yes, that's them! Ah shit man. I have known them for years. Hell, I use to live right behind them," the guy said.

By now Buster seemed eager to give Jesse all the help he could. Without a doubt this information gave Jesse a more relaxed feeling about Buster. From that point they started talking about Miami and what goes on in the Magic City!

* * *

As they rode across town Buster was quite impressed with Jesse, but he didn't pry into his business even though he complimented his car, his clothes, and his entire make up. They started to open up to each other and started sharing bits and pieces of each other's past. That's when Jesse found out that Buster did time in a state prison. The more they talked, Jesse couldn't help but think that this guy just might be worth knowing.

Following Buster's directions, Jesse drove straight to the laundry where Tit was working. As they parked the car, got out and were about to start for the front of the laundry they heard a voice that just brought back memories to Jesse. He recognized Tit walking toward them from the back of the building where the employees take their break.

"Man, what the hell you doing down here?" Tit was saying as the two men met and embraced each other with lots of laughter.

"Man, I saw ya'll pull in and I said 'who's that in that sharp ass Chevrolet? Then I saw that big ass head and I told Johnny that nigga look like my cousin, and damn it's you!" Tit said.

There was more laughter. "How you doing cuz?" Tit asked.

"I'm doing just fine Tit. How about you and Ella man?" Jesse asked.

"Still mean as hell and want to know my every move. You know her," Tit replied.

The three guys were making a friendly scene out there in the parking lot because some workers had now taken the time to stop and stare at the trio.

"What's going on Buster? How you meet my cousin?" Tit asked.

Tit and Buster were shaking hands. "I just met him at the Castle over off Monroe. He was trying to get over here and when he told me who he was looking for, shit I told him we go way back," Buster said. He was laughing and talking at the same time.

"Well, believe it or not man, but this is my cousin that I used to talk about. This nigga here is something else," Tit replied as he was reminiscing of days of he and Jesse's past.

"I can tell you some terrible shit about this nigga!" Tit said.

For some strange reason Buster could not understand, he felt a strange closeness to Jesse even though he'd only known him for a few hours. Little did he know that Jesse had that charming kind of schoolboy affect on some people.

"Man I need to get back to work, but I get off at five. Why don't you let Buster here show you how to get over to my house, if ya'll ain't hanging out," Tit said.

"That sounds good man because I need some rest. I've been up for the last twenty-four hours, but I can't wait to see the rest of this city; but I like what I've seen so far," Jesse said.

He and Tit embraced each other again and Tit proceeded back to work while Jesse and Buster headed for Tit's house. Ella was quite happy to see Jesse when she opened the door. She flashed a big grin and yelled, "Boy, what are you doing down here. Oh my God, you are looking so good, these women gonna go crazy over you. Come on in because your cousin's at work," Ella said.

"I just left him, but hell, I told him I wanted to see you because he's too ugly," Jesse teased.

They both had a hearty laugh.

"How are you doing Buster? I ain't seen you in a while. How you know Jesse?" Ella asked.

She was quite puzzled.

"I just met him a few hours ago but it seems like I've known him for years," Buster replied.

"That's just like him to find somebody that knows us. That's the way he is," Ella said.

"Well, hey man, I'm good right here. This is my area but take my number so when you get some time, give me a ring. Go ahead and be with your people and I'll catch you a little later, alright?" Buster said.

"Thanks for everything man. I'll be in touch with you soon," Jesse said.

Buster and Jesse embraced and off Buster went. Jesse and Ella talked for what seemed like hours before Jesse nodded out on the sofa. She woke him and told him to go into a bedroom and get some sleep. She'd wake him up when she finished cooking, but that was the end of Jesse's first day in the Magic City of Miami.

* * *

Jesse made considerable progress in the two weeks he'd been in the city. He'd gone to the driver's license bureau and portrayed himself as the guy he'd seen in the newspaper. He didn't receive anything but sympathy from the lady at the bureau after she thought he'd lost his house and everything. The he adopted his alias name Al Sims. Jesse also found a job at a seafood restaurant called *Edith & Frenchie*. He'd been working for three days now and the only reason he wanted a job was to conceal the fact that he had a large sum of money. He didn't like his job because he didn't like the smell of fish, but it didn't take him long to win the confidence of Edith and Frenchie because of his willingness to work and his pleasing personality. In no time he was operating the cash register and making purchases from producers. It also didn't take him long to see a flaw in the owners' trust of him because he now knew where they kept the checkbook and the cash.

One night after he and Buster spent a night out on the town from pool halls to nightclubs, they had already been confiding in each other's criminal history and Jesse found out that Buster had been in jail for burglary. Jesse shared a few jobs that he'd pulled, but he never mentioned anything about the cafeteria job.

The next few months you could catch Jesse and Buster together almost every night. They burglarized a few places and were making pretty good moonlighting money. Jesse was getting pretty tired of the fish house job, so he started making plans to leave. One morning when he came in a little late, Frenchie was a little upset and asked, "What's the problem Al? Can't you make it in here on time?"

Jesse really didn't like his tone of voice, but he didn't say a word. He just went on into the kitchen and started taking some fish out of the large freezer. For the next few hours he and Frenchie avoided each other, but Jesse had already come up with his plan. He noticed that Frenchie didn't keep very good records at all. He mainly ran his business right out of his head. Therefore, it wouldn't be hard at all to work a few checks on this place.

A couple of days later Jesse decided to quit and gave Frenchie his resignation, but not before he tore off a sheet of checks from the middle of Edith and Frenchie's business checkbook. The next couple of weeks Jesse and Buster managed to cash all six of the checks around town. They also spent quite a bit of time over in Ft. Lauderdale where Jesse met Mary Hunter.

One afternoon they were just shooting the breeze and riding around. They stopped at a street corner where a crowd had gathered and this loud-mouthed man was shouting to the people, "I'm too pretty to be beat. There ain't a man in the world that can beat me. Sonny Liston, you don't have a chance," the man said.

"Hey man, that's Cassius Clay," Jesse said getting out of the car and walking across the street.

"Take a good look at me. I'm the next heavyweight champion of the world!" the man said.

Cassius Clay was doing a very good job of promoting his upcoming fight with Sonny Liston. He was really putting on a show. Jesse stood there and took a long look at this guy. He seemed so sure of himself. He was invincible, he was great. That was the first time in Jesse's life that he thought he could see some mental similarities between himself and someone else. He too had always wanted to be the best at what he did. He had a burning desire to be different. Jesse knew then that Cassius would some day be the best fighter in the world, but now he was talking shit like he was the best man on the planet. As Jesse and Buster were moved in closer, Jesse came face to face with a pretty black skinned woman who seemed to be staring at him and he returned the amazement. There was some kind of chemistry creating emotions between them. They both seemed willing to go along and let nature take its course.

"You sure are pretty," Jesse spoke to her while they continued to eyeball each other.

"Thank you," she replied with a warm look of flattery on her face. "You trying to blow my head up like that man up there's head is ain't ya?" She asked.

They both started laughing and at that very moment he knew he wanted to know more about her. She had a humorous personality and she was fine too. At that moment Jesse's attention split between Cassius and this lady, and he found out her name was Mary. As Cassius lured the crowd to believing he was the greatest, Jesse and Mary started talking.

"You don't know who that is?" Jesse asked her.

"All I know is he's a big mouth nigga with an ego problem," Mary replied.

They started laughing again.

"That's Cassius Clay. He won a gold medal in the Olympics in '60," Jesse said.

Jesse went on rattling off to her about how bad he was, as if he knew him personally.

"I ain't ever heard of him because I don't know nothing about boxing," she said bewildered.

Buster, Jesse, and another man standing there started really bragging on Cassius, then she asked surprised, "You mean this is somebody famous?"

"He's not as famous as he's going to be if he beats Sonny Liston," Buster said bursting into laughter.

Cassius ended his little charade by inviting the people to his exhibition during his training over in a Miami gym. Jesse invited Mary to the exhibition the following day and she agreed. They saw each other nearly everyday for the next couple of months. A serious but casual relationship developed which had more problems than good times; Also a pretty little girl named Jessica was born.

* * *

By this time Jesse was living in Ft. Lauderdale because the business checks from Frenchie's surfaced and the Miami police were looking for Jesse for questioning. Jesse knew that he had to stay clear of the police by all means. Having two pair of licenses helped him out.

When he was stopped, he would use the license that he thought certain situations and geographic locations would determine. It didn't take too long for the trail of robberies and break-ins Jesse and Buster had been leaving got hot. Jesse had been in Ft. Lauderdale for about six months and he was hot as a firecracker. Nor did it take too long for the heat to follow him there. Jesse allowed his picture to be taken at Frenchie's one night after Frenchie was taking some pictures with a Miami Dolphin football player. Even though it was not Jesse's intention, he was the waiter in the background of the picture as he worked.

The picture was showing up in certain areas. That's when Jesse realized it was time for him to put a few miles between him and Miami. Even though Jesse had been in Florida for less than a year, he had still done a lot of shit and Buster was right there with him. He thought Jesse was a smart nigga and maybe he was. The whole time he was there, he never said one word about the money he'd taken from S & S in Columbus Georgia. However, he met and befriended a woman that he thought was of high standards and class. He really liked her too and he didn't want to blow it with her, because he knew he could never have a woman like this if she knew what he was about.

She even invited him to go to church with her one day. He kind of shined her on, but he was willing to go if he could have this lady, and she accepted him as he was. Her name was Ruby Reed. She was a very beautiful and intelligent woman. She was the only woman that Jesse met in Miami that had her own business. She owned and operated a black art studio. She imported fine black art from Africa and she sold the finest of items, such as perfumes, colognes, jewelry, etc. She had a very good business and what was so inspiring to Jesse was the fact that she was a very business minded person.

They met one day when it was raining and she pulled up to the restaurant and continued to sit in the car waiting for the rain to stop, but Jesse was sitting in the restaurant by the window. When he realized she didn't have an umbrella and he did, he immediately got up and took his umbrella out to her car and gave it to her and ran back inside. She got out of the car real grateful and hurried inside. Once she got inside she walked over to Jesse and smiled and said,

"That was very gentlemanly of you. Thank you very much."

"That's the way my momma raised me," Jesse replied, smiling with the look of approval.

"Ah, seems like your momma is a real nice lady," she said.

"I'm hoping you'll have the pleasure of meeting her one day," Jesse said. Asuby looked him in his eyes with a questionable stare, "maybe so," she replied as she started walking away from the table.

It was obvious that she had a little interest because she kept looking and occasionally smiling. Jesse eventually got up from the table and started for the cashier, but he had another thought. As he turned and walked over to her table he politely said to her, "I hope I'm not disturbing your dinner, but is it possible that I could take you out to a much nicer restaurant for dinner anytime soon?"

He was standing across the table from her.

"Well, the food is good here," she said. She knew that she had blocked his question but she gave in, or gave him some play. "But if you know of a better restaurant, then we can talk about it," she said.

Without further ado, she pulled out a piece of paper and pen, giving him her number. Three days later he called her.

"I thought you'd lost the number," she said into the phone.

"Well, I just didn't want to be a bug, you know," Jesse said.

"Oh, it's no bug. I'd love to try a new taste in food. So what place did you have in mind?" she asked.

"There's this nice place I know of down on Ponce de Leon that I'd like to take you. They have good seafood. You do like seafood don't you?" Jesse asked.

"I love seafood but I can't get away today. Maybe tomorrow, how's that?" she asked.

"That's fine," he replied.

For about three months Jesse and Ruby shared a very casual relationship that never involved sex, mainly because the right time just never arrived. However, they did find a certain kind of trust and confidence in one another. It was more of a relationship about character and honesty that kept them constantly trying to satisfy each other's curiosity. Jesse knew that Ruby would be a good woman to have in his corner because she had good business sense and he felt a loyalty from her that he never felt before. All the time he was in Florida, Jesse and Ruby kept close communication with each other. Jesse managed to keep his private life a complete secret from her, even little Jessica, his daughter by Mary Hunter.

Jessica was now about three months old. Mary already realized that she'd made a mistake with this man. Even though she really loved him and didn't mind having his child, she realized that he was just not the marrying type. He had an elusive way about him that constantly made her wonder just what did he do. Where was he during the many nights she spent alone? Why did she continue, only to get no answer from him whenever he did show up? He was very generous with the money to take care of their little girl, but she knew that he didn't have a job, yet he always had a pocket full of money. That really made her very skeptical of him.

All of these thoughts ran through her mind, only to vanish at the sight of his face.

"The heat is on / Heat waves"

Things were really getting hot for Jesse, not only in Miami, but Ft. Lauderdale too and there had been talk that the police were circulating pictures of him around the Miami area. Jesse knew that if he stayed in Florida it would only be a matter of time before his luck would run out. He had to figure out what he would do with the money he had in the trunk. He made plans to leave Florida in a couple of days. He went to the airport and got a safety deposit box in the name of Jimmy Ogletree, his legal name by birthrights, but also a name that he hadn't been using. He put $68,000.00 in the safe deposit box and walked out of the airport. He only kept $5,000.00 in his possession because he knew that if he got caught it would be easier to explain $5,000.00 rather than $68,000.00 in cash. After making some contacts with a few people, he decided to hit the road for higher ground.

Ruby was his last stop. They met for dinner at their favorite little restaurant where they first met. Ruby wanted to ask all kinds of questions but she couldn't find the right words because she didn't know what it was that bugged her so much about this man. He was mysterious to her and he had this clever way of answering her questions with a question and making her feel somewhat silly.

She drove back to her house in a stupor of confusion. She could feel that something was wrong, but what? All the while they had dinner she could tell that he was deep in thought. It was as if his mind was a million miles away. As Ruby pulled up in her driveway, Jesse drove right in behind her, all the time thinking what and how was he going to tell her he had to leave town. He knew he had to use tact and finesse because Ruby was a very clever woman. By the time Ruby had gathered her purse and keys from the ignition, Jesse was there to open her door with a big smile on his face.

"Gee, that was a quick move," Ruby said.

"Listen, we have to talk for a minute. Do you have any milk? I want a glass of milk," Jesse said.

"Yes, there's some milk in the house. Let's go in," Ruby said.

They started for the house. When they got inside the door, Jesse pulled Ruby to him and planted a passionate kiss on her lips. She was totally shocked because that was the first time he'd ever attempted to kiss her or show any kind of feelings of endearment to her in any manner. She didn't know him to take this type of love attack, but the feeling was right.

"Well, now what was that all about?" she asked surprised.

"Well, I think you already know that I'm attracted to you. I want you to know that, but I just can't show you how much right now because I have to leave town for a little while," Jesse said.

As he spoke he was searching her face to see how she was taking the news.

"There are some things going on back in Columbus that I have to take care of right away. And now is not a good time to tell you," Jesse said.

He had a very serious look on his face and for the first time Ruby began to see or feel a little something different.

"Well, I'm sure you'll tell me when you're ready. So keep in touch when you're away. But you haven't left yet," Ruby responded.

They embraced and went farther into the house. After a few minutes inside, they were becoming very intimate until the phone rang. The phone broke that moment of ecstasy that was building between them. After Ruby talked to the person on the phone for a brief moment, the whole mood of the evening seemed to be back to normal.

"I want you to do me a favor if you don't mind," Jesse said. He was looking her straight in the eyes. "I mean you don't have to do anything. I just want you to keep something for me," he said.

"Something like what?" Ruby asked.

She was now seriously interested. Jesse smiled because he could see that it was time to give up the few answers he could afford to share.

"Baby, all I need you to do for me right now is just keep this key, ok," Jesse said. He was making sure he didn't say anything that would start Ruby to asking questions.

"Jesse, I know we don't have a committed relationship, but I am quite fond of you, and I don't want anything to happen to you. I really wish you'd just shoot straight with me. I want to know what's going on with you," Ruby said.

It seemed that for a minute, Jesse would reveal a side of himself that very few people knew. But just like Jesse, he just smiled again and said in a very childlike voice, "now is not the time to tell you what's going on with me, but I promise you that once I get back, I'll tell you everything ok?" he said.

It sounded more like a deal than a promise, but Ruby also thought that now was not the time to pressure him with her curiosities. So she'd just take what she could get for now.

* * *

Things were really heating up around Miami and Ft. Lauderdale for Jesse and Buster. They knew they had to get out of Florida. Jesse was about to go back over to his place, but as he started to turn down his street, he saw the detectives parked on the side of the street. He slowly kept on down the street and made a right turn. He knew he had to warn Buster, but he wasn't about to go to his house. As he was driving down 35th, he saw a girl that Buster had told him was his cousin. He stopped and got out of the car. He walked over to her.

"Hey baby, have you seen your cousin Buster?" Jesse asked.

She said no, but she had seen his car on the next street over.

"Oh yeah? How long ago?" he asked.

"About fifteen minutes," she said.

"Okay, thank you baby," Jesse said.

He drove around the corner and there was Buster just about to leave. Jesse pulled up on the side of the car.

"Hey man, the fucking detective's watching my place so I'm getting up out of here. What's up?" Jesse asked.

Buster knew that if they were looking for Jesse, they were looking for him too. "Well shit, that means I need to move too," Buster said with concern on his face.

"What are you gonna do? I mean where are you off to?" Buster asked.

"Well, I just wanna get the fuck out of here. Then I'll look for a place to sit down," Jesse said.

"If we hit the road our luck might change," Buster said.

* * *

Later that night Jesse parked his car around the corner and walked all the way around the block looking for anything that looked suspicious. He was very cautious, but he also knew that the detectives really didn't know who he was or if he really stayed there because he was hardly ever there.

He quickly went in the house and grabbed his clothes and stuff and rushed back out of the house. He set his suitcase on the side of the house and went back for the car. He got his clothes and went for Buster. About forty-five minutes later they were on 75 heading north. As they rode and talked they thought it would be a pretty good plan to do a little work while they were on that end. Meanwhile, Jesse had planned to go back through Tampa because he had often thought about the girl he had met when he was on his way to Miami. All the while they were riding, he was thinking if it would be a good move to take that spot off because from what he'd seen that night, they did a lot of volume business.

"Hey man, I know this place in Tampa that might be good for work, but I met a girl up there and I don't know if that would be a good idea," Jesse said.

"Well, let's look it over first because you know man, you never know," Buster answered with much enthusiasm in his voice.

Then Jesse remembered that night he was in that store. He remembered Phyllis had gone down a little hallway that said Private Keep Out. He knew that must be the office. That's when it all came together.

"I got it man!" Jesse said.

Buster could tell from Jesse's voice that he had come up with something. Jesse was still quiet for a few minutes, as though thinking. Buster didn't say a word because he knew now that Jesse won't answer anybody until he's ready.

"Man I really don't want to take the candy stick to this little girl because I really do like her, but I do believe they have some money up in that place. The business is good and security is kind of weak. The office don't look like an office, it's more like a bathroom. It's kind of a sleeper if you don't know. If you think you can trick the lock on the door, I can hold the little girl because the last time I talked to her she couldn't wait to get her hands on me. But it's just my luck the bitch has probably gotten herself fired," Jesse said.

"Well, that don't matter because whoever is there, if you hold them I'll get the door," Buster replied.

These were two criminals who had a lust for living off the fruit of the land and that kind of zest made them very good at what they did. They rode down the street past the store, just looking around and checking things out. Suddenly Jesse said, "Things look pretty good around here. There seems to be quite a bit of business going on. As you know, when we enter the building we don't know each other."

"Hell, we don't know each other anyway!" Buster replied.

They burst out laughing. After looking the place over Buster got out of the car about a half block from the store and Jesse drove off, pulling up on the other side of the parking lot. His view was almost obscured. Then he got out of the car taking his time walking towards the opening door. He saw Phyllis standing behind the counter. As she looked up at the door, she couldn't hide the surprised joy on her face or in her voice.

"Oh my God!" she exclaimed, completely forgetting about the lady standing in front of her. "I don't believe my eyes," she said

They were both smiling.

"I came back to marry you this time," Jesse said, and even the lady at the counter shared in on the laugh.

"Oh I'm not sure that I'm ready for that kind of trouble, but I will give you a hug," Phyllis said.

As she leaned across the counter, they embraced with good feelings.

"I didn't think I'd ever see you anymore," she said.

Before Jesse could answer the woman at the counter said, "So ya'll getting married huh?"

Stephanie said, "He just joking honey. He probably already got a wife."

Jesse put his hand on the lady's shoulder. "You're invited to the wedding so don't be late," he said.

As Phyllis was giving the lady her change, the lady cracked, "Oh no. I don't do weddings and funerals because both of those are a dead end."

As the lady got to the door, Buster was holding it open for her. As Buster walked in he kept straight to the back where a sign read Restrooms. By now Jesse had Phyllis's complete attention and Buster didn't take but about ten seconds to jimmy the office door with a plastic card like a driver's license. To his surprise the safe that was sitting behind the door wasn't even locked. Within two minutes Buster was coming out of the office and went in to the bathroom.

His blood was rushing through his head, but he knew he had to be cool because he had gotten a moneybag out of the safe that was pretty fat. He didn't hesitate at all during the whole job, but once he was in the bathroom, he went straight into a stall and dropped his pants, putting the bag inside his drawers. When he pulled his pants back up, there was no trace anything happened.

He stayed in the bathroom for a few minutes to calm his nerves. He washed his hands and walked back out to the Coca Cola box and got him a Coca Cola. Then he walked to the counter, sat the coke up there and paid for it. He nodded his head to Jesse and said thank you to the clerk and walked out the door. He walked back to the same place Jesse had put him out and sat on the bench at the bus stop.

After a few words with Phyllis, Jesse asked her about a hotel and pretended to be tired and sleepy. He promised her that he would be taking her to dinner the next day. Once they finalized their date for the next day, Jesse squeezed her hand and flashed that smile on her that he knew would work for him. He walked out the store and went to his car. He took his time, started up the car, and pulled out of the parking lot. He drove back to the bus stop and picked up Buster. Buster was waiting patiently for the car to pull up but he was damn sure ready to go.

"Man, that was sweeter than bear meat. Goddamn, I thought I had to work for this but they were waiting for us to take that shit," Buster said, rapping in a spiel of excitement.

Jesse was laughing. "What did we get?" he asked.

"I don't know. It just felt so good keeping my balls warm," Buster replied.

The car filled with laughter. At the same time he was pulling the moneybag out of his pants. Jesse insisted that they get a little distance between them and Tampa. He drove most of the night and stopped off and got a motel room about forty miles outside of Leesburg. Only then did they go into the bag and count the money. The "Creep Job" had netted them $6328.00 which wasn't bad for a stopover. This was also probably the smoothest job Jesse and Buster ever pulled.

* * *

They slept until about two o'clock before checking out of the motel. It was a beautiful day outside and Jesse found it quite pleasant. After they had some dinner at a little restaurant just across the street from the motel, they were on the highway heading for Leesburg. Jesse's second cousin Marcellus, on his mother's side of the family lived in Leesburg and Jesse had planned to stop over for a couple of hours.

When they started into the city limits, Leesburg seemed like a lazy little family town without a lot going on. Jesse knew he couldn't be around here for long. It was too small for him with his problems. After being in the city for ten minutes, Jesse saw Woodland Boulevard, which was where Marcellus lived with his wife Rogers and their two kids Pam and Petey. It was the first time Jesse had ever seen Pam and Petey, but he grew up with Marcellus for years in Crawford, Alabama before he left for Leesburg. He met Rogers the year before Marcellus left for good. She had come to visit Marcellus once.

When Jesse pulled up in the yard and they got out, Rogers greeted him with open arms. She was such a pretty lady, long pretty hair and the Cherokee Indian in her really brought out her subtleness and warmth.

"Well, my, my, what a surprise. Marcellus is going to be knocked off his feet," she said with a grin as she hugged Jesse.

"How's that old man doing? I know he's getting old," Jesse said.

Jesse and Rogers were bursting with laughter.

"And who is this pretty little girl?" Jesse asked, gently picking up the baby and kissing her on her cheeks.

Jesse had a genuine love and affection for children period. After Rogers finished talking about the kids, Jesse introduced Buster.

"This is a friend of mine Rogers. His name is Buster and he's riding back up the road with me," Jesse said.

Rogers reached for his hand in a warm welcoming grip. Then she invited them inside. The house was very neat, clean, and well coordinated. Because she was cooking, she had them come into the dining area of the kitchen where she cut them big slices of cake from half of a cake under its cover. They talked about the families and Marcellus's work. He owned an orange picking business that seemed to be paying off pretty good. Finally Marcellus walked in and all the hugging, grinning, and compliments of meeting old loved ones started all over again. Rogers set up a table that was fit for a king and his royal men. It appeared that she had cooked for a party or something. As they were sitting at the table, Jesse asked, "All this food just for us?"

"Ah, it ain't nothing but leftovers honey," Rogers said.

"You better taste it before you flatter yourself," she said.

They all went to laughing again.

"And all that we don't eat today is gonna be leftovers for tomorrow, ya hear me? Leftovers around here is another family member," Marcellus said.

By now they were having a great evening. After they finished eating, Marcellus took them both downtown for Jesse to meet some more of his relatives. They rode around for about three hours before going back to the house. Once they were back Jesse pulled out a hundred dollar bill and passed it over to Rogers. She looked very puzzled.

"Now Jesse, you know you don't owe us any money. So put that back in your pocket boy!" Rogers demanded.

She went to turn around and Jesse said, "Oh I'm not trying to pay you Rogers. I want you to buy the kids something for me. Whatever they want, do that for me okay?" he asked.

Only then did she take the money. After a little while Rogers bid them goodnight after she tried to get them to stay the night.

"We'll make some room," she'd insisted.

But Jesse and Buster had planned to hit the road later that night. After words of appreciation and farewells between them, Rogers left the room. The men continued talking for a couple more hours before the Jesse and Buster decided to leave. It had been a wonderful day and they were in high spirits, not having the slightest notion things were about to change for the worst. They hadn't been gone five minutes from Marcellus when they were coming out of Woodland Boulevard, getting onto highway 27 north when Jesse noticed a patrol car parked across the highway at a service station. He didn't think anything about it until he made a left turn onto 27 and the patrol car pulled out behind them.

"Heads up man, the cop pulled out," Jesse said.

Buster never moved, but a second later, red lights were flashing with a couple of quick siren sounds to fill the night air.

"We're coming from Miami going to Birmingham, Alabama," Jesse said to Buster.

"Alright," Buster replied.

As the cars came to a halt, the officer slowly opened his door getting out and walking carefully to the driver's side.

"Afternoon sir," the officer said, looking at them very closely.

"How you doing?" Jesse replied.

"Can I see your driver's license? Where you boys headed?" the officer asked.

"Birmingham, Alabama," Jesse answered.

The officer, while shining his flashlight all around in the car said, "Birmingham huh? You boys haven't been drinking have you?"

"No sir. We don't drink," Jesse said.

"Okay. I'll be right back," the officer said

He walked back to the patrol car.

"This shit don't feel right man," Jesse said.

"I was about to say the same thing. It's taking that motherfucker too long just to check you out," Buster said.

They sat there for about ten minutes and they noticed two other patrol cars approaching at a fast rate of speed and proceeded to block them in. By that time the officer got out of the car, he yelled, "Mr. Ogletree, get out of the car with your hands up?"

Jesse made sure that he gave him his Alabama license, but now he felt that could've been a mistake. In all, there were five policemen on the scene now. As Jesse was getting out of the car he asked, "What's the problem officer?"

"Are you sure you don't know boy?" the officer asked. By now the his voice changed. "There's a warrant out for your arrest Mr. Ogletree." Then the questions started coming. They made Buster get out too and read both of them their rights and handcuffed them. The arresting officer then walked over to Jesse and said, "Boy, this must've been bad luck for you. I have me a system where I randomly stop and check every fourteenth car just by habit. You were number fourteen and it seems that you're wanted back in Columbus, Georgia," the officer said.

"What do you have on the other one?" another officer asked. "Well, there's nothing yet, but we better take him in for questioning," another officer insisted. This was the beginning of a long and winding road in Jesse's life, a road that seemed to lead to nowhere, but with no ending. Jesse had given the officer his Alabama license because he thought that if there were a warrant, it would be for the city of Miami, not Columbus Georgia. The officers put Jesse in one car and Buster in another car. As a matter of fact, that was the last time Jesse saw Buster for years. After finding out that Jesse was wanted on burglary charges, the officers didn't have many more questions for him. Jesse knew that as long as he didn't see Buster anymore, they hadn't connected him and Buster with anything from Miami or Tampa.

They finally let Jesse make a phone call around ten o'clock the next morning. He decided to call Rogers. After three rings Rogers answered.

"Hello," she said. "Rogers, this is Jesse. I want you to listen to me very carefully. I'm in Leesburg County jail and I won't be getting out any time soon. I want you to do something for me. You won't be in any kind of trouble. I just need you to do me a favor. Are you listening?" Jesse asked.

His voice was serious, but Rogers was completely dumbfounded.

"Jesse, what's wrong? Why are you in jail?" Rogers asked.

He could hear the nervousness in her voice. Jesse's calm tone of voice calmed Rogers down.

"The state of Georgia had a warrant out for me Rogers. Right after we left your house last night, the police stopped us just as we got on 27 and they found out that I was wanted for burglary. All I want you to do for me is come down to the police station and pick up my belongings for me. I'll write you a letter telling you what I want you to do for me," Jesse said.

Rogers heard herself saying okay, but what was she really saying? She had always been very fond of Jesse and she didn't believe he would do anything to jeopardize her freedom.

"Okay. What do I do?" she asked.

"When you come down, come to the control desk and tell the officer that you want to pick up Jimmy Ogletree's belongings. They'll give them to you and I'll try and get you or Marcellus a visiting pass to come only one time to see me. I promise I'll return you the favor," Jesse said.

Rogers asked herself a thousand questions without answering even one. Was it alright to go down there? Should she call Marcellus? She couldn't. Was Jesse some kind of con man? Is this his way of life? She came to one conclusion before she left the house. She got down on her knees and prayed for guidance and protection.

When she got down to the police station, she asked a policeman where did she go to pick up belongings and he pointed her to the control room. She walked in looking very uneasy and uncertain, but for some reason she wasn't as frightened as she thought she'd be.

"What can I do for you?" a voice asked from behind the dark thick glass which she couldn't see through.

"I want to pick up Jimmy Ogletree's belongings please," Rogers answered.

"What's your name?" was the reply.

"Rogers Hudson," she said.

A few minutes later a side door opened and a tall slender officer came out of the control room with a manila envelope and suitcase. He also had a clipboard with a list of Jesse's belongings on a white sheet of paper. After Rogers identified herself, the officer had her sign the sheet and she gathered all the stuff and headed for the door. It was a lot of stuff, but she didn't want to have to make two trips because just the thought of imprisonment was really claustrophobic for her. When she got back to her car she was numb and sweating, but relieved. Rogers was so excited by the time Marcellus got home, she could hardly tell him what had happened. She'd never had such an exciting day in her life, a day filled with nerve wrenching emotions.

Jesse wrote Rogers a letter that same day but he didn't say too much, only that he wanted her to come see him before he was transferred. As he wished, the county sheriff allowed Jesse to have one visit from Rogers on the first Saturday that he was incarcerated. Rogers walked into the visiting room corridor after being searched, which she thought was quite humiliating. She knew then that this would be her last visit. There was a series of phones on the wall and as she walked down the hallway, a lady called to her.

"Hey miss!" she said.

She turned back and the lady was pointing to a window. She saw Jesse grinning at her as though everything was all right.

"I didn't see you," she said through the phone. "How you doing? What's going on? Why are you in here?" Rogers asked.

She had a lot of questions before Jesse could answer one.

"Well, Rogers, it's a long story, but I'll tell you this much. I'm wanted back in Columbus for burglary, and I don't know what they might try to do to me. But I will keep in touch with you and let you know, but meanwhile, how's Pam and Petey?" Jesse asked.

"They're fine. I didn't tell them anything about what happened." Rogers said.

She never really took her eyes off of Jesse.

"What I want you to do for me is send my clothes and things to my mother's. Was my watch and rings there?" he asked as he gave her the address to his mother's.

"Yes. There was three rings, a watch, two hundred eighty-six dollars and some change," Rogers replied.

Jesse really didn't know if it was okay to say what he wanted to say to her, but he decided to take a chance. "Listen Rogers, very carefully. Take my suitcase and pull the back of it from the inside. There's some money in it, about four thousand dollars. Take whatever you need out of it and send the rest of it to my mother's please. Don't worry about me. I'll be all right. I don't know what kind of time I'm facing, but when I get to Columbus, I'll try to get me a lawyer and try to make bond," Jesse told her.

"Oh no Jesse, I'm not gonna take any of your money. I'll send it all to your mother because you might need it. I'm all right, just glad to be able to help you," Rogers said.

"Well, take some of it and buy the kids something for me. Do that," Jesse said.

He sounded as though this was very important to him, so she said, "Okay, if it'll make you feel any better."

The thirty minutes of visitation went really fast for Jesse. Before he knew it, the officer was telling him his time was up. They said their goodbyes and Rogers was gone. For Jesse, this was the beginning of an eighty-year prison sentence stretch that lasted off and on for approximately thirty-four years. The next day he was transferred to Columbus, Georgia.

"Routine change of Learning"

Muscogee County jail hadn't changed a bit. Jesse had been there before. The first two or three days were interesting. He was just catching up on the happenings around Columbus because he knew a lot of the guys in lockup. Jesse didn't realize the importance of time because his life was about to take a turn for the worse.

Somehow the detectives that investigated the S&S Cafeteria burglary found some fingerprints that matched up with Jesse's perfectly. A warrant for his arrest had been in effect for quite some time. As a matter of fact, the detectives had been to mother's house on two different occasions. When Jesse made contact with the family, he sent postcards addressed to and from the same person, therefore he never heard anything from home.

The Georgia Bureau of Investigations (G.B.I.) had tried unsuccessfully to involve Steve Baker in the burglary, but they didn't have enough evidence to connect them together. Jesse was sentenced to twenty years by the state of Georgia and after the Georgia conviction, Dade County in Miami declined to file the charges against him, which was the only break he had for about two and half years. Jesse had been transferred to a camp in Hamilton, Georgia after he had left the Diagnostic Center in Jackson, Georgia.

The Hamilton Correctional was more of a work camp and the white redneck prison guards just couldn't find enough work for a pretty nigger like Jesse. He looked like he was educated and they wanted all educated niggers to learn the redneck way of doing things. First he was in the pea field for about three weeks and then they transferred him to the farm where they were raising hogs and cows. He didn't like the job at all and he knew absolutely nothing about cows and hogs, but he knew one thing. He knew he had to get the hell out of here. He could not imagine seventeen more years of this bullshit.

Jesse had looked around and thought of every possible way of leaving this camp, but they had dogs that would catch your ass and horses that would run your ass down. So whatever he came up with, it had better work.

* * *

My mother and I went to see Jesse at the Hamilton Correctional Facility and we visited mostly all day. We brought some food, but just sandwiches because Jesse didn't tell us what he could have. It hurt my mother very badly when she first saw Jesse in those prison clothes. She started crying and reciting bible verses that gave her some sort of comfort. She was laughing and crying at the same time and we all wound up in a one big bear hug.

Momma asked Jesse at least a thousand questions about the penitentiary, and he tried to answer every one of them. He had made her a very beautiful shoulder strap purse with matching wallet and key case.

"See Momma, if Jesse hadn't come to this place you wouldn't have all this special made stuff," I said with a big laugh.

The lady sitting at the next table started laughing too. Momma was so glad to see Jesse that it appeared she just couldn't take her eyes off of him for long periods of time. She touched him, hugged him, and then proceeded to start low raiding him for all practical purposes. She told him all about how these kinds of things are really hard on a mother and that this kind of carrying on would drive her to an early grave if he kept it up. All the while momma was talking to Jesse; he just held her hands and kind of smiled. I knew that what she was saying to him was going in one ear and out the other.

The visit was finally over and momma was looking at Jesse as if she'd never see him again. My heart went out to her, but one thing I knew for sure at that moment, was that momma didn't need to visit these places too often. The drive back home was very quiet and peaceful, but I knew my momma's heart was filled with the pain that every mother endures when she sees her son behind bars. Momma said after a while, "I'm gonna cook my son a real special meal in two weeks when we come back up here."

She had that look of love in her eyes and her voice.

"Momma, that place hurts you too bad to see him in there. Do you think it would be a good idea for you to come back in two weeks?" I asked.

"Baby, it hurts just as bad not to come," she replied.

* * *

The next couple of weeks for Jesse were filled with planning and trying to figure out just what he needed to do to make his plans work; because he knew he had to get out of this hell hole of a work camp.

One thing he had to figure out was just how to deal with the guards and inmates here. He realized that they held him in high esteem because his case involved a safe cracking job. They thought that you had to be a real professional criminal to pull off such a job. Besides, most of the guys here had simple cases that involved nothing more than drugs, moonshining, burglary, or wife beating, etc.

Jesse was working on a detail with a guard that had been put out on the farm against his wishes. Before this job, he was just walking around the camp fucking with everybody, especially the black inmates. Then one day there was a disturbance between two inmates and he hit one of the guys in the eye with a Billy club, causing near blindness to the guy's right eye.

Even though the guy filed a complaint against the correctional institution, the only thing that happened was the officer just got transferred to the farm. Due to the fact that most of the guys on the farm were black, the attitude of the officer changed considerably. Jesse thought of everything he could to find a way out of there and he kept coming up blank. He knew that running off on foot was a suicide move because he'd been told that those hound dogs they have at the back of the camp just loved that running shit. They get the chance to eat your ass up. Jesse would lay awake night after night trying to figure a way to get some time between him, freedom, and the law enforcement. He also knew that whatever he did it would have to work, because if it didn't, he would be bound for Reidsville State Prison.

The two-week visit that my momma and I planned to make seemed like a couple of months to Jesse, but finally it was visiting day again. Momma had enough food to feed half of the place. She cooked practically everything that Jesse loved. Not just the food, but also the warm hugs Momma was giving Jesse made him feel like this was a very special day. Even the guards in the visiting room had to have a slice of the caramel cake that Momma had baked.

This guy named Nate that slept in the next bed over from Jesse had befriended him for about a year. And on this day his uncle had come down to visit Nate, and Jesse invited them over to have dinner with us. Jesse and Nate constantly made joking remarks on each other in penitentiary humor. Through small talk, Jesse discovered that Nate's uncle ran a little Bar-B-Que hut, which Nate told him, was backed up by a little bootleg joint. It seemed like he made pretty decent money from it and Jesse could look at him and tell that he was an old country hustler. Nate's uncle was named Willie George and he couldn't stop thanking Momma and complimenting her on the taste of her collard greens.

"Man, now that's the way collard greens suppose to taste with ham hocks in them. Miss lady, you can feed me any day of the week," Willie George said, with a big burst of laughter.

The rest of the day was quite nice until it started getting close to time to go. There were emotions and a few tears from some of the older mothers. Finally, everyone said goodbye and the remainder of the day Jesse just sat real quiet and watched the sun slowly slide down behind the tall pine trees that gave this God forsaken piece of land a touch of life.

Since that visit was the most eventful day that Jesse and Nate had seen for quite a while, it was only natural that most of their night was conversation about the visitors and just the day in general until Nate drifted off to sleep. Jesse was just laying there sleepless and with the whole world spinning around in his head, when all of a sudden he started reminiscing back over some things that Willie George had said about the collard greens and ham hocks. "Ham Hocks" he thought, hell he saw ham hocks everyday and couldn't stand the sight of a hog, but he also heard an old man in there say, "If life gives you lemons, then you make lemonade." Before he realized it, he had a pretty good plan in mind, but he would have to really think it through and figure out his strategy.

The next day Officer Pete (the officer that hit the guy in the eye) came up to Jesse and said, "Ogletree, you're on the feed detail today."

"Got damn," Jesse said to himself.

The feed detail was a sloppy job because they had hog pens everywhere. They had hog pens at least two miles from the camp way back in the woods, but close to an old cut through road that was hardly used anymore. Jesse said to Officer Pete, "Damn man, ya'll trying to break me in right? First this nasty ass farm and now this shitty ass feeding job."

"Well Ogletree, you think I like this shit? Hell, if I didn't have a family to feed, why shit, I'd be looking for me a job tomorrow!" Officer Pete said.

"But shit, you can quit if you wanted to, hell I got twenty years." Jesse said.

"Why hell, you can quit too Ogletree. They'll just throw your ass in the hole," the officer said.

He laughed and Jesse knew he was practically joking, but serious all at the same time. He tried to be cool with the guys down at the farm because he didn't have but a few white boys out there. As time went on, Jesse thought that he could see a way out of there. He began to look forward to the feeding detail and to his surprise; Officer Pete was not a bad guy. The more they worked together, the more they communicated.

The facility was centered on hogs. They had some kind of contract with the state about those hogs. They killed hogs daily and sold them to companies and to the officers and employees of the institution. Jesse also realized that this program was not being operated as it was designed to because he saw lots of foul shit just from being in the know.

* * *

A couple of months later, Jesse found out that Willie George was coming back to visit Nate the following Sunday. So he immediately wrote me a letter and insisted that I come visit him on the same day because it would really help him with his time. l made sure I was there because the only thing I wanted was to see my older brother out there on the street. Visiting had barely begun when I arrived and went inside. I was anxious to know how my presence would aid my brother in this freedom. As we sat there talking, Jesse never seemed to mention anything about his plans of freedom. All we seemed to talk about was what so and so is doing? And is so and so still married to so and so? Suddenly Willie George came into the visiting area and came straight over to our table as he waited for his nephew Nate to come in.

We all greeted each other with humor and laughter because the first thing Willie George asked was, "Where's your momma man? Did she send any more of them collards?" he asked jokingly, keeping the humor going.

But it was quite obvious to me that Jesse had something on his mind because he immediately got serious with Willie George.

"Man, you said you ran a little restaurant, am I right?" Jesse asked.

"Well, it's a little Bar-B-Que place. It ain't much," Willie George replied.

"How much Bar-B-Que could you sell if you could get all the meat you wanted?" Jesse asked.

"Oh hell man, you know ribs cost good money. You don't make a lot off a case of ribs," said Willie George.

He was looking at Jesse with the look on his face asking, "What's the sudden interest in my little business?" Jesse didn't keep him waiting because he didn't want Nate to know or hear anything about their conversation.

"I think you might like what I have to say if we could talk for a minute," Jesse said.

"Okay," Willie said.

"I can get you all the meat you can cook and it would only cost you pennies on the hog," Jesse said.

"Oh yeah. How would you do that?" Willie George asked.

"Well, let me work a few things. We need to talk again on the next visiting day. How about that?" Jesse asked.

"Sounds good to me, just as long as I don't get in no trouble man. You know I leave these places up to ya'll because hell, I can't do this shit man," Willie said.

He laughed. By that time Nate was coming out, so Jesse said, "Just keep this between us, alright?"

"Oh you know that," Willie George said as he was getting up to greet his nephew. "How you doing boy?" he asked Nate as they moved over to another table next to us.

Jesse then explained to me just what I had in mind. He also advised me that it was necessary for me to come back in two weeks so that I could get back on the visiting yard. So for the next two weeks, Jesse spent all of his wakeful hours trying to finalize his plan and get closer to Officer Pete.

"How long you been working here Pete?" Jesse asked the officer.

"Too damn long if you ask me, they don't pay me enough to smell this shit all day. Sometimes I hate to think of coming over here," Pete answered.

"You live around here?" Jesse asked.

"I live in between here and Waverly Hall, about ten miles," Pete said.

Jesse gathered a little personal information for a couple of days on Willie George before he decided to crack Pete. He wanted the timing to be right. Finally, after they had been talking about the cost of living, Jesse decided to crack him.

"Man, how come you ain't making some of this money like the rest of these guys?" Jesse asked.

"Shit, what money? Ain't no money being made around here," Pete said.

"Shit man, look around you, you don't see anything?" Jesse asked.

Jesse felt that Pete was a good candidate for more money, so he didn't have anything to lose. Officer Pete was standing over near a large tree drinking a Coca Cola, when Jesse walked over to him and said, "Pete, if I told you how you could be making good money and not have to worry about getting caught or fucked up, you wouldn't have me locked up would you?" Jesse asked.

He was grinning and looking far away very casual.

"Well I couldn't have you locked up anyway, but what are you talking about?" Pete asked.

"Man I could tell you how to make some real money. Shit, it's simple Pete. I know a man that cooks meat everyday, and he has a pretty good business going. If you could move some of these hogs you could be making a killing!" Jesse said.

Jesse's heart was beating fast with anticipation. Officer Pete's face had the look of interest. Jesse knew that he had won old Pete over when he said, "You ain't got to go back out right now Ogletree. You can do it later."

So Jesse kind of relaxed and started telling Pete all about the plan and how he could operate it.

"Now all I have to do is get you two together and ya'll can work out the rest," Jesse said.

He had Officer Pete all ears. The rest of the week was easy work for Jesse. He had things going his way so far. All he had to do now was make sure Willie George went through with everything. The next visiting day went just fine and Willie George was there just like he said he would be.

I arrived at the institution about the same time as Willie George. That seemed to be something we had in common. I guess we just tried to spend a whole day with the guys since we had to be here in the first place.

Willie George was his usual old talkative self as we greeted each other, and had a few words to exchange as we waited on Jesse and Nate to come out.

As always Jesse came out first, and had about ten minutes of conversation with Willie George before Nate ever came out.

Jesse didn't waste anytime getting into the plans he had in mind. I was sure he realized he didn't have much time.

"Willie George, what if I told you that I could get you as much meat as you could cook out there, would you be interested?" Jesse asked, looking at Willie George as if he was trying to see his thoughts, his strength, or his weaknesses.

Willie George was looking kind of surprised, interested, and cautious as he seemed to analyze the situation, but before he could say anything, Jesse began to explain his plans.

"Man I got a cracker guard that hates these muthafuckers here as much as I do. He's pissed off with the system, and I can work the shit out of him. He's pissed off with the wardens and shit cause they put his ass out on the hog farm, and it's fucked up out there. So you see man, we can make some money!" Jesse explained.

I think the word "money" caught Willie George's attention because at that point, he spoke. "Well, hell yeah, I mean, how safe is this man? You know I ain't gonna get in no trouble now. I'll leave this shit to you and my nephew," he said with a grin.

"Ah really, it ain't gonna be no trouble, all you have to do is buy the meat. These crackers don't know how many hogs they got, or what happens to half of the shit here.

Everybody's getting over on the meat one way or another, but I have a good plan. Are you interested?" Jesse asked point blankly.

"Yeah, hell yeah, I just want to know how you gonna do it, and make sure I can cover my ass. I ain't got no problem making a little money!" Willie said.

Jesse could tell that Willie George was coming around, and the two men started talking more openly. Jesse told Willie George that the guard would let him put hogs in a pen approximately half a mile from the hog pen. All he had to do was leave the money and pick up the hogs about three o'clock in the morning. Willie George would leave fifteen dollars a hog under a rock. Officer Pete would pick it up.

"I got everything straight in here man, as long as you go along with me," Jesse said, "but we'll talk some more later, here comes Nate."

The rest of the day went very smooth, and so did Jesse's plans.

A couple of days later, Jesse sprung the entire plan on Officer Pete. Jesse would take two hogs a day to a pen that the institution no longer used and it was the perfect place for Willie George to get in and out without trouble. Jesse thought about leaving from here, but he wasn't sure that Officer Pete wouldn't blow the whistle on him before he could get off the farm. Therefore, he had to win his confidence.

They had been doing business for approximately three months, and Officer Pete was making pretty good money. And then one day he asked Jesse, "Olgetree, what made you want to help me make money like this? What's in it for you?" Officer Pete asked.

Jesse figured that Officer Pete already knew his game plan, but wanted to hear it from his mouth. So he replied, "Well Officer Pete, I'm hoping that one day you'll let me leave this nasty muthafucker!"

They both laughed. Then he said, "But I'll stay around until you get you another boy to do my job because you can do this shit as long as you're here. They don't have any way of knowing how many hogs they have or how many you sell," Jesse said.

"What you trying to do now, get me fired?" Officer Pete asked.

"Nah man, I got that figured out too. Man I can't do no fucking twenty years in this shit. I got a plan that you can help me with and nobody will ever know," Jesse said.

At this point Jesse had already figured out just how he would leave there, but Officer Pete just walked off as if he didn't want to hear anymore about it. Jesse didn't press the issue. Officer Pete and

Willie George had been doing business for about four months and it was going very well before the subject of Jesse's leaving ever came up again.

Jesse put at least two hundred pigs in the makeshift pen and Willie George was coming down a back road over the woods between two and three o'clock in the morning picking them up. The plan was foolproof. It was so good it almost seemed legal. Nobody was really in any danger of being caught. Jesse's patience was wearing pretty thin by now. He knew he had some good shit on Officer Pete, but he also knew that it was very important to have good timing too, so he just kept planning and thinking.

Finally one day the warden called for Officer Pete to come to the office about a rumor that the guys working in the hog pen were making mash and he was allowing them to drink. Even though it was true, Officer Pete really didn't know anything about it, but the warden threatened to put him on suspension without pay if he heard any more rumors. Officer Pete was really pissed off about that to the point of saying, "Fuck this shit! I can find another job if he keeps fucking with me."

Jesse knew it was time to make his move. The next day, Jesse was moving some newborn pigs from the pen to another when Officer Pete walked over to where he was. Before Jesse could begin to speak of his plan, Officer Pete really surprised him with the words that came out of his mouth.

"Ogletree, I know pretty much what's on your mind and if that's what you want to do, I won't stop you. I won't help you much either. Now, if you have a way of leaving here, I won't report you until they miss you, but we never had this fucking conversation, okay?" Officer Pete said.

At that point he paused and looked Jesse straight in the eyes. Jesse's heart was racing so fast now he had to think before he spoke.

"Give me a couple of days and I'll be ready to go," Jesse said. "And you bet your sweet ass we never had this conversation," Jesse said laughing with joy.

"All I want you to do for me is have Willie George to bring me some clothes to the pickup pen at ten o'clock in the morning on Friday. Will you do that?" Jesse asked.

"I'll think about it, but my name doesn't have to be mentioned okay?" Officer Pete asked.

"Okay," Jesse replied.

The next day Officer Pete made certain to stay clear of Jesse. He never said one word to him. Jesse was just thinking of how he would get out of the Hamilton, Georgia area without any trouble. He knew that he had to get out of the area quick. He barely slept at all that night because he was full of anticipation.

That Friday morning was looking like rain when the man gathered at the back gate to go down to the hog pen. As soon as they got there, Officer Pete walked over to Jesse and told him, "Ogletree, I want you to take them to shoats (hogs) down to the south pen at about 9:30 and be back in two hours."

Jesse knew that this was his cue and Officer Pete gave him a sly look and walked off. Jesse drove the hogs up into the little trailer after hooking it up to the tractor and drove off. Willie George was waiting for him.

"Come on man, hurry up," Willie George said.

Jesse cut the tractor off, jumped down, went over to the fence and ran like hell behind Willie George. Willie George told Jesse to get in the trunk of the '53 Chevy and Jesse didn't hesitate. He jumped in the trunk in one single motion. He felt like he'd just bought him a first class ticket to freedom, and man did it feel good!

The ride in the trunk was something like a roller coaster and moving at this speed after being incarcerated for a long period of time has a real dizzy effect on your equilibrium. Willie George stopped after what seemed like eternity. He opened the trunk with a big grin on his face.

"Man, you have a helluva lot of nerve. How the hell you talked that cracker into letting you leave there?" Willie George asked.

"Shit, it wasn't no problem after he had sold you all them got damn hogs," Jesse said laughing. "Man, where the hell are we?" Jesse asked.

His head was still swimming as he was looking around.

"We are almost in Columbus, Georgia," Willie George answered, "I pulled on this little road so you could put these clothes on."

"I need to get to Phenix City man. I can make it from there," Jesse said.

"That's no problem. Officer Pete told me to make sure I got your ass out of Harris County. Man, you had your finger in that white man's eye didn't ya? When he first came to me with that proposition, I was kind of scared to mess with him. But when he told me how to get the hogs, I knew that this would be a piece of cake because that hog pen where you were putting them hogs is on my granddaddy's land," Willie George explained.

Jesse knew that the next few days were his most crucial and he had to be very careful about how he moved around. When he got to Phenix City, he went to our cousin's place in Fredrick Douglas apartments. Horace and our first cousin Doll Baby had lived there for about twelve years. Jesse was hoping that they hadn't moved. Once there, he took a long bath. Horace went out and bought him some more clothes and later that night he drove Jesse to Crawford.

When the knock came at the door, it was surprising to the family because hardly anybody ever came to our house after dark.

"Wonder who that could be?" Momma asked as she went to the door.

"Who is it?" she asked.

"It's me Momma," Jesse's voice rang out.

"Boy what are you doing here?" Momma was saying all the while she was opening the door. "Oh my God," momma said.

Momma was hugging Jesse so tight we couldn't even get to him, but we were all so glad to see him that we found a way. Horace didn't stay long after he brought Jesse there, and it turned out to be good that he didn't because less than an hour later as we were all sitting in the living room, I saw some headlights pulling up in the yard. We all knew immediately what and who it was.

"It's the police!" I yelled and Jesse was already running for the back door.

"Ya'll go to bed," Momma quickly said.

About that time a loud knock came at the door. Knock, knock, knock.

"F.B.I., open the door," they said.

That was the voice we heard even before Momma could ask who it was. Instead she asked, "What do you want?"

"Ma'am, you need to open the door. We're looking for Jesse Hodge, alias Jimmy Ogletree. Are you his mother?" the police asked.

At that time Momma had opened the door and the F.B.I. detective identified himself by showing Momma his badge, then a picture of Jesse.

"This man escaped from the Harris County Correctional Institution today. Have you seen him?" he asked.

Momma looked at the picture very nervously and in a very quiet voice she said, "Nah sir, I haven't."

"Ma'am I hope that you know that if you know anything about this man's whereabouts you're violating the law if you don't tell us. Do you know that?" the officer asked.

Before Momma said anything two more officers walked in the door. They had gone around the house to cover the back door when they first came up.

"All I know is he's in that place you just said. Now that's all I know," momma said.

Momma was nervous, but she stood her ground.

"Do you mind if we look through the house?" he asked.

"No I don't. Go right ahead," Momma said

I could tell Momma was somewhat getting her composure back.

"What made you think he would be here?" she asked.

"Well, this is just routine Mrs. Hodge. We really don't know where he might have gone, but if you hear anything from him, you would be helping him if you gave us a call," the officer said.

He was passing Momma a card and she took it. In a voice filled with motherly love, Momma said, "Please don't ya'll hurt my child, please."

That's when I saw the tears rolling down my Momma's cheeks and my fear immediately turned to anger. I hoped at that moment that they would never catch Jesse.

"Well Ms. Hodge, that's up to Mr. Ogletree, but you call us ya hear?" the officer said.

The F.B.I. left as suddenly as they had arrived. We watched their car lights as they faded beyond the trees. We were all in a state of shock. Where did Jesse go? Why didn't the two men that went around the house see him? We were puzzled. Momma went to the back door and called, "Jesse! Jesse!"

"They gone?" a voice said with an echo.

To our amazement, Jesse pulled himself up out of the well.

"Oh my God boy, what if you had fell in that well?" Momma asked with more fear in her voice now than when she was talking to the F.B.I.

"I'd rather fall in the well than go back to that place," Jesse said.

When we got back in the house, I think we were the happiest family in the world because we had beaten the F.B.I. at their own game. After we laughed, cried and ate, Jesse told Momma that he had to go because they would probably come back by there in the next couple of days. Momma asked, "Where are you going?"

"I don't know yet, but I'll be alright," Jesse said.

Momma told Jesse to go up to our Cousin Helen's house and spend the night. That way he could get a good night's sleep, and that's where she took him. Even though Jesse got a good night's sleep, it was quite apparent that Helen did not because she and my Momma talked all night long.

When Jesse came in the house the next morning, he didn't stay but a little while. He got the suitcase that Rogers had mailed to Momma three years ago and to his surprise the county jail in Leesburg had left all of his belongings in his bags, even both pairs of his driver's license. Jesse gave Momma $150.00 from the money in the back of the suit case and I then drove him to Tuskegee, Alabama to get a greyhound bus ticket to Miami, Florida. And that was the last time we heard of Jesse for almost four months. He said that they wouldn't be looking for him to be catching a bus out of Tuskegee and apparently he was right.

"Rainy days of sunshine, again"

It was a long and tiring bus ride for more than six hundred miles, but Jesse enjoyed every minute of it. When the bus entered the city of Miami, Jesse had a very good feeling of nostalgia, but he had to be quite discreet here until he could get himself together. Once off the bus, he got a taxi over to Titus's house, and just like before, Ethel was home alone. As Jesse got out of the taxi and started walking up the sidewalk Ethel saw him through the screen door. She rushed to the door with opened arms to greet him.

"Jesse, where have you been? I been thinking about you and wondering whatever happened to you," Ethel said. She was overflowing with laughter and hugs. "You looking so good," she said.

Jesse was just grinning and said, "You looking good yourself Ethel. How's my cousin doing?" he asked.

"Same old fool," she said as they burst out laughing. "But he's doing fine. I heard about some trouble you had. What happened?" she asked.

"This damn old sleepy headed ass police woke up just in time to stop me in Leesburg and the bastard found out that I had an outstanding warrant back in Georgia," Jesse told her. "Of all the fucking cars in the street that night, can you believe he told me he had a system where he stops every fourteenth or fifteenth car and my number came up? Ain't that some shit?" Jesse asked.

"Yeah, Buster told us some of what happened and I think he just got back out of jail," Ethel said.

"Where's he at now?" Jesse asked.

"I think he lives with a lady across town Jesse. Titus knows how to get in touch with him. Let me fix you something to eat and you know where to go if you want to relax or anything," Ethel said.

Jesse and Ethel talked the rest of the afternoon until Titus got home and then they talked half of the night. It was good to be free!!

* * *

Back in Columbus and Phenix City, the local news carried Jesse's picture and a summary of his escape at every news briefing. Being small cities in size, it seemed that everybody was talking about it and because Jesse had left the state when he robbed S & S Cafeteria, and now had escaped from the state of Georgia, the case was turned over to the F.B.I. Momma seemed to be quite annoyed at what people were saying, but for me, I was real excited and proud of Jesse. For some strange reason, it seemed that Jesse was some kind of hero. To me, Jesse lived on the edge of some kind of adrenaline that most people never dreamed of. Grownups would say stuff like, "That boy Jesse got more nerves than Billy the Kid. Man, Jesse is something else." And when I heard these things it gave me a real charge just to be his brother.

* * *

Jesse didn't want to be too visible in Miami the first couple of days and he knew he couldn't stay there, so he had to make some contacts and get out of Miami as soon as possible. Titus located Buster for Jesse and they immediately started planning to do something. This was their first time talking to each other since that night in Leesburg, and they had a lot of talking to do. However, the police never locked Buster up that night. Instead they let him go to his surprise and he caught the bus back to Miami. His parole officer revoked his parole as soon as he got back and he wound up doing two years and a couple of months and had only been out a few months.

"Man, I have a few people to see, and it might take me a couple of days but we need to get together if you want to hit the road. I can't stay here," Jesse said.

"Hey man, I'm ready when you are. Now that I'm off that paper, I'm free to float," Buster replied. "But this time let's go for the real money."

"That's my plan and we won't stay anywhere too long," Jesse said.

Jesse's next move was to get in touch with Ruby because he needed some money so that he could move. When he walked into Ruby's shop she could hardly believe her eyes and she started smiling.

"I'm gonna whip you," she said playfully hitting him and hugging him at the same time. "Why haven't you called me?" she asked.

Ruby was almost in tears of joy. After hours of conversation, feeling and touching, Ruby closed the boutique and spent the remainder of the afternoon with Jesse. The following morning Jesse got $3000.00 from the airport safety deposit box and eventually found his way over to Mary's house in Ft. Lauderdale. Mary couldn't believe her eyes when she saw Jesse getting out of the taxi. The first thing that came out of her mouth was, "Jessica, here comes your father. Go give him a hug."

Jessica was looking real puzzled at Jesse when he picked her up and started kissing her all over her face. "What you been doing sugar plum?" he asked.

"My name Jessica!" she stated.

"Your name ain't Jessica. You trying to fool me," Jesse replied.

Jesse played with Jessica for a long time and then he, Mary, and Jessica walked down to a supermarket not far from Mary's house. Jesse was never one to really tell you the whole truth about anything, especially when it came to his business. So even though he and Mary did a lot of talking, she never knew that he was a wanted man. All he really told her was that he had some business to take care of and he would be in Miami, but only for a few days and he would be going up north. Jesse gave Mary some money to buy Jessica some clothes and shoes. And just as suddenly as he'd come, he was gone leaving no forwarding contacts whatsoever. Mary could sense that something was not right, but she didn't want to think that something was wrong either. Jesse was such a mysterious person you really couldn't say what was going on with him.

Buster bought a 1957 Ford. It ran very good and Buster told Jesse that he bought the car with some of the money that they had taken that night in Tampa.

"So that means that half of this car belongs to you," Buster said.

That comment brought about their first real healthy laugh.

"You mean they didn't take that money from you?" Jesse asked.

"Hell nah man. They didn't even search me cause I told them I was just getting a ride with you to show you how to get downtown. Them muthafuckers told me I could leave and I went back over to your cousin's house and he took me to the bus station. I got the hell out of town and about three months later that parole officer of mine got pissed off at me cause I wouldn't get a job and sent me back up for the rest of that time I had to do," Buster explained.

After Jesse and Buster made some last minute contacts they were on 75 heading north. Once they filled up with gas in Miami, they drove about 300 miles before they stopped to gas up again, which was in a little town just outside of the Jacksonville, Florida exit. They got back on 75 to Tifton, Georgia before they decided to take a rest break.

Their conversation was all about casing some banks. Jesse undoubtedly knew that he would be caught at one point or another because he'd read a Columbus, Georgia newspaper and saw a small article in the paper about his escape. There was no picture or anything indicating where he might be, but he would stay clear of Georgia and Florida. After the rest break, they drove straight for Birmingham, Alabama, stopping only for gas and a Denny's restaurant for food. Once they entered the city of Birmingham, they rented an Extended Stay motel room with a stove and refrigerator and a completely furnished living room with two beds. The little place was a cozy little laid back motel. The first couple of days they just slept and rode around looking at banks, exits and freeways.

Jesse had met a guy in Hamilton Correctional named John Wesley, who was serving time for armed robbery that was from Birmingham. He'd left Hamilton about a year after Jesse got there and they spent countless nights talking about what they were going to do once they were free. The second day in Birmingham, as they were riding down a street in the black section of the city, Jesse saw a pool hall called *Rack & Cue*. He told Buster to pullover.

"Man, you think you sharp enough for these muthafuckers? You know it's been a while since you hit them balls," Buster said.

Jesse just laughed. "I might be rusty, but it won't take me but a few days to clean up my game. So I'll just set up some game now," Jesse said.

Buster had seen Jesse run racks of balls plenty of times and he knew that when Jesse's game was on and he was in the zone, couldn't nobody beat that nigga on that pool table. As a matter of fact, the pool table was Jesse's best hustle. Jesse seemed as though he could command the balls to go in the pocket once he hit them. Jesse was so sharp when he walked in the Rack & Cue; he couldn't help but demand attention. Them niggas were looking at him like he was the second coming of somebody great. They walked over to the bar and sat on a couple of stools. The bartender walked over to them and to Jesse's surprise, the bartender said, "Man, the only nigga I know be clean as you is known as Bro. Gunn. Man, that nigga be clean," the bartender said.

"Where is Gunn? Man, I'd like to see him if he's in town," Jesse said.

Gunn was a con man, the best. Gunn could talk a radio out of its music. He was interesting just to be around because of the way he heard shit. He found game in damn near everything. Jesse immediately got into conversation with the bartender after he introduced him to Buster. A little while later, Jesse got a pool table in the corner and started hitting the balls by himself. That went on for about an hour before a tall slim man asked Jesse if he wanted to hit a few. Jesse took him up on his offer with pleasure. Even though Jesse wasn't hitting the balls as good as he could, he still felt the confidence of skinning just the average player, but Jesse said it was mainly because of his willingness to play for any stakes. The higher the stakes, the calmer Jesse was and he had a smooth way of putting on the pressure by betting on hard shots. They rolled the balls for the break and the slim man won. They started playing for two bucks and they traded back and forth for a while with the slim man leading by a few dollars, which was exactly what Jesse wanted. All the while they were playing; Jesse was steadily trying impossible shots. He was still practicing, and then out of the blue the slim man said, "Man, we just trading money. Let's make it a little more interesting. Whatcha' say?"

Jesse asked, "What do you have on your mind?"

"How about five dollars, my man?" he asked.

"That's cool. You wanna raise the stakes?" Jesse asked.

They each dropped five dollars and folded them snuggly under the table's edge. Jesse was an old pro at this game and he had no intention of winning any games today. He knew that all eyes were on him. After about three hours of play, the slim man had won about seventy-five dollars off of Jesse. That's when Jesse tightened up a little and won about three straight and that's when the slim man found something that he had to do, so he called it quits.

For the next few days Jesse would go to a little pool hall downtown and practice half a day before he would go into the *Rack & Cue*. It didn't take long before he was kicking ass, but he still wasn't putting all of his concentration into the game as he would when the money got right. Jesse was playing some guy that played pretty good and Jesse was playing him the old 2-1 game, you win two let him win one. Then all of a sudden the tall slim guy that he'd played a few days ago came into the poolroom and walked over to their table.

"Well man, I see you got my hustle," he said to the other man.

"Oh, so I'm your hustle?" Jesse asked.

"Well, if you want to hit a few with me, you know that ass belongs to me!" the slim man said.

It was something about those words that really got under Jesse's skin. He knew that it was time to get the respect that he knew he deserved, and to seek out the real player with the money around here. Jesse won the next couple of games and the guy folded.

"This time we're playing for money. How about ten dollars a game?" the slim man asked.

"That's what you call real money?" Jesse asked.

"I thought you're talking money, just don't over play yourself because I don't want you to quit after a few games. I'll tell you what, twenty a game," the slim man said.

Jesse looked over at Buster with that grin Buster had seen many times before, and then he said, "That's fine. Let's hit the balls."

Jesse won the break. The next four games, before the slim man won a game or had anything to say, Jesse started winning at will, talking a little stuff at the guy and kicking his ass.

"So I'm your hustle huh?" Jesse asked.

The slim guy would come back with a few words but Jesse was steadily breaking him down and from that point on, Jesse made a real statement in Birmingham on the pool table. After Jesse had skinned Slim for about three hundred dollars, Slim had decided to hang it up until Jesse said, "Hey slim, one shot. Double or nothing, I'll play this ball all the way down the table past, the side pocket in the corner for the same money, deal?"

Slim looked at the shot Jesse had set up on the table. "Ain't no fucking way," Slim said, "Bet!"

With a lot of low bottom English and the right angle, Jesse shot the ball straight in the pocket because it was a shot he'd been shooting every since he started playing. Slim was so dumbfounded that he thought it was all just luck, and even though he didn't have any more money at the moment, he knew he had to get Jesse back. What he never realized was that he was out of Jesse's league. For about the next couple of months all Jesse and Buster did was hang out around the pool hall and go by a couple of banks everyday, just looking around. They kept a very low profile. They were never really visible where they went because they took turns looking things over and comparing their views.

In the meantime, Jesse made a real statement on the pool table. Guys from everywhere were coming to try and beat him and the more they came, the better Jesse got. It even got to the point that some of Birmingham's best players wanted Jesse to spot them at least one ball, but whenever he gave a spot, he owned the break. If he made anything on the break, which was ninety-five percent of the time, he ran the remainder of the rack. Sometimes he'd play four or five games before ever giving up a shot. One night after Jesse had won over three thousand dollars off of a guy that drove a Coca Cola truck for a living, he turned around and betted two thousand dollars on one shot, which was the same shot frozen on the cushion above the side pocket. Just like before, the ball just slid straight down the table for the end corner pocket. After about three months, it was about time to make a move.

Jesse and Buster had talked to another guy named Lester about their plans for the bank and he was willing to do his part, which was driving the getaway car. So now that they had made their plans, they would just wait on the first rainy day. They didn't have to wait long. Actually less than a week it was raining pretty hard on that Wednesday when Jesse, Buster, and Lester decided to rob the Birmingham First National Bank.

It was about 5:54 p.m. when Jesse and Buster entered the Birmingham National Bank with skull caps pulled down over their faces. Before the guard could react to anything, Jesse immediately apprehended him by taking his gun. Buster then threw a coat over the video camera mounted up in the corner of the walls. With the nickel plated .38 pistol in his hand, Jesse yelled out, "Alright, everybody on the floor where I can see you, cause everybody knows what it is."

The people seemed most willing to cooperate, by doing just what Jesse said.

"You," Jesse shouted, while pointing to a very pale looking white lady behind the counter. "Fill this bag with money, and be quick about it."

The lady began running from the teller window packing money in the bag. "Hurry up, I don't got all day!" Jesse shouted. The bag was stuffed with money as Jesse snatched it from her. He and Buster ran from the bank door, and to their surprise, all hell was about to break loose. Somehow somebody must've alarmed the police. A car was coming down the street when they came out, running for the car. That's when another form of panic came in. The damn car wouldn't crank. Instinctively, Jesse just kept running past the car and down the street as fast as he could.

When he reached the corner, there was a man and two women in a car at the traffic light. Jesse snatched the back door open, jumping in the car, and yelling to the driver to drive off, as he flashed the pistol, and dropped a handful of money on the front seat. The man was looking real frantic until he saw all that money, then his whole demeanor changed. He pulled off almost burning rubber in the old car, running through the red light.

"Just get me out of the area man; I ain't gonna hurt nobody ok?" Jesse said. The man took a second glance at the money as he increased the speed. Jesse told the man to stop and let the two ladies out of the car. The man did just that. "Ladies, don't say a word to anybody about this, not today ok?" Jesse said. They were both shaking their heads. Jesse really never knew exactly what happened or how Buster and Lester got caught, other than the fact that the car wouldn't start and it would be almost two years before they would see each other again.

Jesse had made a clean getaway from the bank but had made a very costly mistake. When the pale white woman in the bank was filling the bag with money on one end, Jesse pushed a window open at one of the teller windows and grabbed a handful of money out of an open drawer and left his fingerprints on the window. The F.B.I. collected enough of Jesse's prints to make a positive ID of the bank robber.

As Jesse and the man rode, Jesse went into the bag again and counted out five hundred. He reached over to the man holding the money in his hand and said, "I need to get to Calera, just outside of Montevallo, Alabama."

"I know where it is, no problem," the man said.

Strangely enough the man seemed to be enjoying himself. When Jesse said to him, "I want you to go back and call them. Tell them I held you at gunpoint and made you take me north of Birmingham and stick to your story."

"Don't worry about me bro, I know what to do. I ain't mad at you for taking them cracker's money because they been taking from us for four hundred years," the man said.

* * *

One day when Jesse and Buster were eating at the waffle house, Jesse met a girl named Charlotte and she lived in Calera. Jesse had taken her home one day and she begged him to come back to see her. Jesse didn't have a problem finding Charlotte's house again. Charlotte lived in a small apartment in a little run down neighborhood. Because of the way she worked she didn't have much company. When Jesse knocked on her door, she opened the door with great surprise and bewilderment. She was glad to see him, but she could sense that something was wrong.

"I need a place to stay for a few days. Can I stay with you?" Jesse asked as he slid his arms around her waist.

Charlotte couldn't think of anything else to say but, "It's okay."

She had a thousand questions, but she didn't know how to ask them, so she simply said, "Is everything alright?"

"No, everything's not alright. Listen to me. First of all, I'm not gonna let anything happen to you, understand?" he told her.

Jesse knew that this was a critical moment, so he thought he might use the power of persuasion. He pulled out about five hundred dollars and gave it to her. Charlotte's heart started beating very fast. She had never felt this way before. She was excited and scared at the same time.

"I only need to be here for a couple of days. Can't nobody know I'm here and please don't tell anybody, okay?" Jesse said.

"Okay, okay," Charlotte said not knowing what to say or do.

"Can you call in sick today and just stay at home?" Jesse asked.

"I don't have to work today, but will you please tell me what's going on?" she asked in a frail voice.

Just before Jesse could speak, a special report came on the TV. "A bank robbery at the Birmingham National Bank this morning left one man wounded and in police custody, yet another man fled the scene with an undisclosed amount of money. The identity of the lone gunman is not known at this time. There will be more news at twelve."

When Jesse heard this, he just went numb all over. He just sat there motionless for a few minutes. He knew that Buster had been hit, but it never occurred to him that Buster was apprehended? How long would it take them to find out who he was? How much did Lester know about him? All kinds of questions started racing through Jesse's mind. He sat there trying to figure his next move under the circumstances, because he was certain that things were about to get real hot.

For a few minutes Charlotte couldn't say a word because her heart was beating so fast. What was the penalty for harboring a fugitive? A bank robber and little did she know, an escaped convict on top of that.

"Jesse please don't get me involved in no trouble. Please!" Charlotte begged.

"Don't worry about that. They don't know who I am or where I am. And before they know or find out anything about me, I'll be gone. All I need is a few days for things to cool off. Right now let's just stay inside the house and be cool, okay?" Jesse said.

His mind was so preoccupied with the news of Buster's capture that he'd completely forgot about counting the money. This was the worst tragedy that had ever happened to him, but when you're in the game, you have no other choice but to play the hand that you're dealt. Now is not the time to start bitching up and crying! These things do happen.

It took the F.B.I. about twenty-four hours to find out who Jesse was. When they did, an all points bulletin went out across the country:

> *Jimmy L. Ogletree, alias Jesse Hodge alias Al Sims, is at large and wanted in connection with the Birmingham National Bank robbery that left one man wounded and another in police custody. Police said Ogletree is believed to be armed and extremely dangerous. Any information leading to the whereabouts of Mr. Ogletree is urged*

> to contact the Birmingham police or the F.B.I. Mr. Ogletree escaped from the Hamilton Georgia Correctional Institution approximately six months ago and has been at large since that time. There is a substantial reward for his arrest.

* * *

My mother almost fell to the floor when I yelled to her, "Momma, Jesse's picture is on TV 'bout a bank robbery!"

It was quite obvious that everybody was watching TV at six o'clock because people started calling to see if we were watching TV also. Momma just bowed down on her knees and started praying for her son and the parents of the other sons (Buster and the other guy) with him.

"Lord that boy's gonna be the death of me yet," Momma said immediately after seeing the news.

We knew it wouldn't be long before the police would be back at our house. Jesse caused the biggest news bulletin that Crawford, Alabama had ever heard of. People from all over were talking about the robbery. All momma could say was, "I'll just leave him in the hands of the Lord cause I've tried everything else."

Just as we suspected, the F.B.I. was at our house again later that night with the same shit.

"Call us if you hear anything from Jimmy, because we have orders to shoot him on sight if he doesn't surrender," the agent said.

But Jesse was as quiet as a mouse in a box of corn flakes. He didn't make a single move for nearly twelve days. He stayed inside the house and went out only two times, both times at night, however, he was pretty sure that he wasn't suspected of being in the area. After Jesse laid with Charlotte for more than two weeks, he felt that now would be a good time to move around 8:30 a.m. on Saturday when the traffic was pretty heavy. He had taken Charlotte's '53 Plymouth after giving her a thousand dollars to buy her another car.

"If the police ever ask anything about your car, just tell them that a man offered to buy a car that you wanted to sell and that was all there was," Jesse said.

She didn't know who he was. He schooled her on a lot of do's and don'ts if she was questioned. Jesse knew that hardly anybody could connect them together because they were never really seen in public. What he didn't know was Charlotte was pregnant!

* * *

Jesse had on a dark blue suit and tie and a pair of "My Three Sons" Stacy Adams shoes.

He looked much more like a preacher than a prisoner, a clergyman rather than a convict.

Jesse's personality kind of took the thought of him being a bad person away from you. He never looked like he'd harm a fly. As he traveled up the freeway headed to South Carolina, he never told Charlotte where he was going or in what direction.

He drove straight through, only stopping for gas and getting snacks as he filled up. The old Plymouth ran very good and it definitely wasn't the kind of car that got your attention, so Jesse felt real good about driving it. Maybe only on two occasions did he even see a police cruiser during his entire trip. Jesse thought about Buster quite a bit. He even thought of calling Titus and telling him about the situation, but he soon abandoned that idea. By now he didn't think that it would be a good idea for him to contact anybody. He was sure that the police department had found out who Buster was and where he was from and contacted his family. He said a silent prayer for Buster and let bygones be bygones.

Jesse stopped in a little town called Munch Corner, South Carolina that didn't look to be much bigger than a football field, but he thought he'd stay over for a night or two just to figure out what he'd do next. But what he was really looking for was a woman who had her own house or apartment where he could hold up for a while. He was straight for money, so he didn't have to do any hustling for a minute. The bank job had netted approximately $13,000.00 and he was still more than $38,000.00 strong. He checked in at a Red Rooster motel on the outskirts of the city, which seemed to be a cool little spot, however, it didn't take him but a couple of days to realize that this cool little spot was a little too small for him. There weren't enough people and everybody seemed to know everybody. He did stay there long enough to read four of the newspapers that he thought might carry something about him or the bank robbery, but he was so relaxed that he hardly even thought about being an escapee anymore. Jesse made sure he read the paper everyday and so far there was nothing in the newspaper about him, but he still kept a very low profile. As he left the little small city of Munch Corner he headed for Greenville, South Carolina. He thought that city should be big enough for him to lie for about a month and then he'd make another move.

His thoughts had constantly rested on Buster. He still wondered if he should call someone in Florida and say something about Buster, but he didn't want to take any chances of giving himself away. Besides, he felt like the F.B.I. would be expecting him or someone else to get in contact with some of Buster's people, and that would be some form of a lead for them. So he just forgot about the idea of calling anyone for any reason. Jesse got into Greenville, South Carolina just before dark and he rode around for a while before he stopped anywhere. He rode until he found the ghetto part of the city where the "ho's" were walking and talking shit. He knew that this is where he needed to be for a while. Once he found the ghetto he would find out what and where the action jumped off at in this city, like dice games, card games, or anything else that was illegal.

Jesse saw a Bar & Grill that had a pool hall in the back and after he walked in and looked around for a minute, he walked over to the corner of the bar and ordered a Schlitz beer. He just stood there on the corner of the bar sipping on the beer for a long while, checking the place out. He walked inside the pool hall and had some conversation with a couple of guys before playing a few games where he played very reserved and controlled. He missed a few balls and made some good shots, but still very controlled.

He found out about some of the card games and where the after-hours crowd hung out at after the clubs were closed. A couple of days later Jesse had found a nice room in a nice section of the city with an elderly lady that rented neat and clean rooms to (what the ad read was to "Good Respectable People"). The room that Jesse rented had a side door entrance just ideal for him because he could come and go without disturbing anyone. His landlord was a very neat and serene looking little lady that he thought might be a Gichee. She was short with beautiful black skin and pretty hair. She was a lovely little lady.

Bobby Hodge

* * *

About three days after Jesse had been living there, one day as he was coming in the yard, he noticed Mrs. Williams, his landlord, was looking out the window at him. He thought that this was sort of strange behavior for her because he usually didn't ever see her during his travel in or out of the house. A few minutes later there was a knock at his door and without even looking out he knew that it was her. His first thought was, had she found out something about him in the papers or seen something on the news? A lot of things rushed through his mind. Jesse opened the door and invited her in. Mrs. Williams walked in and she had a pleasant smile on her face.

"I like the way you keep your room clean and neat," she said.

"Well, that was what you asked for in the ad right?" Jesse said.

She just smiled. "I came in your room just to see how you kept it and I received some strange vibes when I came in here," she said with a quizzical look on her face.

This really caught him by surprise. "What do you mean?" he asked her.

"My feelings tell me that you have a very dark path and that you're in trouble with the law. Am I right?" she asked.

Mrs. Williams was looking him straight in the eyes. He was so shocked that he didn't say a word at that moment. "Don't worry. I'm not here to hurt you or cause you any harm. In fact, I'm here to help you," said Mrs. Williams.

"What made you feel like that about me?" Jesse asked, not knowing what else to say after hearing her words.

Mrs. Williams calmly laid her hand on his arm and closed her eyes. For a few moments she didn't say a word and Jesse didn't quite know what to think.

"Captivity is in your future. You will have some restless nights in fear of being caught," Mrs. Williams said looking at Jesse again.

"How can you help me? Are you a fortuneteller?" he asked.

"I can feel things and I can see things. I can guide you away from danger. I can give you peace in your life," she said to him.

Jesse didn't know if he was scared, weak, or just plain stunned, but he knew he couldn't find any words to say.

"I'm gonna ask you some questions and you must be honest with me before I can help you," she said.

Jesse felt like it would be in his best interest to tell her the truth, but maybe not tell her everything, only what she asked him. After what seemed like forever, Mrs. Williams asked Jesse some strange questions and he was quite truthful about everything. Mrs. Williams told Jesse to go out and buy him a piece of cloth garment that he could keep with him at all times and to bring it back to her after midnight. As Jesse rode down the street in the car, he didn't know what to think about the recent encounter with Mrs. Williams. He'd never believed in fortunetellers before and didn't see how this would help him, but then, he thought, how did she know all this shit? How did she know about Buster? How did she know he was on the run? And if she knew all that shit, then surely she knew about the money!

Jesse found a real nice scarf that he could wear around his neck or be used as a handkerchief and bought it. Jesse didn't know why he deliberately stayed out until after midnight, but he did. He ranged Mrs. Williams's doorbell, but it seemed as though she was standing at the door because it opened immediately. He gave her the scarf and just as sudden as the door opened, it closed. Mrs. Williams never said a word and neither did Jesse.

The next morning Mrs. Williams knocked on his door about seven o'clock in the morning. She was holding the scarf in her right hand as she gave it to him, she said, "Don't ever be caught without this scarf. If you do, I can't protect you. Now I don't charge no certain amount of money so you do what you feel in your heart, okay? You can bring it to me later today. Don't be in no hurry."

With those words, Mrs. Williams was gone. Jesse gave Mrs. Williams two hundred dollars and she didn't seem surprised or disappointed. She just smiled and said, "Stay in touch with me. Okay Jesse?"

Jesse was shocked again because he never told her his name was Jesse didn't have the slightest idea of what he had just bought for two hundred dollars, but he felt that Mrs. Williams knew absolutely too much about him for him to take any chances. He still didn't know how she knew what she knew. It didn't take too long for him to find out.

A couple of weeks had passed and Jesse had been playing the pool halls, the late night card games and winning very good money. Then all of a sudden, one night, the door of the house where they were playing cards at around four o'clock in the morning, just came crashing open.

"This is a police raid!" a voice shouted out. "Everybody lay your hands on the table."

The police continued to collect the money off of the table and handcuffed people and started taking them out to the patrol car parked in the front of the house. They locked up the entire house, including a couple of people who obviously was not playing. They were sitting on the sideline.

The most shocking thing that happened was that Jesse had just gotten up from the table and went to the bathroom. And once he heard the commotion, he got over into the bathtub and closed the curtains, but no one ever came into the bathroom to look in. So once the house was clean, Jesse eased out of the house and got into his car and rode off. Now maybe the scarf had meant something or maybe it didn't, but Jesse couldn't help but wonder either Mrs. Williams knew her shit, knew exactly what she was talking about or, if it was just the hand of faith that caused him to have to use the bathroom at that particular time or not. Another surprising thing to him was that when he pulled into the yard at approximately four o'clock in the morning, Mrs. Williams was standing in the window looking at him. He never knew her to stay up so late before.

That was the first of several episodes that happened to him in a similar fashion when it came down to that scarf, but it did leave an undeniable impression on him about Mrs. Williams. The next couple of days she acted as though she didn't even know him. She didn't say a word other than to speak to him. Things really started to get better for Jesse. He was playing the pool halls and winning cash money every day, it just seemed as though he couldn't lose. Even though he had to spot almost everyone he played a ball or two, he'd still win. When he went into the dice games and card games, he usually won big because he would out bet everybody and it seemed that he had this winning aura around him. Jesse had such a character about him that was so strong, so confident, and so masculine that whenever he entered a room you'd think the president of the United States had walked in. Everybody took a second look and on the second look they stared. It seemed that he knew something that nobody else knew.

Jesse thought one time that his stay in Greenville was about over, but he hadn't had any trouble around here and he was keeping a pretty low profile, however, he was still becoming too well known by the people in the street because of his winnings. His skills were not going unnoticed. He was becoming a little too relaxed for his own comfort because after all, he was still a wanted criminal. These days he found himself thinking about Buster quite a bit, but he never mentioned Buster's name or the incident to anyone. The situation also made him a little reluctant to work with anybody else like that because it gave you too much to have to think about. Life for Jesse was going pretty good for a while. He had met a couple of ladies that he would spend a little time with, but nothing serious ever evolved from either one. Neither one of them really understood him, they just liked him because he was Jesse.

Then one night Jesse went to a gambling house on the south side of town where he'd been once before with a guy named Ben. The night was very cloudy with the skies threatening to rain, but the weather was very warm and humid. When Jesse got out of the car and walked towards the house, he decided to take off a sweater he had on underneath his coat and put his coat back on. In the process he unthinkingly left the scarf lying on the front seat of the car. As he entered the room, there were about eight people in there and right off Jesse didn't get very good vibes from a man sitting at the table. He made some kind of snobby remark but Jesse didn't pay him much attention. He waited until one of the players got up and Jesse took his seat.

"I hope you didn't bring any of that bullshit with you tonight muthafucker," said the man looking at Jesse.

"Whatcha mean nigga, if you ain't got no fucking money to lose, then you should get up from the table," Jesse replied.

The man never said anything else at that time. There were a couple of guys there that Jesse recognized from the pool hall and the streets. The houseman spoke up, "There ain't gonna be none of that shit from you T, so either play or leave." The man still didn't say anything. The game had been going on for about an hour when the man called T, got played out of the game. That motherfucker there got that same shit. Jesse had won about $400.00 and as he started to say, "Muthafucker why you keep fucking with me?" The man T had come out of his pocket with a knife that was already opened and before Jesse could get out of his way, T stabbed Jesse in his upper right shoulder in the back. The pain was excruciating but Jesse managed to fall from the table on his left side. As he did, he pulled his coat with him and as the houseman grabbed T, Jesse pulled the nickel-plated .38 out of his coat pocket. As he rolled to get up, he fired the .38 into the man's chest and the force from the bullet knocked the man about five feet back as he fell to the floor.

By this time everybody was running out of the door, but there was a lady standing behind the door as though she was in a state of shock. Jesse said to her, "Would you please pull this knife out of my back?"

At first she said I can't do it, but then she just grabbed it, pulled it out and then started to regurgitate. The houseman said to Jesse, "Man, get the hell out of here. I don't know you. Just get out of here. The nigga brought it on himself."

Jesse didn't know if the man was dead or not. He just left. The pain was almost more than he could stand, but he knew that he had to get out of the area, out of the city, and out of the state. When he got back to Mrs. Williams' house, she was standing at the door as if she knew that something was wrong. As Jesse got out of the car, she could see that he was soaked in blood.

"Oh my God! What happened to you Jesse?" she asked. She was very hysterical. "Are you alright?" she asked.

"I got stabbed in my back. Can you help me?" Jesse asked.

"You need to go to the hospital," she said.

"I can't go to the hospital. They'll be asking too many questions, but if you can just help me with some bandages I can make it. I got to leave right away," Jesse said.

By now Mrs. Williams was a bundle of uncontrollable nerves, but she soon gathered her composure and started helping him undress. The wound was opened and she could barely stand to look at it but somehow she found the courage. She ran back into her house and got some towels, peroxide and a jar of alum. She cleansed the wound as best she could and then realized that the bleeding was not quite as bad as she thought it was. After putting on all the medications, she said, "The only way to stop the bleeding is to apply as much pressure as you can stand. So I'm going to wrap this bandage around you real tight and I think you should see a doctor as soon as possible. This wound ain't gonna heal by itself."

"I shot the nigga Mrs. Williams. I don't know how bad I hurt him, but I know I've got to get out of town right away. I know a place I can lay for a while but first I must get there. The police will probably be looking for me, so if they come here just tell them I left owing you a full months rent and you don't know anything about my whereabouts," Jesse said.

Mrs. Williams wanted desperately to talk Jesse out of leaving town because she was quite fond of him, but deep down in her heart she knew that Jesse's situation was a lot more serious than he had told her. She also knew that if he stayed around, it would eventually bring the police to her house. She didn't know what dark demons lurked in his past, but for some reason she just knew that he was a wanted man. They talked about the situation that had just occurred and other things. As Jesse packed his clothes, Mrs. Williams helped him load them into the car. Even though Jesse's rent was paid up, he went into his pocket and gave Mrs. Williams an additional $200.00. She refused, but he insisted. Jesse had come into her life like a thief in the night and without stealing a thing, he was now driving out of her life just before dawn.

"Flashing life, Memories of better times"

The pain from the wound was slowly restricting movement in Jesse's shoulder and he could feel himself getting weaker, but he knew that he had to make it to Salem, Alabama. He hoped he could do it before he bled to death. As Jesse rode down I-85, he made sure he didn't draw any attention to himself. He drove the speed limit and kept drinking the hot coffee Mrs. Williams had made for him. He didn't plan on stopping for anything, but gas and that was at a full service station so that he wouldn't have to get out of the car for anything before he got to Alabama. He gave lots of thought as to his situation as he drove, but he was thinking about Buster because he felt that they could have devised a better plan than the one they had. He actually thought that the robbery was a costly mistake that could've been avoided. It really gave him something to think about. As long as he'd been a member of the street he'd never had anything like this to happen to him.

Jesse drove in one position for so long it was almost impossible for him to find any comfort of any kind in any other position because the stiffness was really setting in. After what seemed like hours and hours of almost unbearable pain, Jesse saw a sign that said Opelika, Alabama, 27 miles. With that sign in mind, he knew he could make it because Opelika was only ten miles from Salem. He was going to our Aunt Essie Mae's house, the lady who had practically raised him. Right now this was the only place he knew he could go and get some help without the police being involved and Momma could be at his side.

When Jesse finally pulled up in the yard, he was so weak he couldn't get out of the car without Aunt Essie's help. When she saw his condition, she almost lost it.

"Lord have mercy boy, what done happened to you? You 'bout to bleed to death! Jesse, come on and let me get you in this house. You need to see a doctor right now. Boy, you hurt bad," said Aunt Essie said.

"Aunt Essie, I can't go to the hospital. They gonna lock me up if I do that. I don't want anybody to know I'm here but my Momma," he said.

"I'll get your Momma up here right now, and maybe she can get Mrs. Callie to help us," she said.

Aunt Essie told her daughter Doll baby what to do and she quickly jumped into the car and went to go get my Momma and Mrs. Callie Jones. Mrs. Callie was a midwife and just about delivered most of the people in that county and was as good as the doctor. Around there I remember when my younger brother was born. Mrs. Callie stayed with us for about a week and she was a very strict person. You did what she said and that was that. Her favorite meal was black coffee and biscuits even though she didn't have any teeth in her mouth. Mrs. Callie ate whatever she wanted to: apples, skins, peanuts, you name it.

Doll baby finally got back with Momma and Mrs. Callie and the first thing Mrs. Callie said as she came in the house was, "Lord let us pray!" She started to pray as she kept right on walking into the next room. Momma was almost running to the bed where Jesse was laying. She was saying, "Lord have mercy boy, what you done did now?" She was turning the cover back as she talked.

"Honey, that don't look too good from here, but you alright huh?" momma asked. She was looking directly into Jesse's eyes.

"Yeah, I'm gonna spank your butt," Mrs. Callie said and continued, "I brought you in this world and I done spanked you before," she said laughing.

She was just laughing, then got serious and she went to work on Jesse. She cleansed the wound and put something on it that made Jesse almost shit and then she actually sewed him up. Finally, what seemed like a lifetime, because nobody was talking enough and it was much too quiet, Mrs. Callie said, "I think my baby's gonna be alright if he just didn't lose too much blood. If we can get some good food in him after a while, that boy'll be back on his feet in no time."

Then Aunt Essie started telling them what Jesse said had happened. Then everybody understood why he couldn't go to the hospital and why it was a must that his presence in this house remain a secret. Jesse stayed in the back room at Aunt Essie's house for about three weeks and nobody knew he was even in the state of Alabama, let alone the neighborhood. Even I'd forget he was back there because I would want him to come out and talk to me; tell me something about what's been going on. Everybody seemed to know but me! Jesse laid around the house for about a week and a half before he started moving around and talking a little. I just thought that everything Jesse said was gangster like and I thought that was so cool.

I really wanted to be like him for some unknown reason and I couldn't get enough of being around him. Jesse's being at home was probably the best-kept secret in Crawford and Salem. There were very few people who suspected that Jesse was here after he'd actually left. Only after he was gone did Momma and Aunt Essie talk about Jesse's situation and what happened in South Carolina.

After Jesse began to feel his old self again, and knew that he could handle the soreness, he realized that it was time to move on. Jesse had been thinking of where he should head once he left here, and he thought that Savannah, Georgia might be a pretty good spot for a little while because they had a lot of mixed races and not a lot of crime. He thought there wouldn't be a lot of police looking for felons down there. Whenever Jesse would start out on the road moving from city to city, he would normally leave around six in the morning so he could blend in with the early morning work traffic. He always thought of what Uncle Robert had told him one morning when it was time to go plow that ole mule Daisy. He said, "If you get up early in the morning you got a jump on a sleeper and that's when you can make some money." But he also knew that the police were least likely to stop that early in the morning rush traffic.

Even though Jesse had a nationwide warrant for his arrest, he kind of felt that if he stayed out or away from the police, he would pretty much be alright. He felt that if he dressed really neat and maintained a professional like attitude, people were less likely to see him otherwise.

So he would look like a preacher or a professional person, but not a criminal.

Just before he left Salem on his way to Savannah, Georgia, he saw Eugene Anderson standing in his front yard, so he pulled in. Eugene and his brothers Jewel and General all went to school with us. Their mother died when they were little boys, but their daddy did a good job raising them. As Jesse was getting out of the car, Eugene was recognizing his face and couldn't believe his eyes.

"Jesse, man where you been?" Eugene asked

"Here, there, everywhere Gene," was Jesse's reply.

They embraced in a big friendly hug. "Man, I done heard so much about you getting money, breaking out of jail, and all sorts of stuff. Man, you're a helluva dude man. How you do that stuff Jesse?" Eugene asked. Eugene was laughing as he asked Jesse question after question.

"Gene, I ain't been doing all that shit they say I been doing man," Jesse said, "but you know man, a man's gotta do what a man's gotta do just to stay alive out here right?"

"Yeah, you right Jesse, but I just don't see how you have the nerve to do some of that stuff. I'd be scared shitless," Eugene said. They both burst out laughing.

"Man, they said you broke out of that penitentiary in North Georgia. Is that true?" Eugene asked.

"Yeah, that's true. Well, I didn't really break out. There was an old red neck guard there that I talked into letting me go. They were screwing him around and I just persuaded him to see things my way. They probably fired his ass after I left," Jesse said.

"And I heard you robbed a bank in Birmingham?" Eugene said.

Jesse looked at Gene for a brief minute, quickly remembering Buster. "Oh, that was a mistake. We never should've fucked with that bank. At least not that day," Jesse said.

Jesse quickly changed the subject. "How are your daddy and your brothers man?" he asked.

"They're all doing fine man. As a matter of fact, here comes daddy now," Eugene said.

Jesse looked up to see an old pickup truck pulling into the yard on the side of his car.

"Well I be dog gone." That was Mr. Anderson's favorite saying. "Boy, Lord have mercy, where you been? They tell me you a real hell cat," Mr. Anderson was saying, laughing and grabbing Jesse's hand at the same time.

"You something else," he said to Jesse.

The conversation continued for a few more minutes, mainly questions about stuff they'd heard about him, and he knew that they were gonna have a lot to talk about for the next few weeks or from now on for that matter. They were acting like he was a John Dillinger or Pretty Boy Floyd. Mr. Anderson finally went into the house, leaving the two men with their talks. Jesse walked to the back of the car and opened the trunk and Gene walked back there with him. Jesse opened a suitcase, pulled out the inner lining and there was about $30,000.00. Jesse told him to get him some money and Jesse just stood there looking at Eugene. Eugene had just frozen in his tracks, his eyes bucked, and his mouth open and he could not speak for a few seconds. When he did, his words were only, "Got damn man! That's real money ain't it? I ain't never seen this much money before in my life," Eugene said.

"Get you some money man," Jesse said again.

"Jesse, I just ain't got the heart man. I could never spend a penny of that money Jesse. I'd be too scared," Eugene said.

"Scared of what?" asked Jesse.

"Man, I might get caught with some of that stuff man. And I wouldn't know what to say," Eugene said.

He appeared to be caught up between being scared and stupid. "Man, ain't no trace on that money," Jesse assured him.

But to no avail Eugene wouldn't take any money. So Jesse knew then that it was time for him to go. He even thought that this could've been a bad move on his behalf. Immediately Jesse slammed the trunk down and after a few more words of bullshit, Jesse bid him farewell and left. For some strange reason Jesse didn't feel like Eugene would ever say a word about what had just taken place because he felt that he was too scared to have any knowledge of the ordeal. Jesse thought maybe he should get out of the Columbus and Phenix City area without trying to come into contact with anyone else. Who knows how many people felt the same way Eugene did. So at that moment he headed south on highway 80 for Savannah. Jesse had just given Momma, Aunt Essie and Mrs. Callie about $12,000.00 and none of them had a problem taking the money so he couldn't understand why Eugene had. Then he began to remember from days gone by that he thought a lot of people in this area had a low mental attitude about the kind of life that he found so rewarding.

It took Jesse less than four hours to get to Savannah and immediately after he arrived he knew he was going to like this city. It seemed real quiet and not to be an area having a high criminal rate, but little did he know that the road he'd been traveling was about to come to a bitter end.

* * *

Jesse had been in Savannah for about two days before he met Brenda Larkins, a real nice slender dark complexioned lady approximately thirty years old. She worked in a dry cleaning laundry and when Jesse walked in the laundry one morning to have a couple of suits dry cleaned, they started talking. Jesse knew right away that she would be someone that he needed to know even if for nothing more than cleaning services, but it turned into a beautiful relationship.

"What is Savannah like?" Jesse asked her.

"Well, it's a nice place to me. There's a lot of fool people here," she answered. "Where are you from that you don't know about Savannah?" Brenda asked.

"From a lot of places you might say, but I was born in Tennessee. Memphis, Tennessee to be exact," he lied.

He didn't see anything wrong with what he said because she would never know anything about him. That definitely wouldn't be in his best interest.

"Well then, what are you doing in Savannah?" she asked.

"Well, I'll tell you what, what if you promise to have dinner with me and show me around this nice city? I'll tell you everything I know about me, whatcha say?" Jesse asked.

"Oh I don't know about that. Besides, how you know I ain't married or have a boyfriend?" Brenda asked.

"Well I don't wanna have dinner with ya husband, and if you have a boyfriend, then maybe it's time for a beautiful woman like yourself to get yourself a man," Jesse replied.

They both began to laugh. "Well I see how you have a silver tongue," she said with a big grin.

"What do you mean by that?" Jesse asked.

"You know," replied Brenda.

"What I know is that I don't know anyone here in this city and all I'm looking for is a friend. What's so silver tongued about that?" Jesse asked.

He was now looking straight into her pretty brown eyes. She had a charming smile that would unarm the average person. She had a shapely figure that complimented the rest of her beautiful body.

"I only work a half day tomorrow, so if you really want to take me to dinner, then you can be here tomorrow at one o'clock," Brenda said.

Jesse was there at a quarter to one. Their dinner spilled over into a relationship that quickly moved him into her apartment in three days. Brenda was so excited about Jesse that she wanted all of her friends to meet him. He was simply fascinating to her. She had never known a man with such flare and good taste; to her he was a real gentleman. She showed him off every chance she got and marveled at being his woman, but she couldn't tell anybody anything about this very handsome man because she didn't know anything about him to tell.

Jesse was in Savannah for approximately three months before he really started to get out. He'd been keeping a very low profile, only going to the pool halls, which he used for recreation and exercise for his shoulder. His shoulder was still quite sore. One night when he groaned in pain after Brenda had lain on his shoulder, she was curious to know what had happened. Jesse told her that he'd gotten hurt on a job in Tennessee and had gotten some compensation from the incident. He felt that would explain his having money without a job and it worked.

Jesse often thought about the trouble he had in South Carolina and the man he shot because he still didn't know if he killed him or not, but he really didn't lose much sleep over that. That man was really trying to take him out and he had to do what he had to do.

* * *

Savannah was a much laid back kind of country town with a lot of things going on, but Jesse had enough money to hold him over for a while. His pool game down here was really paying off well for him even though his shoulder was still sore. He played everyday to make sure he could continue his normal game, and the constant play really allowed him to try things that he had never tried before.

His game was getting so good that he really didn't see any reason why he needed to candy stick for a while. His game was really up to par. Brenda was buying him everything she thought he wanted and he was living rent-free. She was enjoying him and he was enjoying her hospitality. Oh man, what a life.

One night they went out to a smooth little jazz club. The music was great and the crowd was mostly middle aged people who appeared to be very relaxed. Brenda introduced Jesse to one of her girlfriends who happened to be a waitress, her name was Martha Bennett.

"It's good to meet you Martha," Jesse said.

"Likewise," was Martha's reply.

Before the night was over, Jesse had the distinct feeling that Martha didn't like him too much from the signs of her body language and he didn't know why. Every time she would bring them a drink over, she would obviously direct her conversation strictly to Brenda and then slightly give him a brush-off look. At one point she made a smart comment about how most men just wanting to get into women's pants. When he asked her what she meant by the remark, she boldly said, "I would think that you would already know what I mean!"

She walked away from the table and Jesse asked Brenda the same question of her intent. Brenda just smiled and said, "Ah, she's just like that. Maybe she's been hurt a time or two."

Finally Martha came back to the table and Jesse asked her, "Do you think you might know me from somewhere sweetheart?"

"Honey, I don't know you from any other man. I just know you're a man!" she said.

"So you're saying that I want to get in your drawers? I don't even like women like you." Jesse's words had a certain fiery tone.

"You could never get in these drawers honey!" she smirked.

"Hey, what's going on here? Why are you two judging each other?" Brenda asked.

At that time Martha walked away from the table.

"Don't pay her any attention. She's just jealous," Brenda said.

"Or maybe she's just gay," Jesse said. "Maybe she wants you for herself."

Jesse started laughing. Brenda snapped her head around in shock. "I know you're bullshitting. I don't go out like that. Shit, you must be crazy," she said.

"But maybe she does," he replied. "She's mad at me for some reason. I just thought she was upset about seeing you with a man," he laughed.

"You crazy Jesse, she ain't gay," Brenda said.

Jesse started kissing her on the jaw and rubbing on Brenda. "It doesn't matter. She can't have none of this," he said.

Brenda was blushing and smiling while she told him to stop, but it was obvious she was loving every minute of it. Jesse was convinced Martha didn't like him for some reason, but the feeling was pretty mutual because he didn't give a damn about her either. However, the night continued to be a romantic flavor of good jazz that filled the place with electrifying sounds, while the mixed drinks and beers created the mood for the rhythm of the night.

Jesse found a nice little skin house game that he'd visited a couple of times, but he hadn't sat in on a game as of yet. He kept thinking about his last game more often than he cared to think of.

For more than three months Jesse didn't' do anything but play pool and he was winning more than his fair share. Everyday was a good day for him because Brenda was handling everything that had to do with the house and the bills. All he had to do was be there and be himself. Jesse had almost forgotten about the candy sticking game and the cards for a while. He was just enjoying life. One night he decided to go down to the jazz bar where he and Brenda had gone. He sat around for a few minutes before he ordered an orange juice because he was not about strong drinks, never had been. Martha came over and asked Jesse where he was from.

"I'm from a lot of places. Why do you ask?" was his reply.

"You just look so familiar to me," Martha said.

"Well, where do you think you know me from?" Jesse asked.

"I didn't say I knew you, I said you look familiar, like I seen you before," replied Martha.

Jesse couldn't help but be concerned about her statement, but he never showed any emotion. He continued to drink his orange juice and listen to the music as he pondered her words. The rest of the night he didn't have anything else to say to her and for a while she stayed her distance. Finally, she came back over to the table and asked if he wanted another orange juice.

"No, I'm fine. This'll hold me," he said.

"Are you a police?" Martha asked.

Jesse was kind of troubled by her question, but answered her sharply. "I used to be. Is that how you know me?"

"I still didn't say I knew you, I said you look familiar to me and I thought you were a police or something. Maybe I was wrong," Martha said.

After finishing the orange juice Jesse got up and started out the door when two policemen approached him and asked for some I.D. About that time Martha walked over to them and said, "He said he was a police, but I saw his picture in the newspaper. He's a wanted man," Martha said.

Before Jesse could show any I.D. or say anything one of the officers drew his gun and said, "Turn around and put your hands on top of your head. You're under arrest."

"What's the charge officer? I know you're not taking me to jail for something this crazy ass woman said?" Jesse asked.

Even though he was getting real angry, he still complied with the officer.

"First of all, for perpetrating a police officer, but if you don't have anything to hide then you don't have any problems now do you?" the officer replied. "But we're taking you down and clearing this little matter up."

Jesse had given them a driver's license with the name Ray Sims on it, which he'd made in South Carolina.

"What are you doing in Savannah if you're from South Carolina?" the officer asked.

"I didn't know it was against the law to be in Savannah," was Jesse's answer.

Jesse looked at Martha without saying a word, but his stare left her no doubt that she'd never want to see him again. Once the officers got Jesse down to the precinct they ran every search warrant they knew on the name Ray Sims and came up empty handed. They took his fingerprints and after two days and a thousand questions they were about to let him go for lack of evidence. The perpetration of a police officer really didn't carry any weight. Suddenly, bingo, the fingerprints come back and the entire police department went into hysterics. They finally realized that they had a full-fledged criminal in their jail!

Warrants from Georgia, Alabama, Florida, and South Carolina came back on Jesse. They didn't know who had first priority, but the arresting officers both received expert performance awards for his arrest. He stayed in the Savannah jail for three weeks before being extradited back to Columbus, Georgia because that was a Muscogee County case that he escaped from in Hamilton, Georgia. Therefore, they had jurisdiction on his release from Savannah.

It was months before Jesse saw Brenda again however; he had gotten her a couple of letters out through one of the jailers in Savannah. He had instructed her of where to send his clothes and stuff. Jesse had been at Jack T. Rutledge for four months before Brenda could come to see him. She told him that Martha had read about the Birmingham bank robbery in the newspaper and remembered his face. He thought of all the millions of people reading the paper everyday, this one bitch would remember his face! What a streak of bad luck!

Brenda said that they had a real falling out about the whole thing and they would never be friends anymore and to Jesse's surprise she also confirmed the fact that Martha was a lesbian!!

"Auburndale"

Jesse had been in Jack T. Rutledge for about fourteen months before he was given a security clearance to work outside of the compound. He was finally given a job on the road, which was hard work and he knew that it was only a matter of time before he would try to leave this red-necked place.

One thing that Jesse didn't understand was the fact that he was able to get back out of the institution on a work detail. Maybe they hadn't gotten his records of previous escapes, or were they trying to set him up to get killed by running? The warden had a rule at Jack T. Rutledge that hardcore prisoners must work hard labor and long hours with a one hour lunch break and two ten minute breaks all day. Regardless of how hard the work was he knew this made his plans of escaping a lot easier. Jesse had been on the road detail for more than six months and had seen a couple of possibilities but the timing would have to be right or they would lock him down for sure, and he'd do everyday of his time. He spent most of his days working hard and his nights reading and planning. Very few people knew that he was in Columbus, Georgia doing time and he wanted it that way.

One day when they were working in the neighborhood the school bus stopped to unload some kids, and Jesse knew that the freeway was just a short piece through the woods. It had just started to rain pretty hard when the guard was about to call them in. Jesse made a break across the road in front of the school bus towards the kids because he knew that the guard was not going to shoot in the direction of the children, but to his surprise the guard didn't even see him run. Once he hit the wood line, he just cast faith to the wind and ran like hell.

He went across the freeway into the woods on the other side and continued to run. He knew that he would be hard to track because the rain would make his scent and tracks very hard for the dogs and the police to follow. Jesse knew that he had to get out of Columbus, Georgia, but first he had to get to Crawford, Alabama. That's where his money was stashed in his suitcase, but his biggest problem at the moment was to get rid of the prison clothes he had on.

Even though Jesse was in the woods he still kept sight of the freeway so that he wouldn't get lost. He stayed in the woods until about 11 p.m. that night before he saw a service station that was pretty much lit up in the front area, but the back of the station was pretty dark and unreserved. Jesse eased up behind the station and hid behind a dumpster for what seemed like hours, but what was more like thirty minutes, before a work truck that looked like a plumber's truck or some kind of construction truck with a lot of junk on the back. The driver pulled down on the side of the service station where there was an air hose. He got out of the truck and started putting air in his rear tire while he left the truck running. Once he finished putting air in the tire, he went inside the store and it gave Jesse the perfect chance to get on the back of the truck where he camouflaged himself under a wheel barrel.

Shortly after that the driver came out of the store and got into the truck and pulled off. He made a right out of the service station and headed for the downtown area. He was going down streets that Jesse was not too familiar with. While he was still going in the downtown area, Jesse was trying to think of someone he knew around the area they were in, and if they would still be living there. The truck finally pulled up in a driveway somewhere up in Bibb City. At first Jesse didn't know where he was. The driver turned the truck off and got out. Jesse was sure hoping he didn't come to the back of the truck and just as he had hoped, the man slammed the door and walked towards a house.

Jesse laid on the back of that truck for about two hours after he saw the lights go out in the house. Before he made a move, he eased off the back of the truck and went to the passenger's side. He eased open the door and first thing he saw was a jumpsuit on the seat. He eased the door back shut and went out of the yard before he slipped into the jumpsuit. It was a bit too big but that was good because it gave him a much different appearance. Jesse had also taken a toolbox from the front floor of the truck. Even though it was pretty heavy, he looked like a man walking to or from work.

Once he looked around and saw Bibb's Mills he knew exactly where he was, so he walked down First Avenue, which was quite common for mill workers. After a couple of blocks Jesse felt pretty comfortable walking but he was still looking for a ride. Then bingo a brother stopped at a red light and Jesse didn't hesitate to ask for a ride.

"Say mister, would you mind giving me a lift down to Eighth Street if you're going that far? These tools are heavy as hell," he said.

"Sho' man, get in," the man said. "I don't mind at all."

Jesse went to telling him about a job he'd been working with a cracker and he didn't want to pay him right, so he just got his tools and quit. The man then commented on irate people who want to work you for pennies.

"Some folks just want you to get them some money, they don't care nothing 'bout nobody but da'self," the man said.

A few minutes later they were on the corner of Eighth Street and Ninth Avenue. Jesse got out on the corner and thanked the man dearly for the ride.

"Oh I'm glad to be able to do you the favor. God bless you Son!" was the man's words as he pulled off.

Jesse's ex-wife Ruth lived on Ninth Avenue and that's where Jesse had planned to lay and recover for a minute. Ruth was totally shocked when she opened the door and there stood Jesse with a big grin on his face. Ruth knew that this couldn't be good. She didn't know how bad, but with her blood rushing through her veins at super speed she thought her head would explode. However, she was glad and scared to see him at the same time.

"Oh, my God Jesse, man, where are you coming from? How did you get out?" Ruth asked.

Ruth had a million questions, but subconsciously she already knew the answers.

"How did you get out?" she asked.

"I ran!" Jesse said.

"Ain't they looking for you?" Ruth asked.

Little did Jesse know that his picture had been on Crime Stoppers on the 11 o'clock news. There was an all points bulletin about his escape. Lucky for him no one other than the man that gave him a ride had seen his face, but he didn't know what the man would say if he saw his face on the news. Jesse knew that he couldn't stay here, but Ruth didn't have a car and he didn't want anyone around here to know he was in the area. He was even uneasy just being here because he didn't know if they knew that he was once married to Ruth, or if she lived in Columbus.

"I need some clothes and shoes right away. If I can get them I'll be out of here," Jesse said.

"Are you hungry?" Ruth asked.

"Yeah, but I need to get in touch with my cousin Little Robert Aunt Essie's son. I know he'll get me out of the area."

Ruth was preparing some tuna sandwiches and asking questions at the same time while she was on the phone trying to locate Little Robert. They talked for quite a while until the phone rang.

"Hello," Ruth said and paused then said, "Hold on a minute." She turned towards Jesse and said, "It's for you."

"Yeah," Jesse said.

"What the hell you done did now nigga?" the voice on the other end said and Jesse knew it was Robert.

With a little grin Jesse began to speak. "Hey man, how you doing?"

"Naw nigga, how you doing?" Robert replied.

"Oh, I'm okay, but listen man. I need to get out of here. I need a car and don't worry about no money. I just need to get away from here. I need you to go to Momma's house and get my clothes. Tell her to send my suitcase," Jesse said.

Robert had always been Jesse's favorite cousin because he was just as devious and conning as Jesse was. In fact, a lot of his traits could be traced back to Robert because he was always stealing Uncle Robert's car (his father). Jesse and Robert literally grew up together in the cotton fields of Alabama where they smelled mule shit and dry dust all day long. Uncle Robert owned a farm.

At last, Jesse began to feel a little better about his situation because he knew he could count on Little Robert to help him out. They had always done little things in the past like stealing from some building. They didn't talk on the phone for long at all, in fact, their conversation was pretty brief and Robert got right on the job. As Jesse waited for

Little Robert, he and Ruth had their intimate moments but there was no time for any silly shit! He wasn't thinking about anything but getting out of town quick.

Little Robert had gone by momma's house as instructed and picked up the suitcase with the rest of his clothes. Little Robert finally knocked at Ruth's door. Jesse was listening so hard he thought he heard footsteps and he did. Ruth answered the door as Jesse was moving towards the kitchen door.

"Who is it?" Ruth asked.

"Robert," the voice answered.

Ruth opened the door. "Where's that damn rabbit at?" he joked.

Ruth laughed and said, "In the kitchen fixing to run."

Ruth and Robert both started laughing as Jesse was walking back into the living room grinning too.

"Man, you'll run like hell won't cha?" Robert said as he was reaching for Jesse's hand and shoulder, in greeting.

"What you did boy?" Robert asked.

"Man, I had to leave them goddamn red neck's out there. You just don't know. That was the hardest time I ever did. Them crackers will work your damn brains out. They don't give a damn about nobody!" Jesse said.

"How much time you have to do Jesse?" Robert asked.

"Twenty years for Georgia right now, but they might bring some more charges against me from Alabama and South Carolina. They just ain't put me with that shit yet cause man these muthafuckers still don't know exactly who I am. They still think it's two of me. They just ain' put it together yet. But listen, as soon as I get a bath and put on some clothes, I want you to get me out of town. I got a little money," Jesse told him.

He knew the word "money" would have a whole different meaning than what it did to Eugene. Robert was sitting in the living room when Jesse came out of the bedroom with a nice brown suit on. He had his suitcase in one hand and some money in the other hand. Robert was never told that the suitcase he was carrying had $25,000 in the back of the inside cushion of the case. He held the money out in front of Robert. He had $400 in his hand. As he held the money out he asked, "How much of this money you need nigga?" Jesse asked.

"All of that!" Robert answered.

"For a car?" Jesse asked with a grin.

"Well, it won't be a good one you can bet on that, but I can probably help you out with something to get out of town in. And you can count on it to get you where you're going," said Robert.

He gave Jesse the keys to a 1959 Chevrolet six cylinder, but it was just right for Jesse. It served its purpose because the old car ran very good. Jesse gave Robert another three hundred dollars for the old car and once he left Robert's house, he headed for highway 431 to Dothan, Alabama.

* * *

Even though Jesse was heading for Miami, Florida, he figured going to Dothan, Alabama and then taking 231 into Fort Walton Beach would be the best way to go under the circumstances, so he eased the old Chevy right on into Miami without any problems. Once he got to Miami he immediately called Mary in Fort Lauderdale and asked her about the baby, Lil' Jessica. He had only really seen her when she was a very small kid and now she was a tall brown skinned pretty little girl that he wanted to be around for a while. He wanted to be really low key for a while because he knew too many people in Miami. Besides, he knew that some people around would be asking what happened to Buster and he wasn't ready to explain or talk about that incident because he had never come to grips with the situation himself. He was not ready to say anything about the incident and he basically kept quiet about the whole thing regardless of who asked him about it. Luckily there were not many people around who'd heard of what happened in Alabama.

After Jesse spent some quality time with Lil' Jessica he thought it might be a good idea to ease up on Ruby because she didn't know that he was in town or anything. He rode by Ruby's house a couple of times before he decided to stop in. She was simply shocked to see him because they hadn't been in contact for a couple of years. Jesse made it a point not to write many people that he'd been involved with over the years for safety reasons. That way if the institutions were checking his mail, they wouldn't know too much about the people he had reasons to contact. Whenever he'd write Ruby he'd use a fake name because she knew his handwriting.

"What are you doing here?" she asked while looking him over from head to toe.

"I'm looking for you baby! Is that alright?" Jesse asked.

"Yes, you know it's alright. Why haven't you gotten in touch with me? Are you free now?" Ruby asked.

Her voice was full of excitement.

"For the moment, you know how that goes. I left a work camp in Georgia a couple of days ago but they won't be looking for me down here. However, I won't be here but a few days," Jesse answered. "I just need a little money to do a few things and I'll be out of here," Jesse explained.

Ruby was really glad to see him but for obvious reasons. The sound of him leaving in a few days sounded better than him staying because she wasn't accustomed to harboring a fugitive. Ruby never knew Buster so there was no conversation about him; in fact, the only person that he talked to Ruby about was his cousin Titus.

"How's your business going?" Jesse asked.

"The business is going good. I'm thinking about a new location," she answered.

"Well, who's been making love to you? Don't tell me that's alright too," Jesse said.

He was smiling as he slipped his arms around her waist, pulling her into him and kissing her with a deep passionate tongue-fondling kiss. He could feel her caresses and before they could regain control, they were pulling off each other's clothes. It had been more than three years since he'd seen or touched her body.

The remainder of the evening was filled with foreplay, hugs, kisses, and lots of questions, but mostly the ecstasy of love. As the evening filled the sky with darkness, Jesse and Ruby lay in the bed looking out the window at the glow of stars that hung over Miami. They both realized that they shared a very special kind of relationship even though they rarely communicated with each other. Maybe it was the rarity that kept them in sync with their kind of relationship.

"I heard a lot of things about you once you left Miami and I couldn't believe my ears," Ruby said.

"Things like what?" he asked.

"Like you were a bank robber and stick-up man, that you had a little girl in Fort Lauderdale, and that you had broken out of jail in

Georgia. Is any of that true?" Ruby asked as her eyes were searching his eyes for some hint of the truth.

"All of it is true, but what does that have to do with us?" Jesse asked.

"Well, where was I when you were getting a baby in Lauderdale? And why didn't you tell me about her and your other woman?" Ruby asked trying to look serious.

"You were here in Miami and besides, that happened before I met you. I didn't say anything about it because I already have enough trouble in my life," Jesse said.

"So you had a woman when I met you, huh?" Ruby asked.

"Let's just say I have a baby by a woman in Lauderdale, and I love my baby very much. Now, can we forget about that?" Jesse asked.

Ruby didn't want to make him angry; after all, she'd waited for this moment for years. After a long silence Ruby said, "Would you tell me how to find her and I'll buy her some things. I'll make sure she'll have whatever she wants or need, if it's okay with her mother."

"It'll be fine with her mother. After all, we're better friends than anything else, but let me talk to her," Jesse said.

The rest of the night was filled with more questions and conversation.

"You ain't spent my money have you?" Jesse asked her.

"Now why would you think I'd do a fool thing like that? All I do is pay the P.O. Box fee. I haven't even been down there. I was really scared that somebody might be watching it," she said with a grin.

"What make you think that someone would be watching it?" Jesse asked.

"Well, once I thought about it. I wondered why you would leave that much money with me and I kind of thought it might have been stolen because you've always been so secretive with me. You never really told me much about your business or whatever," Ruby said.

"There are things in my life that won't help you at all to know about me, but I'll promise you this, I'll never hurt you in any way. I'll never cause you any trouble and all I want you to ever do is to just listen to me, okay?" Jesse said.

He was looking her deep in her eyes as if he could see her feelings for him deep down in her soul.

"Okay," Ruby heard herself saying. "I won't ask anymore questions. You know, it seems like you just scare me into loving you. Does that make sense?" she asked.

She was sounding half serious and half jive, but he knew exactly what she meant. Instead, he just started laughing at her and again they embraced each other and drifted off into slumber.

The next morning Jesse was up early on his way to see the guy he knew could help him out with a fake I.D. Before twelve o'clock he had a driver's license with his picture on it and the name of Raymond Bell. He'd gotten the key from Ruby and went to the P.O. Box for some cash. He took out $5,000. After he'd counted the money and saw it was all there, he thought about how he had constantly wondered if Ruby had crossed him for some of the money, or all of it. Now he knew that his hunch was right that he could trust her. He spent most of his time between Mary and Ruby's house. He knew lots of people there but he didn't know where his picture had been posted or what news station had aired his escape.

Jesse stayed for approximately two months before he decided to make a move. He'd seen a guy that used to run around with Buster one day and even though they never spoke a word to each other, just the sight of that guy gave him some eerie feelings. So he thought this might be the time to move. The last two days he spent with Jessica. He even took her to meet Ruby and they took her shopping and to the park. They also went to watch the Miami Dolphins at their work camp. Jessica was the happiest little girl ever, but little did she know that this would be the last she would see of her father for a long, long time.

* * *

Jesse left Miami and headed to Auburndale, Florida where there was a guy living there that he'd met when he was in the county jail in Leesburg, Florida. Richard Milton, he and Jesse had become good friends during his stay. They'd talked about their lifestyles and the things that got them there. Jesse thought that he might just see what he was all about. It took him about three and a half hours to get to Auburndale, and when he did reach the city limit he had to pull over into a service station to check the water in the car. It was running hot. Jesse got out of the car and opened the hood only to find the water hose had burst. Oh well, not so bad after all. It took him very little time to locate Richard. He lived with his mother.

Mrs. Milton was a very frisky kind of woman that ran a bootleg house. It was a big house and it seemed as though people were around this house quite a bit. Richard couldn't believe his eyes when he saw Jesse getting out of the car. He ran out.

"Oh shit! It's my man, ah ah, Jimmy!" the man yelled. "Jimmy man, it sho' is good to see you. Man you wasn't lying about coming down was you? Man I thought you'd be down for some years with all that shit they had you for. How'd they let you out?" Richard was almost yelling.

"Well, they didn't really let me out Richard. I kind of just walked off," Jesse said.

The sound of that really excited Richard, but his mother came to the door. Jesse quickly said, "I'll talk to you about that man, just you and me okay?"

"Oh yeah Jimmy, hey momma, this is a friend of mine from Leesburg. Remember the guy I told you about that won everybody's money in the county jail? Well, this him! This my momma Jimmy, Alberta Milton," Richard said.

"How you doing Mrs. Milton? It's good to meet you," Jesse said.

"Likewise, this boy talked about you so much, I finally get to meet you. He didn't tell me you were this handsome," Ms. Milton said with a big grin on her face. "Boy, these women round here gonna run you crazy," she said.

She was still laughing and looking him over. Jesse could tell right away that he and Mrs. Milton were going to get along just fine. She liked money and she was a woman wise beyond her years.

"Do you have any family here in Auburndale?" she asked.

"No I don't. I'm more or less just passing through, but I'll be here a few days. I'm going on down to Miami," Jesse said.

"Well come on in the house and make yourself at home. You're welcome to stay here with us as long as you like," Mrs. Milton said.

Mrs. Milton had a pleasant cheer in her voice and Jesse couldn't believe this woman had just given him the comforts of her home without even knowing him from Adam's house cat!

* * *

Auburndale was a small town that had its own little flavor twist that suited Jesse just fine and he and Richard really got to be strong friends. Richard had done about as much as Jesse without as many breaks. They rode the remainder of the evening just talking and going to some people's houses and by this time he knew that he was going to like this little town and its people. When Jesse and Richard finally got back home, Mrs. Milton simply refused to let him go to a motel. She had already prepared a bedroom for him.

"Now don't give me a hard time because you just as welcome here as you are anywhere in the world. And don't you forget it," she said.

"Well, I can't beat that can I? I want to at least pay you for my keep," Jesse said.

Before Jesse could say anything else, she was yelling, "I wish you would try to pay me baby! I just wish."

Jesse just sort of sat around and watched everything the rest of the night. When the people began to thin out, the conversation became more personal between Richard, Alberta, and himself.

"Well, tell me Mr. Jimmy, what kind of work you do that let's you be so sharp?" Alberta asked while washing some glasses in the sink.

"Well, I'm a cook by trade but I haven't worked in that field for a while. I'm also a professional waiter. I've worked in some of the finest restaurants, but right now I'm in between jobs and just kind of floating around," Jesse answered.

"Momma, don't let that nigga fool you. He's slick as hell with a deck of cards. I told you he won everybody's money in the county jail, everybody's." Richard was saying with a bit of bragging in his voice. "I'm telling you Momma, he slick as hell with those cards and dice. He ain't no joke with them cards. He came down there and took over the houseman's job with them cards. Have you been doing it much lately Jimmy?" Richard asked.

"Well, I did a little shinning up in Virginia a couple of months ago," Jesse lied.

He didn't want to get Mrs. Alberta all excited about his breakout.

"Well, if you all of that, then we need to get us a system because these people around here like their card game like you wouldn't believe it. So Jesse, tell me something about yourself. Where you from and what you doing down here in this part of the country?" Alberta asked.

Jesse could see that Alberta was real cool so he felt the best thing to do was to level with her so she would know what she was up against. So he came clean with her. "Alberta, it's like this. I can't be around here for too long cause I'm really on the run, but they're really looking for me up north. I'm still on my P's & Q's cause you never know just what's going on with them," explained Jesse.

Jesse went on to explain to her the whole situation later on about him because he felt that he could trust her. She was easy to talk to and very understanding about things like that.

He felt that if it ever came down to it, he could really depend on her because she was a woman with a flair for money and the hustle game. She made her money on the cards and cutting the games. She made good money and she never thought about a job. These were the kind of people Jesse had been around practically all his young to mid adult life. He had learned to survive off of the kind of people who supported the game.

"Well, I would like to have a few hands at the game before I have to move on cause I don't want to bring any heat down on you. This would be a nice little place for me for a while if I got a little money going on around here," Jesse said.

Jesse never let on to having much money. He was playing everything by ear. And sure enough Jesse's money began to grow the first night he sat down at the card table at a "skin" game. He won about four hundred dollars and Alberta cut about two hundred fifty dollars, which was pretty good money not to include the beer she sold. They had a neat little thing going on and it was on the perfect side of town. The police didn't come in the area too much. It appeared that they were more interested in the marijuana smokers and drug dealers.

Jesse was pretty comfortable here for about three months and then he decided to go back to Columbus to take care of some business with Ruth, his ex-wife. That's when all hell broke loose.

* * *

Jesse had just gotten in Columbus when he saw a guy he knew from the old pool hall days here, but he never said anything to him or even stopped the car. He never even thought anything of the guy. He never remembered that was the guy that he'd once hit in the head with a pool cue. As Jesse walked into Ruth's house she was cooking some chicken and rice.

"Oh my God Jesse, you always scare the shit out of me!" she exclaimed half screaming and half laughing, but completely overjoyed to see him.

She grabbed him in a bear hug. "I been waiting to hear from you," Ruth said.

"I didn't want to write or call. I had planned to come back anyway, but only for a minute," Jesse replied.

Ruth had fixed her and Jesse a plate. He walked out on the back porch and sat in a chair. Jesse had only been there about thirty minutes, about to take a bite out of the chicken leg when it seemed like the police came from everywhere out of the clear blue sky. Some came around the side of the house, two came through the front door, and about five came around the other side of the apartments.

"Get down on the floor!" the police yelled, "Get down now!" Jesse got down on the floor and that was the beginning of a long nightmare for him.

The next day the Columbus Ledger read: *Escaped convict apprehended while eating chicken.* The news spread like wildfire. It was like they had caught "Billy the Kid". It was a sad day for Jesse because as of now, they had more charges pending on Jesse and they were very angry with him. When Jesse went to court in Birmingham, the judge made some kind of blatant statement for making an example out of him. Jesse eventually ended up with nearly eighty years and they sent him straight to the federal penitentiary in Atlanta, Georgia. There, Jesse remained for quite a few years.

"SAM AND ME"

I was floating down the freeway headed for Miami when I suddenly had a change of plans. I instead decided to go to Leesburg for a few days. I went straight to Rogers and Marcellus's house. They were very surprised and glad to see me.

"What brings you down to this part of the country?" Rogers asked.

"Well, I was really going down in the bottom (Miami) to see if I liked the place and if I did I might stay for a while. But when I thought about that little girl next door, Karen, I thought I'd come through here to see how she was doing," I said. Marcellus and I were laughing at each other.

The evening went very smooth because Rogers' whole talk was about Jesse and how he was doing. We talked about the stupid things that Jesse had done in the past, the jobs, the breakouts, and the alias names, the whole nine yards. We talked about the familiar and the old times, but what they still didn't know was that they still had a criminal in the house. I even thought that Rogers would probably faint if she knew that there was stolen bank money in the car outside, or that there was a possibility that the police could've been looking for me at that very same moment. But for the most part, the afternoon went very pleasant.

It didn't take me long to get over to Karen's house because my cousin Wilbert and I had been down here a couple of years earlier for a couple of weeks. Karen and I were kind of sweet on each other anyway, and I certainly felt like the new kid on the block.

I remembered that when Wilbert and I were down here two years ago, we got into it with some guys from another neighborhood and we got the support of the guys right here in Woodland Park, so that made me feel pretty good. I knew no one was really gonna mess with me because we had guns that night and the other guys were just running their mouth. Karen and I went out to a drive-in movie, which we could almost be seen from her house. We got physical and emotional right there in the car.

The next day I took her downtown and she did a little shopping. We did a lot of laughing, kissing, playing with each other, and finally got a room. It also didn't take me long to realize that this situation could easily get out of hand because Karen was a young girl and had never been this far before. The day after, me and one of my cousins, who was making a living here from Crawford, Alabama spent the whole day together. We even went to Ocala, a small city about thirty minutes from Leesburg, but the third and fourth day I went out to the orange orchard with Marcellus and picked fruit.

I did it for two reasons: first of all, I didn't want anyone thinking that I already had money in large amounts. Second, I wanted to just hang out with Marcellus and kind of pay my room and board. I had been in Leesburg for about seven days when I finally called home to talk to my mother. She was so very glad to hear my voice.

"Baby, how are you doing? Ya'll just leave and don't tell me nothing' bout where you going," she said.

"Momma, I'm fine. Remember, I told you I was going out of town for a few days," I said

"Yeah, but you didn't tell me where you were going. You had me so worried about you," said momma.

"Well, I'm sorry Momma. How are you and the rest of the family?" I asked

"We all doing fine, but you got a letter here from the U.S. Army. I think it's a draft letter," she said.

My heart just stopped beating for a minute and I didn't know what to say or think. I was just dumbfounded. "Man, I don't know what to say," I thought.

Right off I knew that the Army wasn't anything to be playing with, so for the first time I started to look at life in a much different manner than I'd ever done before. After taking a while to think, I thought that maybe I should be heading for home to take care of that because I knew that draft evaders were looked upon as really bad and I didn't need that.

Then I really started to see things in a different way. The military would be the best place to be right now I thought. I could really move around and do my thing. This could be the beginning of something exciting.

I gave everybody my so longs and goodbyes and I decided to get back on the road and head for Alabama, which I thought was my best move. After I got back home and opened my letter, I knew exactly what the next move was. I had to go to Montgomery and be tested for military duties, but to my surprise, Wilbert had the same letter! At least I would be going with my best friend, but Wilbert had already made up his mind that the Army was not the place for him and he said that regardless of what they say, he was going the other way. If they said red, Wilbert said blue. If they said four, Wilbert said two, and his game plan kept him out of the Army. However, it was a different story for me. I was really ready for a change of lifestyle. I was thinking, what could be a better cover than the Army. I was drafted into the U.S. Army and I had never dreamed of such an experience.

My first duty station was Fort Benning, Georgia for eight weeks of basic training. And to think, I thought that the induction process was tough. Basic training had me sore and aching in places I didn't even know I could hurt in. The 5 a.m. wake-up calls, the five-mile runs and two hours of calisthenics were enough to make you want to go A.W.O.L. (Absent With Out Leave).

My second duty station wasn't any better than it was. The only difference was it was in Fort Knox, Kentucky, It was another eight weeks long plus, an additional six weeks for military recon training after A.I.T. (Advanced Individual Training. Fort. Knox turned out to be okay because we could go downtown on weekends. We had the freedom to do whatever we wanted after five o'clock if we didn't have any additional duties.

* * *

The war in Vietnam was claiming lots of lives and it seemed that everybody that was in the Army was going to Vietnam. Everybody had the jitters about going over there. Jacob Bennett, a school friend of mine, had been drafted approximately four months before I was. Jacob had been sent to Vietnam where he was killed during my A.I.T. training and for the first time in my life, I found myself being really scared about going to Vietnam. This part of the Army was something that I had never thought about in real detail until now. Just the thought of it gave me cold chills. By the time my fourteen weeks were up in Ft. Knox, I already knew that I was not going to Vietnam. I just didn't know how I was going to get out of it yet.

After .A.I.T. everyone got a fourteen-day vacation before they were to go on to their next duty station, however, you know where you're going before you leave. The same day that I got home on my fourteen-day furlough before going on to Fort Dixon, N. J., I found out that Jacob had been killed in Vietnam. In fact, he had been buried the day before and even then I already had orders for Vietnam. Before I heard about Jacob I was scared to go to Vietnam. I was sure I wouldn't make it back, but after hearing about Jacob, I knew I was not going over there. I just knew!

After telling momma my feelings about Vietnam she just started to cry. "Baby, just trust in God and pray. He'll never leave you, I promise," momma said.

I remembered reading somewhere that the Bible said, "Watch as well as pray." I knew that meant watch out for yourself.

Wilbert Hood had spent most of the fourteen days with me and we had a lot to talk about. Wilbert was steadily saying, "Man, I told you not to go to the Army. That shit ain't real." And for the first time I thought that what Wilbert was saying was making more sense to me now, that maybe I should've tried to get out of going to the Army. Maybe it wasn't a good move, but then I remembered that I wanted to get out of Crawford, Alabama, out of the south. I wanted to make something out of myself and I was really not cut out to be the kind of criminal that my brother Jesse was. I knew that and besides, I thought that being a soldier was really cool. I'd always wanted to be a soldier, but after basic training and A.I.T. I had a very different view and understanding about the Army now. This thing was not all it was cracked up to be. From day one it was hurry up and wait, shit head this and shit head that, but at the graduation ceremonies everybody was grade "A" soldiers and you did a superb job. The only ones making promotions were the white boys and they were getting the best authoritative positions. By now I realized that Wilbert might've been right, but what could I do about it now?

After the fourteen-day furlough, my sister Doll, Aluester, Wilber's brother, and Wilbert all drove me to the airport. Wilbert told me, "I'll see you long after you leave here. I'm gonna watch you out of sight."

All of this stuff sounded kind of strange to me but I didn't think much of it at the time. However, Doll wrote me later on and said that Wilbert stood out on the runway at the airport and watched the plane clear out of sight and that was the last I would ever see of Wilbert again. Wilbert was killed in a car accident exactly five months later and even now, Wilbert continues to remain my very best friend.

When the plane landed in Ft. Dix, N.J., there was snow everywhere and this was the first time I had ever seen so much snow. It was very difficult to walk in. There were guys in Ft. Dix from just about every Army base in the country going to different duty stations, but mostly Vietnam. Everyone seemed to be a little frightened, except for a very few heroic white boys that would probably freeze up at the first sight of a little blood. I tried to shake the feeling of fear but it was too strong. Everyone had to be inoculated before leaving the country, so it was a very, very sore arm day. Some guys got sick after taking so many shots, but for me, the shots were nothing, Vietnam was the problem.

The time finally came when they started reading off the orders of duty stations and when I heard Vietnam I almost fainted but managed to keep my composure, at least for the moment. They started shipping everybody out to their designated areas and that's when it seemed that it was now or never I thought. There was a Mexican guy that was in Ft. Benning with me and we met again in Ft. Dix. He went to infantry training after basic training and I went to an armor unit 11-Echo. Gomez and I immediately started talking to each other and feeling good about seeing someone else we knew.

Gomez mentioned to me that he had a joint of marijuana. "How about we get a buzz before we leave here man?" Gomez said.

At this point anything sounded good to me so I said, "Yeah man!"

We went into the bathroom and fixed up the joint. I pulled it hard and waited on the sensation. It seemed that was all I remembered for what seemed like a smooth transition from one world into another.

"Oh, hells yeah, fuck Vietnam man. What's the shit? They don't know me and I don't know them. That's what Muhammad Ali said!" I told him. By now we were both laughing like hell.

It seemed that everything was going through my mind now but for some strange reason I was not afraid anymore. I didn't care anything about Vietnam now. It was like I had another plan, but what was it? Shit, I didn't know and then reality started slowly occupying my mind once again.

"Oh shit, how long have I been in here? Where's Gomez?" I thought. Then I remembered Gomez saying something like, "Come on Hodge let's go!"

"Go where?" I said.

It had seemed like a big game and I didn't know the rules to it. After a while I gathered myself and remembered what I was there for in the first place. I ran back out in the lobby area, which had been full of soldiers before I went into the bathroom with Gomez. Now everybody was gone. I saw my duffel bag sitting in the same place I'd left it. I ran to the ticket counter and gave the cashier my ticket.

"That's your plane leaving the runway now soldier!" the cashier said.

Not only did the sound of those words create a lot of chaos, but also the M.P.'s were called. I was placed under barrack's arrest for the next twenty-four hours in which I waited to see the post commander. I didn't know what was going to happen, but I knew that it'd be better than going to Vietnam.

The next morning I had to see a Lt. Colonel who had a stone face and he looked every bit like the real mascot of what the Army should be. When I saluted him he never gave me at-ease, he just started cursing and saying some very degrading things about a soldier who was a deserter and how they should be shot on sight. His choice of words really started to get under my skin and I didn't see why I should have to stand there and take this bullshit because I knew I hadn't done anything wrong. Before I realized what I was saying, I was going back at the Colonel, telling him exactly what happened.

"Sir, I wasn't trying to desert the Army or run from Vietnam. I just went to sleep and I didn't hear my flight being called and when I woke up the plane was leaving the runway. That's when I went to the ticket booth and called the M.P.'s and for that I don't think you have to talk to me like I'm a dog or a sorry man because I'm a man!" I said.

It seemed that the Colonel was so shocked by my sudden outburst that he started talking real soft and respectable and his whole persona changed. He actually started talking about the possibilities of getting my orders changed to Germany. I was shocked. I thought it was some kind of trick. How was this man going to do that? But he did it!

That was the first I ever realized the power of standing up for what you believed in, standing up for your manhood. Was it the marijuana that triggered something in my head or was it the will of God that opened my eyes to the world of my own manhood. The Colonel stood up and he walked over to me, looking me straight in the eyes and said, "Welcome to your manhood soldier." Now I was really confused, but proud of myself. Maybe I'd just saved my own life.

Then he saluted and dismissed me. I was so stunned by what had just happened that I was kind of reluctant to even move. After all, I was thinking more like an article 15 or something but instead I got orders to go to Germany and when I called home to inform my mother she said, "See there baby. The Lord hears all and knows all. He knew you were scared," she said.

We laughed. Not only was this incident enlightening for me, but also in the last few months I'd grown in leaps and bounds! Once again I was glad to be away from the petty life of robbing and stealing and now I was getting a chance to see the world and meet people of all races and nationalities. Army life wasn't really so bad if there was no Vietnam.

When I landed in Frankfurt, Germany I felt light years away from my known civilization. Nobody seemed to speak the English language. Seeing all those white folks took some getting used to because the German people look at you like you're from another planet. They just stare at you straight in the eyes with a solemn smile without breaking their stare.

There was so much snow and ice; that I knew it was going to be a long, long winter. it was cold from the time I got there and it wasn't any warmth in the place still, everybody was drinking beer which was served ice cold. From Frankfurt my next stop was Stuttgart, where I stayed in the officer's barracks for two weeks. I didn't have to do anything during that time but wait for my P.D.S. (Permanent Duty Station) orders. Stuttgart was more like a false alarm because none of the remainder of my duties in Germany was like Stuttgart. Stuttgart was sweet. Finally I was stationed in Amberg, Germany. When I walked into the hallway of

I Troop the first day, I met the 1st Sergeant coming down the hall. First Sergeant Franks said, "Smith, what are you doing in dress greens?"

The comment puzzled me, but before he could speak the clerk of the orderly room looked solemnly at me and said, "Top that's not Smith!"

The 1st Sergeant stopped and looked at me for a long moment and said, "Well, I be damned if you don't have a twin in here soldier." He just walked off.

"How you doing man? Where you from? Oh, my name's Specialist Andrew," the clerk said.

"My name's Private Bobby L. Hodge Jr.," I said.

"You know, Top was right, you look just like Smith. That's what everybody calls him," the clerk said.

After getting signed into the unit at least three more guys told me that I looked like Smith, but so far Smith hadn't shown himself. One of the things that I noticed among the black guys in this unit was an unconditional kind of affection for each other; I want to say love for one another. There were fists of black power everywhere. You saw brothers giving up dap to one another. It was a long sequence of hand slapping and arm folding body movements that completed the formality. Every black man seemed to have a dying brotherly love for one another, whether they had ever seen each other before or not; it was a feeling that made you feel secure. It made you feel safe, like you were a member of a race of people destined by God himself. It made you feel very proud to be a black man.

I had never dreamed of anything like this. Just as I walked through the hallway doors I looked down the stairs to see a brother that I could immediately identify, coming up the stairs. It was Smith.

"What's up brother? You must be the brother everybody's saying looks like me," Smith said.

"Yeah, I think so. Man I think we do kinda look alike," I said

We started dapping each other. Smith had the kind of personality that reminded me of myself. He was very outspoken. As soon as we walked into the hallway Smith yelled out to some more guys that were coming up the hallway.

"Hey fellas, this is my brother that I've been telling ya'll about is just like me. He gets the best of treatment. Everything!" Smith said. The words made me feel very good.

Everybody started coming around welcoming me into the unit. For the first time in my life I really felt like I was a part of something that was not only real, but also powerful. It was strange the way white boys gave black guys the utmost respect, almost as if they were afraid. It seemed that we were on top of the world.

Germany turned out to be a fascinating experience. I found out quickly that it was very necessary to learn to count the money and speak the language. Smith and I became running buddies because everybody thought we were biological brothers and we never told the German women (fraulines) any different. Even though the white boys told the German women that black men had tails that actually came out at night as a joke, They didn't tell them that the tail was in the front and it didn't go back in after dark. Those German women were wild about black guys. My friendship among the 2nd Brigade went very wide through all the ranks. One of my very best friends was Lt. McRae from Houston, Texas. As a matter of fact Lt. McRae and I went to see Jimmy Hendrix in Munich, Germany in that same year. Lt. McRae's favorite words were "Hodge, don't call me Kenny during work hours and I won't have to bust your ass."

"Ah fuck you man," was my response.

There was a warmth and affection among all black men regardless of their ranks. We had a way of communicating that only the brothers understood.

Germany turned out to be a lot of things that a country boy from Alabama wouldn't expect it to be and a lot different from American culture. One of my most memorable moments was one day while on guard patrol with two other white boys in the jeep, we stopped in a little country town and the whole city ran up to see me. One girl actually ran because she'd never seen a black man in that little town. At first I was kind of pissed off at the white boys for stopping at this little brothel, but then I started to see the amazement in the eyes of these people. Everybody wanted to touch me and one lady held up a yellow flower against my arm and said in German, "*Prema.*" It meant beautiful, I think, because she was very nice to me.

That's when it dawned on me that these people thought I was something very special. So even if the white boys were trying to get them a good joke, the whole thing backfired on them, sweeter and sweeter. Graferfeil, Hornsfelt, and Phillipsroit were field duties where all the troops in the battalion kept occupied at all times. Driving for the company commander, while on field duty was my job. I made lots of trips back to the company while we were in the field, because each unit had thirty days at a time. Sometimes it got so cold out there that you needed some hash just to make it through the day or night, and we kept some hash.

One day it was twenty-four below degrees zero with a freezing wind chill factor and would you believe that the 1st Sergeant came out into formation in short sleeves? And just like Smith he yelled out, "First Sergeant, are you really that cold sir?" Smith said and the whole battalion died with laughter.

Even the 1st Sergeant found it amusing. Time moved slowly. The snow was very plentiful and the cold weather never went away. It was easy to see all four seasons in the same day. The German women seemed to be everywhere the brothers were and getting hooked up was never a problem, especially with me. One Saturday, Al Woods, Nolen Smith, and Larry Hill were on pass from the barracks. We went down in this little town where they were having a carnival. Larry Hill told one of the girls that we were the Jackson Five and before we knew it there were people everywhere all around us screaming. We were shocked so silly that all of a sudden Larry started singing, "A.B.C. doe-rae-me, A.B.C. one two three baby you and me girl!" We all started stepping in rhythm and the whole thing turned out to be a gas because every one of us had a girl.

As the carnival began to die out we all wound up at the nightclub that was located in the inner city. We found that upon leaving, all four tires on the car were flat and no one had a clue as to what happened, so we complained to the management who turned around and called the police. When the police arrived and talked to the manager they came over and asked for our ID. When they found out that we were American soldiers, not only did they apologize, but they had another truck to come out from somewhere. They had four new tires and they put them on the car (sweeter and sweeter and sweeter). Incidents such as these were far too many.

For instance, we were traveling through a small town and we had a flat tire, on a Sunday afternoon. It just so happened that we stopped at a service station which was about to close, but the guy took pity on us. As we fixed the tire, but he charged us enough to buy a new tire.

When we started to complain, he said something in German, and out of nowhere came these two big ass rockweilers like hell on wheels. We damn near tore the doors off the car because we'd never seen dogs that big. They looked like cows and when we got in the little V.W. Bug, the dogs just jumped all over the hood, windows, everywhere. We got the hell out of there but as we left, the guy was standing out there just laughing and waving us goodbye.

Even though we had a lot of fun there, the military still maintained its original level of racism. The white boys still made the ranks and were often times sought out for the better jobs. One cold winter night two black guys were downtown and they saw two white G.I.'s (Government Issues) go into this bar called "Silver Palace", which was supposedly off limits to G.I.'s, but it had been rumored that the white G.I.'s had been going in there. So these two brothers went inside and were immediately escorted out. Well, this created a problem for the white G.I.'s because they put them out also. The white boys were so upset they decided to jump the black guys just to teach them a lesson.

One of the guys got away and ran all the way to the barracks. Mostly all the guys were getting ready to go downtown for the regular get down, but this ordeal put a whole damper on the afternoon. The brother ran up the stairs and yelled out loud, "They jumped us man! The white boys jumped us!"

"Hold up man, what's going on brother? What's up?" Everybody was asking. And finally Jackson, a brother in "I" Troup yelled out, "Them white boys jumped us man, down at the Silver Palace. Another brother and I went in because we didn't know it was off limits to G.I.'s and some white boys from this unit jumped us." His mouth was bleeding. A brother from Texas yelled out, "Ya'll know what time it is brothers. It's time to get some respect. These peckerwoods need to learn that. This is a new day and that shit's out man!"

Everybody just started to get excited. It was as if they really had something that needed to be expressed and for the first time in my life I felt the powers of black unity. These brothers just came together like it was real and natural and anybody would've wanted to be a part of that. A white platoon sergeant came walking up the stairs and that's when Johnson yelled out, "That's one of them right there!" And before I could even think of any reason why I reacted the way I did, I just turned and hit the platoon sergeant in the mouth. It seemed that everybody wanted to kick a white boy's ass and before we knew what was happening there was a riot underway.

White boys were getting beat up everywhere and anywhere you saw a black man, you would see the unity fist going up in the air. For that whole weekend the brothers were steadily popping white boys in the mouth. The brothers had locked down the whole compound and you couldn't see a white person anywhere until they called the MP's to the barracks. The whole thing was kind of scary and fun at the same time. The thing that bugged the hell out of me was why did I react in the manner that I did when I hit the platoon sergeant? I couldn't even explain it to myself because I'd never been racist like that and I had quite a few white friends on the compound and had never had any real wrongful feelings about them before. Was this some kind of hatred that had been stored up every since the beginning of my time or had I really learned just how white people really felt about black people? Racism was never a secret in America but since we were in Germany there had been more of a truce between the black and white races, but there was really never a time when you couldn't see it for what it was.

Once the M.P.'s and officers came and somewhat got things pretty much back to normal, the black G.I.'s and the whites all sat down for a meeting of the minds. The white folks admitted they were wrong and there were no more repercussions behind anything else, except the brothers remained so close that it was like being born in a special race and for the first time in my life, I was very proud to be a black man. For once the Black Panther party sounded like the organization to be a part of.

* * *

That weekend had completely changed my views and thoughts of life in terms of skin color, but I still wondered why it made such a difference. This weekend substantiated all the issues by definition. Only the Hispanics were out in force with the brothers. The whites, the Irish, the Jews etc., all stayed to themselves and out of sight. It took about two months before the compound got back to normal, if you want to say that it ever did. For life, that weekend changed things for everyone involved.

One day during a company football game that we had instead of running, 1st sergeant Franks asked me had I ever thought of becoming a boxer. "No I haven't," I replied. "Why are you asking me that Top?"

"You have the body of a good prize fighter and the way I heard you knocked Sergeant Bivins down the stairs, well, hell he's a big man. Maybe you should think about it," Franks said.

I was shocked that "Top" would know about that and his reply was simple. "How did you know about that Top?" I asked.

"Well Hodge, you know the word gets around," Franks said.

"Oh, so ya'll been talking about me behind my back Top?" I asked smiling.

"Ah, no one was talking behind your back Hodge. We were just talking," Franks replied.

Well, I never really considered boxing as a career but what the first sergeant said to me made me realize with a great amount of confidence that I could handle myself in any situation.

Lots of things happened in Germany. Situations arose and throughout all of the turmoil there was never a dull moment. Brooks Benton steamed up the airwaves with his hit "Rainy Night in Georgia" and the memories of back in the world were just enough to set a love crazed mood in the guesthouses and night clubs, and the closer my E.T.S. (End Term Of Survive) date came the more we partied. The night before my departure, there was a party that lasted all night long and the day of my departure the whole I Troop took off work and went down to the Bonhaus to see me off. Surely there would be some lip from platoon leaders but it won't mean a thing because I knew that the hardest thing I had to do was say goodbye to all of these guys. In a way it was much worse than leaving home for overseas duty.

* * *

The plane finally landed in Ft. Dix and I actually saw the same person at the ticket counter that told me that my plane was in the air and I felt very compelled to walk over and speak to him. There was a lot of laughter between us and it kind of eased the pressure on me. I had a Kool cigarette pack stuffed with Lebauesse Blond Hashes and I managed to walk straight through with it.

Getting discharged from the U. S. Army seemed to be a good thing for me because I'd never really learned to like the Army. For some strange reason though I felt that I was going to miss the Army and I was right, once getting back to Phenix City, Alabama. Things just weren't the same. The people didn't seem to understand me anymore and it just seemed that this place was just too small now.

I had been working at Swift Textile Mills for about two weeks when I actually realized that I could never do this again. The straw that broke the camel's back came one morning when I went up to the service station in Crawford and while I was standing there, I saw a guy walking up to the store named Curtis Reese. Curtis was cursing Mr. Lavert, the service station attendant and he was saying some harsh things. When Mr. Lavert, attempted to ignore Curtis, Curtis picked up two soda bottles sitting in a crate near the door and he threw one of them at Mr. Lavert, hitting him hard in his side or shoulder area. It was obvious that Mr. Lavert was afraid of the man as he ran inside the store and went behind the counter. He got a .38 Revolver from underneath the counter and ran back to the door.

"Reese, leave my property before I kill you. Please just leave," Mr. Lavert begged.

It was obvious to me that something was very wrong with Curtis Reese because his eyes were as red as fire and he was acting like a mentally deranged man that was beyond reasoning with. Curtis then threw the second bottle at the man hitting the man on the arm as he shielded his face. What sounded like the world coming to an end, Was the .38 ring out as the bullet hit Curtis in the chest, spinning him around, as he fell to one knee. Just as suddenly as he fell he began to get up and charge Mr. Lavert again and the .38 rang out again hitting Curtis again in his upper left chest above his heart. Curtis took off running across the street where he fell dead.

I continued to sit on the hood of the car in dismay because I just couldn't believe what I'd just witnessed. I'd just spent the last two years in the Army during war time and came back home to see a killing. This ordeal along with trying to get a decent job had left me pretty much drained for understanding about the whole human race. It seemed that everybody was tripping in their own world and there was no togetherness among the people. They didn't see the love train of blackness or the powers of togetherness. I felt more like an outsider than ever before.

Even though Curtis Reese caused his own death and no white person was at fault for that, there was still something missing among the sisters and brothers here. I didn't go to work that day, in fact, I never went back. Instead I rejoined the Army in Ft. Benning, Georgia in July of '71 in which I was duty stationed there for eighteen months or until I was arrested for armed robbery on the reservations and sentenced to ten years in a federal institution. After being stationed in Ft. Benning for twelve months, I took a T.D.Y. (Temporary Duty) duty in Miami, Florida as a recruiting officer in Miami Beach. That's when I miraculously met Ruby.

It all happened one day when Ethel had taken me down to the same little restaurant that Jesse used to eat in and had taken Ruby several times. As Ethel and I enjoyed our dinner and talked about being back in Alabama, I decided to try a slice of potato pie that I saw sitting on the end of the counter.

"May I have a slice of that potato pie and a glass of milk please?" I asked the lady as she walked past our table.

"Why you sho' can Mr. Soldier," the lady replied with a big grin. "You guarding our country, you can get all the sweet potato pie you want."

People in Miami didn't see many soldiers and they treated them with a great deal of respect and admiration and I found that very pleasing. At the same time I noticed a beautiful lady sitting at a table alone, slyly watching me and I didn't know if it was me or the freshly pressed military uniform I was wearing, but on two occasions our eyes met. I excused myself from the table and went to the bathroom and on my way back this fine lady was walking toward the cash register when I intervened and said, "Would you let me handle your check today, so when I see you here again we can have dinner with each other? By the way, my name's Peil," I said.

Ruby was kind of surprised by my approach but accepted my offer. "I'm Ruby and I think that's the least I could do for our country," she said smiling and walked out. Even though she was obviously older than me, I knew right then that I wanted to see her again and I would make sure of that. Miami was a real different life from anything I'd ever thought of. The women here were so loose and vulnerable to the game and I was having my fun just being myself.

I had been conversating with a young lady from Manhattan, New York before I ever left Germany and she had written me a letter with a phone number and I put that number to work from the recruiting office in Miami, which turned out to be a bad move. The phone calls to Gloria in New York are what finally got me removed from the Florida office back to Fort Benning, but before I left I had an amusing six months there.

* * *

I made the restaurant a daily stop looking for that sexy looking lady I'd met there. About three weeks later, on a day I least expected to see her, she was sitting in the same seat where I first saw her. I walked straight over to her table and asked sharply, "Hey pretty lady, may I join you?"

Ruby looked up from the table only to look right into my eyes, remembering the day we met. "Sure you may. I thought you were gone back to the war," she said.

"Oh, so you been thinking 'bout me, eh?" I joked.

Ruby kind of smiled and said, "Well, I just hadn't seen you and you did pick up my tab. You know, you just don't forget people like that," Ruby said.

That dinner sparked a fiery relationship between Ruby and me. Maybe because I was so young, so self-assuring, and as I liked to think, I was quite amusing too. Well, maybe these attributes started Ruby's bells ringing, but I knew that those big pretty legs, that shapely firm body, and of course, that pretty face is what lit my fire.

For the next three weeks we spent all of our time with each other. We had dinner, went to movies, and even caught a Miami Dolphins, Buffalo Bills game at Joe Roby Stadium. One day as we sat in the restaurant I ordered a slice of potato pie and a glass of buttermilk when Ruby replied, "I know a guy that used to come in here. He also liked potato pie and buttermilk. Is that some kind of coincidence?"

"Well, he got to be one of the last real soul brothers if he likes it like this," I said.

It never crossed my mind that Ruby could've been talking about my brother. The first night that I made love to her I knew that I wanted Ruby in my life forever. She was warm, smart, loving, and sexy as hell. If a man didn't appreciate a woman like her, he had to be gay I thought. The first weekend that I drove back to Ft. Benning, Georgia to visit my family in Crawford, Alabama; I brought with me two kilos of marijuana and three ounces of cocaine.

I knew I wouldn't have any problems getting rid of the drugs because I knew all about the drug scene in Ft. Benning and Columbus, Georgia and things went just fine. However, once I returned to Miami, the recruiting office had found out about the telephone calls to New York and had already decided to terminate my contract of T.D.Y. I was immediately ordered to return to Ft. Benning within five days and that really broke my heart because I had really begun to like Miami and especially Ruby!

I had to move fast with a few things before I left Miami and one of those things were to re-up on the drugs because I knew it would be a while before I'd be able to come back to Miami. I might be getting an article 15. I had given a friend of mine at a tire store twenty-five dollars to put the drugs in my spare tire and pump it back up with air. It finally came time for me to leave Miami and because I had invested all of my money in the drugs, I asked Ruby for some money to get back to Ft. Benning and she never hesitated to give me five hundred dollars. I hit the highway for Ft. Benning even though I'd been up almost thirty-six hours and Ruby begged me not to go before I got a few hours of sleep, but I knew I had to report in at seven the following morning.

As I drove down the freeway, about one thirty in the morning my eyes became so heavy that I could hardly see. As I drove through an area where the freeway was being reconstructed, all the traffic was traveling on one side for what seemed like miles. When the traffic resumed, I was so sleepy that I never really noticed that this big truck heading straight towards me was on my right side and it was me who was about to cause a traffic accident. Finally I came out of a sleepy nod just in time to hear this loud horn that scared the hell out of me. I jerked the car so hard that I almost lost control, but God was with me. The almost fatal accident scared me straight awake and I drove the remainder of the trip without stopping for anything other than gas, but to my total surprise, when I entered Ft. Benning, Georgia the M.P.'s (Military Police) were

Break and Run

waiting for me. They had somehow gotten word that I had brought drugs to the area on my last visit and as I entered the base about three thirty in the morning I was stopped by the M.P.'s. The car was searched thoroughly for drugs and the dogs were brought in to also search the car.

"What's going on here?" I asked the husky M.P. officer.

"We were informed that this car was carrying drugs. Just stand over there please," he said.

"Man, who told you I had drugs in my car?" I asked.

I got no response. After what seemed like hours, they finally let me go. I drove straight to the battalion office and complained to the company commander about the harassment. The company commander informed me that a soldier had been busted with some marijuana and had reported me as the supplier, and after that incident with the phone calls in Miami the M.P.'s were alerted to be on the lookout for my vehicle over the weekend.

I was so upset about the ordeal that I asked for the day off to repair a door panel that one of the M.P.'s had damaged because they never found anything in the car. Once I left the base I went straight to a tire garage and had my spare tire broken down. Even though the M.P. went through my car with a fine tooth comb and the dogs never touched the spare tire, it held two kilos of marijuana and approximately three ounces of coke. To be honest, I was a nervous wreck mostly all day or until I got rid of the drugs. After that I went back to the barracks and fell deeply into a long and peaceful sleep. Within the next year I was transferred from the 69th Armored Brigade to Headquarters platoon to another Company. It seemed that everywhere I went there was trouble. One day, I found out just who the guy was that snitched on me about the drugs and I vowed to get even with him.

As my army career suffered from lack of promotion, things only got worse. One night as Charles and I were riding on post, we saw the guy that had done the informing pulling guard duty. We decided to put a little whipping on his head and take his money, but that turned out to be a very bad move, even though the soldier had more than four thousand dollars on him. To our surprise before we could get off post we had been identified, apprehended, and arrested for armed robbery on a government reservation. Both of us received ten years in the federal penitentiary.

December 1, 1972 was the beginning of a long and horrible nightmare for me.

* * *

After spending six months in the county jail, I was transferred to El Reno, Oklahoma where I stayed for four months that really felt more like four years. The violence and rival fights between the gangs there was unbelievable. About every month someone was killed or seriously hurt and the weather didn't help much either, it was freezing. I requested a transfer closer to home and was granted.

After four and a half months in Reno I was transferred to Tallahassee Federal Correctional Institution. It took me another ten months to get there because my next stop had Was Ft. Leavenworth, Kansas Federal Penitentiary, in which I stayed for four months. Because I was not twenty five years of age, I could not go out into the general population, and was under constant lock down with the exception of the three times a day we went to the cafeteria to eat. With a one hour break on the recreation yard, life for me now was at an all time low, but the kind of people I was coming into contact with was enough to keep my antenna high. Jesse and I wrote each other letters through our sister because we couldn't write directly to each other.

There was a riot in Ft. Leavenworth in which a guard was killed and everybody in the joint was locked down, however; before the lock down was my most frightening moment in the penitentiary. The fight broke out on the first tier of a three-tier dorm and I was on the third tier. As the inmates tried to overpower the guards, they started setting the mattresses on fire and that cotton smoke was very heavy in the entire dorm. As you know, smoke rises to the top and that's when things got spooky.

It became very difficult to breathe and the smoke was burning people's eyes so I grabbed my blanket off of the bunk and wet it in the face bowl and wrapped the blanket around my head so that I wouldn't breathe the smoke. It was a horrifying experience that lasted much too long, but thank God for the riot squad. They finally got things back under control.

After looking and watching, and heeding advise from Jesse, I just about learned how to maneuver myself around the place, after all, I'd already been around men in the military and I found that the situations were the same regardless. A man is a man anywhere he goes. But Leavenworth also had its positive points such as the 51 year old man that I played hand ball with everyday and never could win. He was a great source of inspiration and knowledge to me.

First of all the first day we spoke to each other, the old man said to me, "you're a smart young man with a good life ahead of you, you don't belong here. So when you breath free air again you make the best that you can for yourself, cause these prisons ain't nothing but wasted life!" he said, "I been watching you, you gonna be alright."

The words he spoke, will forever be with me, and when I was about to leave, he said to me, "Read everything you see, if you find a word that you don't understand, look it up and define it. Find out what it means before you go any further. And pray to God everyday religiously." To me, these were words of wisdom that every individual should live by. But still the strangest thing was that I could never beat this old man at handball.

Finally I was transferred to Atlanta Federal Prison where I stayed for approximately six months before being transferred again to Tallahassee. In Atlanta, I met Bobby Sanders, a hustler from Detroit, Michigan who inspired me to start writing poetry and playing chess, When we were both in lock down together, That was a good way to past the time away. Bobby had communications with the ladies prison in Ohio, and before long a young lady named Carmen was writing me. We kept in contact for more than two years and everyday Carmen would send me a newspaper clipping called "Love Is". It always had these neat little love poems. I would always write her back with a love poem that I would make up from the top of my head. I actually got good with the writing process, as a matter of fact; I was so good that once I got to Tallahassee, I started sending poems to the radio station. A female D.J. would read the poems every night at 10:00 pm along with the theme song of her introduction and a soft instrumental tune in the background, the whole joint would be tuned in. The guys would pay me to write them a love poem and they would rewrite it and mail it to their girlfriends and wives. I was making money with my pen.

Atlanta penitentiary was pretty quiet. One night about three o'clock, they came and took Bobby Sanders away ; that was the last time I ever saw Bobby.

The very next day they brought a tall skinny hippie looking white boy and put him in the room with me. Immediately the guy started acting crazy. He would sit there and stare at his food for fifteen minutes or more. He would also put his shoes underneath his pillow at night, but he never said a word for about a week. Then one day he started staring at the light bulb for about ten minutes. Then all of a sudden he touched me on the shoulder and asked me if I saw a man in the light bulb? Before I knew what happened, I had grabbed him in a half nelson, a wrestling move, and slammed him to the floor. I started choking him and yelling at the top of my voice, "I don't see no fucking man, and don't try to show me no fucking man, cracker, you understand?" I yelled. The guys face had turned red and his eyes were bulging as he was completely helpless, because I was a very healthy and strong man. Only after the guy started trying to apologize did I let him up.

I jumped up in a self defense stance, still starring at the man as he slowly go up off of the floor and sat on the side of his bed. "I'm sorry man, I didn't mean no harm," he said, voice trembling with fear. For the rest of that afternoon neither of us spoke, but later that night, the man started to talk. "They think I killed an FBI agent man, and my only defense is to get my case turned over to being mentally insane, otherwise I'll spend the rest of my life in here!" he said. I never looked up from the book I was reading, or said a word.

For the next two weeks we never said a word to each other, and just like Bobby Sanders, around three a.m., the Federal Marshals came and transported me to Tallahassee Federal Penitentiary.

After I packed my belongings and started for the door, I paused briefly and looked at the skinny-framed man lying on the bunk and said, "No hard feelings man, good luck to you." I reached out to shake his hand and then I walked out. Leaving Atlanta Penitentiary was like making parole, or some other kind of freedom. For some strange reason, I just knew that from here on out, the time I had left would be much easier to cope with.

We arrived in Tallahassee around 3 p.m. on a pretty sunny day during the summer of "74". I was delighted to see a prison compound that looked like a college campus. The average inmate here was from the age of 20 to maybe 33 years old. There were all kinds of technical programs and trades to get into, but the only program that I was interested in was the school program.

I immediately enrolled in the Tallahassee Community College program, in which I studied Biology and Psychology and because of my grade point average, I was given the job of work release driver. Whenever some one was released from the institution, I drove them to the bus station or to work if they were on the Work Release Program. However, none of these things came so easy; it was a constant battle of proving your rehabilitation.

I was also voted in as President of the East Tallahassee Jaycees, an organization that allowed me to attend a breakfast conference at the Ronald Reagan inauguration in Lakeland, Fl during the summer of "76".

Tallahassee was the learning center for the "gift of gab". As far as I was concerned, I started writing people from all walks of life, I even wrote Arthur Ashe and expressed my love for the game of tennis and my need of a racket. Mr. Ashe sent me a tennis racket. My tennis game became almost semi-professional because I played all during my spare time when I wasn't running. The recreation program held tennis tournaments with Florida State University and I was on the tennis team.

Tallahassee continued to be a great source of education for me during the remainder of my time and when I was paroled in "76", I was only 14 hrs short of an Associate of Arts Degree. And to my surprise the credits were transferable.

However, Tallahassee was not only a source of education for me. In fact, my entire time of incarceration really changed my life and my way of thinking completely. I constantly studied my history in depth. I read Nat Turner, W.E.B. Du Bois, James Baldwin, an numerous early American Black history books. I even read Shakespeare, but I was an avid and continuous reader and studier of the Bible. God became a never-ending campaign in my life.

After collectively reviewing my life up to this point, I knew that incarceration in any form was dehumanizing and was no life for me. Therefore, I promised the Lord that if he found it in his will to grant me my freedom; I would never again be incarcerated through an act that I willfully committed.

"Jesse's Escape"

I was released from the Tallahassee Federal Correctional Institution on December 1, 1976. I'd been locked down for a total of four years. After making parole, I moved back to Phenix City, Al with my sister and I enrolled in Columbus Technical School as a seamstress and completed my course, but I never really cared too much about tailoring once I found out just how time consuming it was.

Around the 10th of December, my brothers James and Willie and I went to visit Jesse in Reidsville State Prison. Jesse expressed his itching desire to get out of that place. He also informed us that he would be transferred to Staton State Prison in Elmo City, Alabama to start on the time he had for the Alabama convictions. Jesse had now been locked up for almost seven years, the longest he'd ever been locked down at one time. Jesse was really ready to go to Alabama because he'd heard that they made you work there and he wanted anything that would put him outside.

It took almost one year later for Jesse to finally be transferred to Alabama. He began serving time on the forty-five years he'd been sentenced to by the State of Alabama.

Because he'd been under maximum security ever since he'd gone to Reidsville, he was in Staton for two years before he got the security clearance that would allow him to work outside of the prison.

I had visited Jesse on numerous occasions over the next couple of years and Jesse had expressed the fact that he had a good plan for leaving once he calculated just how things worked around there. Knowing Jesse, he had already looked that place over.

I'd enrolled in cosmetology school and graduated with honors. I worked in a beauty salon for a year and now had opened my own salon in Columbus, GA. Business was good.

One day Jesse called and wanted me to come and visit him, because I hadn't been to see him in months. I went to see Jesse the Sunday before the forth of July, and we laughed and talked for quite a while before Jesse spilled his scheme.

"I know a good way to leave here and it's as simple as walking out the door, but it has to be done right. There can't be any mistakes and I need your help," Jesse said. He was looking me straight in the eyes as he talked. I was looking at Jesse as if he'd lost his damn mind!

"Man, you been locked up too long!" was my response with a laugh. "That's why I need you to help me leave here," Jesse said and we both burst out laughing.

"Seems to me you're doing good out here cause you got jokes," I said. Then Jesse's smile disappeared and that serious tone re-entered his voice. "Pete", that's what Jesse sometimes called me, "I got forty-five years to be here, man do you know how old I'll be in forty-five years?" Jesse asked with sincerity in his face and tone. "But you won't have to do the whole forty-five, you'll make parole in about fifteen years won't cha?" I said still treating the situation like it was a silly joke.

"Are you down with me?" Jesse asked. "I don't even know your plan, so what can I say," I replied. "I know one thing, if it jeopardizes my freedom, I aint down, cause I don't plan on ever coming back inside of one of these places to do any time," I said.

"You won't even hardly be involved; I just need you to help me just a little," Jesse said. By that time the officer called out that visiting hours were over, and I was glad to hear those words.

"Don't come back for a month and we'll talk about it in detail, ain't nothing to it," Jesse said.

"I'll see you in a few weeks man!" said Jesse. We shook hands and walked over to the door. "Give Momma a hug for me and tell her I'll see her soon," Jesse said with a smile. "Yeah right," I chuckled.

As I drove back down the highway, I thought that bastard really thinks he's smart. He chose his time to speak on his plan and knew he wouldn't have enough time to explain. He just wanted to plant the seed right now and give me enough time to think about it.

But I was thinking about my promise to never go back to Jail, and now my brother, whom I thought so much of, is asking me to take a chance on my freedom so that he might be free even if it was only for a little while.

I was actually mad at Jesse for even putting me in this position of having to make such a decision. What if things don't go right? What if he ended up with more time than he had at first? Sometimes, the biological love between family members can be stronger than the love that exists between a man and a woman. Sometimes when the love of childhood grows into adulthood, people can do some strange things.

* * *

The next couple of weeks were very gloomy for me. The more I thought of Jesse's plans, the more I thought of the perfect methods of escape. Even though the plan to help Jesse escape was a dangerous endeavor, it was also kind of exciting.

Jesse did very little communicating with me for the next few weeks and then I received a letter from an unknown address and sender. When I opened the envelope, there was another envelope inside with the handwriting that I knew all too well; it was a letter from Jesse.

The letter didn't have much to say, only that he'd like for me to visit him on the following Sunday and we would talk. The words on the paper started my blood to race through my veins. I didn't want to read the rest of the letter; however, I still complied and finished it.

The following Sunday, I went to visit Jesse and we talked in intricate details about the plans. "Man this is a hellava task you're asking of me, what if things don't go right," I asked.

"Everything'll go just fine if you do what I tell you to do. There ain't no danger involved; all I need you to do is be in place to pick me up. You don't even have to get out of the car," Jesse said. "Well talk to me like I'm a two year old, and don't give me any bullshit." I said with a slight hint of disgust in my voice.

"O.K.," Jesse said, "I'm working outside about a mile from here, when you leave today, I want you to drive down that road and you'll cross the bridge. We go back to work in the afternoon at 1:00pm. I want you to drive across that bridge at exactly 2:00pm. Drive one way for five minutes and turn around that should give you five minutes to get back to the bridge. I will time you so that I will be at the bridge at 2:10pm. Then I want you to stop on the bridge, get out and open the trunk and then the hood as if something's wrong with your car. But don't cut the car off, as soon as you open the hood, I'll be in the trunk. Slam the hood, then close the trunk and drive off at regular speed. Now do you think you can do that?" Jesse asked staring at me as if to see if I comprehended what he'd just said.

"Yeah, I got you, but let's do it tomorrow before I change my mind," I said. I was mad and excited at the same time.

"Let's set our watches and everything must go just like I just told you. Seconds are important and minutes will fuck everything up, understand?" Jesse asked.

"You just have your ass there, cause I ain't turning around to come back for you!" I snapped.

I was more nervous going out of the prison than I was going in, but as I turned and drove down the road, everything was just as Jesse had said it. So I drove across the bridge at 20 miles per hour for five minutes and I was crossing the bridge coming back in exactly ten minutes. I even estimated the time it would take me to get to the bridge from the road and now the plan didn't seem so bad.

I decided to spend the night in the next county. I got a motel room and spent the rest of the afternoon just riding around Montgomery and visiting a couple of night clubs. I even met a woman that showed me around town.

I must have drank four or five mixed drinks that night, but I never even felt the effects of the alcohol. Most of my next twelve hours plus was spent thinking of the next day. The young lady and I capped the night off with breakfast at Denny's.

The next morning, I got out of bed around 8:00am and went for about a three mile run before getting a long shower and checking out of the motel. The closer the clock ticked to 2 o'clock, the more my adrenalin was present and leaving a lump in my throat. Finally, the time had arrived.

I was driving my sister's brown '74 Cadillac coupe, I'd timed the beginning of the plan just right. Because I was driving across the bridge at exactly 2:00pm and I could see the inmates down in a field, but I couldn't tell what they were doing other than maybe just cleaning off a field. I adjusted my speed to 20 miles per hour and I did that for five minutes and came back. And just as I was approaching the beginning of the bridge, I saw Jesse and another man lying in the grass just under the side of the bridge. I stopped the car and casually got out. After opening the trunk from the glove compartment, I proceeded to walk to the back of the car and lift the trunk as if I was getting something out of it. I then walked to the front of the car and raised the hood; I leaned over into the engine compartment as if checking for something. I slammed the hood back down and hurriedly walked to the back of the car and closed the trunk. But what had just taken place was enough to make me want to put a stop to this plan at this very minute.

As I got back into the car and pulled off, I almost fainted when I saw a Guard Patrol truck coming towards me. My heart skipped a beat. But the man in the truck just waved at me and proceeded on down the road.

When the man didn't try to stop me, it made me feel like the plan was working just as we had planned, but I was mad as hell at my brother Jesse.

For the first few miles, I drove the speed limit, but as soon as we got out of the county where we'd just left, I let the hammer down on the Cadillac.

After about fifty miles, I pulled into a wooded area and opened the trunk from inside the car. As I got out of the car I was furious. "Who's this fucking cracker man?" And what's he doing with you? Why didn't you tell me he was coming with you Jesse?" I inquired. "Cause you wouldn't have went along if you'd known he was coming, it was his plan. The guard that let us go was his cousin and if I had told you that, now tell me the truth, would you have did it?" Jesse asked. He had a very sincere look on his face that said, you know I got your back!

This took a lot of pressure off of me, but the pressure wasn't absent for long, you see, after they had got in the car and had traveled down the road, I asked the white man what was he in for and he replied, "I got a kidnap and murder charge, but I'm trying to get my case back to the courts. I got double life!" he said.

That's when my pressure went to its peek, what kind of time would they give a man for aiding an escapee from a state institution? Then the reality of what I'd just done was vividly clear, I could wind up with just as much time as these two convicts. Nobody would have ever known that there were three people in the car; they were both almost lying down in the car before I would tell them that the coast was clear.

I took Jesse and the white boy to a girl's house that Jesse used to trim when they were growing up. She lived alone, so they both stayed at the girl's house until night came and after she had got them clothes, she took them both out of town that same night.

That was the last time that Jesse and I had any contact for more than a year.

* * *

When Jesse first left, he went to Florida for a while and I didn't really know where he was for quite a while. Momma would get a postcard every now and then but never a hint or clue of where he might be. And then all of a sudden one day as I was working in the salon, the phone rang and it was Jesse. He was calling from Atlanta, Georgia and I was so shocked when Jesse told me what he was doing that I couldn't stop laughing. He told me that he was on the Atlanta police force!

I started laughing so hard that I couldn't stop. I went to Atlanta and we spent some time together at a lady's house name "Elsie". She was a woman that I thought was too lonely or just crazy as hell to fool with Jesse, but she thought that she'd been saved by her knight in shining armor. Little did she know she was being used like a wet rag!

When Jesse told me how he had gotten on the police force, I had to admit that it was very cleaver and definitely took a lot of nerve. Jesse had talked to a man who applied for a job on the force and had been approved, but before he took his oath of employment, he'd decided that he would be moving back to his home town of Charlotte, NC. Jesse then started asking him questions about the job and the man gave him some very valuable information about the personnel channels and the hiring practice.

"After I decided to go back home, I just took all of the information I had turned in with me," the man said. The man got the paperwork out of a brown manila folder and showed it to Jesse. The first thing Jesse thought about upon seeing the application was that he needed this application, because Mr. Griffin had his fingerprints on it and all he had to do was to get his picture on a drivers license with this man's name on it.

"Listen man, if you're leaving town, would you take a $100.00 for this application? You see I have a situation where I need this for a job in security. All I need is your information and prints and I promise you that no harm of any kind will come to you. If I get busted, just say somebody got a folder out of your car, but you didn't remember the application being in there. To be honest with you man, I'm on the run and if I get caught with it, they would just think that this is the kind of shit that I do anyway and that alone would clear you of any wrong doing," explained Jesse.

"Hell yeah, I'll take a bill man, cause they probably won't ever think of checking any fingerprints," the man said. Isaiah told Jesse that a little short white man took his application, but there was a black lady in the office also who did the same thing. Therefore Jesse wanted to catch the black chick, just in case the white man remembered his name or this person.

Jesse was glad to give the man a hundred dollars for the application because the only thing he had to do now was get him some license in Isaiah Griffin's name and that was one thing he knew how to do all too well.

Exactly three days later Jesse had Georgia driver's license in Mr. Griffin's name.

The following day, Jesse went to the Fulton County Police Department and applied for a job on the force and a red headed white lady around fifty years old gave him an application and pen. She instructed Jesse to go into a room and fill out the application. Once he completed the form, he took it back to her and she instructed him to take it to another department for fingerprints and bring it back to her. That's when Jesse went back down the hall and out of a side door. Things were going just fine.

The next morning, he brought the application back to the department with Mr. Griffin's fingerprints on it and turned it in to the lady he'd talked to the day before. He told her that when he'd come back to her office the day before, she'd left out. He told her that was the reason that he had to come back. The lady just smiled and never asked any questions.

She scheduled him to take a physical and talk to the Chief of Police, and he did both. The next thing Jesse knew, he was in a policeman's uniform with a badge pinned to his chest. Jesse felt very comfortable about being in this uniform; he kind of had a feeling that he was now "above the law", who would ever believe that such a thing was possible?

His first job was as security reinforcement at the Atlanta airport. There was a very wealthy family that had invested heavily in the concession stands and restaurants inside the airport and there were a lot of issues surrounding the situation because there was a scandal in full operation and the security was very tight. On his third day, he was surely surprised when he was instructed to keep in close proximity with Mayor Maynard Jackson, who was touring the airport.

It was quite obvious that there were some real power leaking around the place and if that was the case, then he would probably be pretty safe around here.

Jesse worked at the airport approximately two months before he was transferred downtown to the Underground. Everything was wide open down there, drugs were plentiful, and prostitution was so rampant that you'd think it was legal. Anything else you could imagine was going on there to. Immediately, Jesse realized that this was the place for him to be because the money was flowing like water.

One day Jesse observed a tall skinny guy for about forty-five minutes from across the street and he noticed that every time the guy thought he had his eye on him, he would make a move over near a garbage dump. He would then come back to the same spot as if he'd never moved. Jesse knew that the guy was selling drugs and he knew that he was making good money because he was moving around too much, but he was sure the guy didn't know he was watching him.

One night Jesse targeted this guy all night and when he started to get his stash, Jesse walked out from behind the garbage dump and said, "Put your hands on the wall, this is a shake down. I have reasons to believe those are drugs you have in that bag. So you have the right to remain silent until I decide what the hell I want to do with you," said Jesse.

Jesse began to frisk the man down and as he did he found a gun in the man's left hip pocket. He took the gun and stuck it inside his belt; he then made the guy get into a more vulnerable position and made him spread his legs. Jesse then read the guy his rights.

Jesse also got a bag that contained about three different kinds of drugs and the man also had about $2700.00 in his pocket. The man immediately started begging for a chance. He said that he was already a two-time loser and this would surely get him more than a few years in the slammer.

This was exactly what Jesse wanted, because he never had any intentions of taking anyone to jail. Shit, that's against his creed!

After they had a few minutes of 'what will happen to me if I go down' versus 'what's gonna happen to you if I take you down' Jesse finally said, "Listen, I'm gonna give your ass a break, but at anytime you don't like the deal, you just say so and I'll just lock your ass up, ok?"

"I'm taking all of your money and your gun, you understand?" Jesse asked in a deep voice. "I'm gonna let you keep the drugs, just as long as you cut me in on everything you do down here you understand?"

After Jesse had gotten all of his information on a phony book just to make the man think that he was really on record, the man started agreeing with everything Jesse was saying. The man was "piss in his pants happy" from the words he was hearing from Jesse's mouth. Eventually, Jesse let the man leave, after telling him of a couple more spots in the Underground that turned out to be good business spots.

That night started a trend for Jesse because he was the only cop on the run that he knew of.

* * *

Jesse found himself making money so easy that he knew he had to be very careful. The only time he would enforce the law upon a person was when he was with another officer or where the situation dictated no other choice. Jesse had been working the Underground Atlanta for about four months before he started to get that little itchy feeling that it was about time to move on. Not that he'd seen anything in particular, but he knew that he'd been shading some real wrong doings since being down here in the Underground and common sense just tells you that you just can't continue to do the same wrong things and be able to stay in the same area. But another incident that jarred his senses was one morning when Jesse walked into the Chief of Police's office and there he sat looking through some most wanted profiles.

Jesse acted as though he had no interest in what the man was doing as he talked to him about a security job they were sending policemen to in Florida, but he never stopped looking at the pictures. After that day, Jesse didn't find many reasons to go into his office again.

Jesse was working one night when he met a lady named Elsie. She was from some part of Alabama, but had been living in Atlanta for a couple of years with her son Jalon. Jesse met Elsie one day when she locked her keys in her car. Jesse had gotten a clothes hanger and slipped it through her door and jimmied her lock and opened it. She was so elated by what he'd done that she offered to pay him, but he declined the money and asked for a good old country cooked meal, and she obliged him.

And sure enough the very next day, Elsie cooked a meal that would be fitting for a king. Collard greens, macaroni and cheese, potato salad, baked chicken and a butter crusted apple pie. Jesse was very complimentary of her cooking skills and Elsie was totally overwhelmed by his mannerisms, charms and good looks. As a matter of fact, that very dinner was the introduction to a relationship that took on many crooks and turns.

The very next day Elsie came down on his job around the time he was getting off and they had an evening out on the town. After that night, Jesse moved in with her and her son.

Elsie walked blindly into a love triangle that really just confused her in a lot of ways. She had absolutely no way of knowing what kind of a man she was dealing with, the police uniform really deceived her. His charismatic personality left her absolutely nothing to go on; even though he seemed to be everything she ever wanted in a man. He was romantic, caring, humorous, supportive and very handsome. But for some strange reason, Elsie knew that this was a man of seasons; when the weather changes, he would probably be gone. But for now she was definitely going to enjoy the mysteries, fallacies and the comforts of this man.

She hardly knew anything about him, his background, his life style, or his goals in life and even when she asked him questions, Jesse was so cautious about answering them that she only got a real smooth lie. The police uniform really threw her clean out of the ballpark of knowing who and what he was.

Elsie was steadily becoming more and more vulnerable to Jesse's wants and needs. She was always trying to please him and Jesse was taking cold advantage of her hospitality and generosity.

"Elcie"

Elsie had never had a relationship that really gave her the endearing affection that she knew she deserved. They all seemed to take advantage of her generosity and feelings. Jalon's father had left her for a white woman and Elsie had never quite gotten over what he did, but at least her desires remained with black men.

One very beautiful sunny Saturday morning, Jesse took Elsie and Jalon to Savannah, Georgia with him and she thought that was the bomb. She was so happy she had a glow on her face because she'd never been treated like this before. But for Jesse, he just wanted to look like the average black family when he went into the city. After all he did get busted there and he couldn't afford to be running into certain people.

But Jesse was going to Savannah to talk to some people he knew about doing a job. Jesse knew that he wasn't going to be in Atlanta too long, he was feeling that itch and he wanted to pull a job before he headed north.

Jesse really didn't like taking them to many places with him, because of his spur of the moment life style. He wasn't married and had no interest in living like a married man. When he had to move, he had to move and couldn't afford to truly be obligated to any particular person or thing. But shortly after their weekend in Savannah, Jesse was riding in Elsie's car one Friday night somewhere on the south side of Atlanta, when he ran a stop sign. Blue lights came on from behind him and he knew that he had to come up with something quick because he had two other guys in the car with him and they had been drinking a few beers.

Break and Run

The squad car was now right on his bumper and Jesse pulled over. Jesse immediately got out of the car and started to tell the officers that he too was a police officer, but the officer ordered him to get back into the vehicle, he knew then that he was about to have some trouble out of this redneck cop. He was already calling in the tag number. When the officer finally got out of the cruiser, he walked to one side of the car as his partner walked to the back passenger side with his hand on his gun. They didn't want to hear no shit. Jesse tried again to tell the officers he was an officer also. But the officers replied, "Shit, that still don't give you the right to be runnin stop signs, officer! His words were harsh and his tone of voice was very sarcastic. Then he requested to see some I.D. from everybody. The situation was so tensed you could feel the vibrations of nervous energy in the air.

First of all, Jesse knew that the officer really didn't believe he was an officer or he just wanted to harass a brother, because the first thing he asked Jesse for was his badge number and he insisted on seeing his shield. Well the first thing that ran through Jesse's mind was that these freaks was gonna take him down, because the officer on the passenger side was now shining his flash light all threw the car. And before his thought had time to transcend into reality, he heard the officer yell, "We got something here," he was coming out of the car with a gun that Jesse had underneath the seat. That's when they pulled their guns and ordered them to lie down on the ground and they all were handcuffed while Jesse tried to explain.

He told the officers that the gun had been confiscated from a guy he'd apprehended on the street, which was true, but at this point, these guys were only talking precinct. Even though this was the last place Jesse needed to go, he felt that he still had a chance of getting out if they didn't find out who he really was and he was going to try like hell to keep them from fingerprinting.

However, Jesse had been fingerprinted so many times that he thought he had a pretty good system for beating the fingerprinting thang, cause he would constantly shave his fingers with a Gillette razorblade. This alters the print and makes them flat; his own prints have come back negative.

The tag came back registered to Elsie and the officer wanted to know if the car was stolen. Jesse explained to him how he was legally in charge of the car. Once they got to the precinct, Jesse was pretty upset at the officers because they had treated him like a common criminal about the gun and he had requested to talk to the Chief of Police, but was told that the Chief would be unavailable for three days. Fingerprints were never mentioned since he already had been fingerprinted as an officer.

The next morning, he had a preliminary hearing and the judge gave him a $2500.00 bond on each count to be followed by an investigation of why he had not turned the guns in if they were confiscated. As soon as they allowed him a phone call, he called Elsie and told her what had happened and that he needed her to come down and bail him out and get her car. Jesse knew he had to get out of here and fast.

* * *

Elsie assured him that she would be down to get him, but first she had to borrow the money from her uncle. At 11:20am the following morning, Jesse was being released. She didn't even inquire about her car. She was just so glad that her man was out of jail. "What happened?" she asked. Along with a million other questions, but as always she was lead to believe that it was a bullshit case of some red neck cops trying to get a black man fired.

Things took a drastic turn after the night Jesse was arrested. Actually the whole police thing was becoming too intense and emotional to continue to deal with. He was too much in the limelight and his personality was totally different from that. He felt he needed to be a lot more discreet than the job allowed and he also knew that it was time for him to leave this city behind.

* * *

Trying to explain to Elsie that he had to be leaving the city for a while was like speaking Greek to a German. She just couldn't force herself to even try to understand this whole thing about leaving her behind. It just didn't sound right. Elsie was not too concerned about anything but going with Jesse. He had to plain just say no, no, hell no you can't go!

Elsie was devastated, all she had invested in this man, all the love she had shown, all the money she had spent and the most hurtful, all the fool she had been. This relationship was turning out just the way her previous one's did, with a broken heart and a man not leaving a forwarding address. It was really kind of hard for Jesse to leave Jalon and Elsie at that time because he had really started to like them quite a bit. After all, they were the closest thing he'd had to a normal family life in years, but the road of a criminal's life was not the road a woman and a kid need to travel.

After a couple of days out, Jesse knew it was time to move and that's just what he did. Elsie was really hurt and humiliated and this time it seemed as though it really hurt more than before. She really thought that this one would last. She was so in love with everything that Jesse said, but what she didn't want to hear was that Jesse was now gone out of her life for good. In the back of her mind though, she knew it wouldn't last too long because it was too sweet. She didn't have a clue as to where he was going. All he said was that he would call her and let her know where he was in due time, but she was already lonely for him and she didn't have a clue as to if she would ever see him again.

Jesse had been gone for about three weeks before two detectives came to Elsie's house and showed her pictures of Jesse and asked her if she knew this man. Elsie was shocked numb by the words and accusations these people were saying about this wonderful man. It had to be a mistake, they had to be crazy!

The detective told her that Jesse was a wanted man by the state of Alabama and Georgia for bank robbery and escape. Elsie was completely blown away by these charges.

All she could say was, "This man here couldn't be wanted, he was a police officer right here in Atlanta, he couldn't be wanted."

"Do you know where we can find him?" the detective asked.

"No, I do not know, I haven't heard from him in about three weeks," she said.

"Did he say where he was going?" the detective asked.

"No he did not, I've been waiting to hear from him," she replied.

"Do you know the penalty for harboring a fugitive?" he asked.

The words alone started Elsie to perspire caused she'd never had any kind of dealings with the law before.

"Mr., I've told ya'll all I know about this man, he lived with me and my son for about three or four months and he left here about three weeks ago. I ain't heard from him since and that's the truth," Elsie said. She was almost in tears, how could this be?

"Listen, here's my card, if he contacts you in any way, I urge you to call this number at once and I must inform you that any information you withhold can be used against you in a court of law. So you should make sure you call if you hear anything o.k.?" the detective said.

"Yes sir!" she said.

* * *

It seemed as though Jesse had ESP because less than two hours later, he called Elsie. "How are you and Jalon doing?" he asked.

No, hell no, you mean how the hell are you doing, don't you?" Elsie said. Her voice was very hostile and it sounded as if she'd been crying. "Some detectives just left my house looking for you and they told me so much about you that I just can't believe it," Elsie said.

"They said you was wanted by the police in two states, baby please tell me that's not true, please!" she begged.

"Elsie calm down baby listen, I wanted to tell you, but I really couldn't take the chance of telling you what's really going on with me, it would have been too stressful for you and Jalon, that's why I couldn't take you with me, now do you understand?" Jesse said. He tried to explain, but Elsie was too hysterical to listen to or hear anything he was saying.

"What did you tell them and what did they tell you?" he asked. At this point, Jesse was very skeptical about what he said now, because he knew how the detectives could frighten Elsie into some strange things. He would never tell her where he was calling from.

"They asked me if I knew where you were going, did I know your whereabouts and how long did you stay with me," she said.

"And what did you say?" Jesse asked.

"I told them I didn't know where you were and that we stayed together for about three or four months and that I didn't believe those things they told me!" she said.

"They also told me to call them if I hear from you," Elsie said.

"Are you gonna call them?" he asked.

"Call them for what?" she said. "I don't have anything to tell them folks, cause I still can't believe what they said, please tell me it's not so," she said. Elsie's voice was considerably calmer now. It kinda sounded like some of them old loving feelings were creeping back in.

Nevertheless, Jesse wasn't about to tell her where he was and he was glad now that he was at least a one hundred miles from the city when he decided to make this call, because if they traced the call, they would still be a good distance away from him.

"When am I gonna see you?" Elsie asked.

"I don't know baby, I got to figure out some things and I'll be getting back with you ok," Jesse said.

"Well, baby tell me something, don't leave me like this, I need you!" Elsie said.

"Listen, I'll be getting in touch with you. Read the want-ads, you'll find me!" Jesse said.

"I need to go, ok. Give Jalon my regards," Jesse said.

Elsie was more confused now than before, because Jesse never did deny any of the charges that were lodged against him and that didn't set too well with her. This time she really felt used, betrayed and just plain played on.

Was there a reason that all her relationships had to turn out in such utter disappointments? Was there any real love in the cards for her? Would she find love at the end of the rainbow? These thoughts and more ran through her mind. The more she thought of the situation, the angrier she became with the thought of men!

Something had to give. She didn't want to continue being screwed too many different ways by these "just between the legs freaks". It was time to do something!

"Betrayed by love"

For the first time in her life, Elsie was becoming more and more angry. She wanted to get even, especially after Jesse wouldn't tell her where he was. Her first thought was that he must've been with some woman that he was using just like he used her. Jesse was in Tampa, Florida when he called Elsie, but he was on his way to Auburndale, Florida where he had friends.

Alberta and her son were both glad to see him and were really amazed at the story he had to tell them about the jailbreak and the job on the police force. They thought that was the biggest joke ever played on the law.

It didn't take Jesse long to get back in the groove of the things he normally did cause he'd always stop by the pool hall for a few games, just to keep his edge sharp.

After about four months in Auburndale, Jesse had been thinking of maybe heading out for New York City. He felt that he had a much better chance of concealment in a city with millions of people.

One day as he was coming from St. Petersburg, Florida with a girl he'd met in Auburndale, he decided to stop and call Elsie. "Hello?" said Elsie. Her voice was very pleasant and then the voice from the other end spoke into her ear, a voice she recognized as Jesse's. "How are you baby?" Jesse asked. "Oh you finally left them bitches alone long enough to call?" Elsie said. Her voice had changed with the sound of his voice. "Are you angry Elsie?" Jesse asked her.

"What the hell do you expect me to be after all this time and I haven't heard from you?" she said. She was almost crying as she screamed into the phone.

"Got Damn Elsie, you really don't get it do you? I'm on the fucking run! I'm sure you know that by now, so what's this bullshit baby? Either you're done with me or you're not, now what's up?" Jesse said.

Before she could answer, Jesse continued, "Baby, there's no room for you in my life right now. I don't know what tomorrow may bring to me, but I have to stay on the move, can you see that?"

"Then why don't you give yourself up and one day we could be together!" she said.

Even before she was finished with her sentence, Jesse was laughing at her statement. "If I was gonna give myself up, shit I might as well have stayed in prison!" he said.

This conversation went on for a few minutes before it really turned sour. "Well when will I see you?" Elsie asked.

"Well seeing me might be out of the question for awhile, but I'll let you know, ok?" Jesse said.

Elsie could hear the tone of his voice and she already knew the answer. This thing with Jesse was just like the others and it ain't no fun being the fool all the time.

Jesse realized that it was time to lose this woman's phone number because she was too into some other kind of world to know what this had to be about. So at that point Jesse resumed looking out for number one.

About six months had passed and Jesse was keeping pretty low in Auburndale, Florida. The only thing he was doing was gambling at Alberta's house, but if you didn't know what was going on, you never would know. Because the people that came there were all a very select group. That way they controlled just who really knew about their escapade.

One weekend during the summer of '80, Jesse decided to come up to Alabama to see the family. He brought a woman up with him from Auburndale. She was a beautiful young lady with a fantastic body, but maybe a few years younger than she actually looked. But that Saturday turned out to be the worst night for Jesse in a long time.

The young lady that Jesse had brought with him, Eldora, had wanted to go out to a club just to see what really went on around Phenix City, Alabama.

Because they were staying with our sister, Doll, there was a club just up the street that was really popping hot in those days. The crowd would always end up at the H&D club in the wee hours of the morning because it didn't close until 5:00 am and they served food.

Jesse decided to take Eldora there for a while. Very few people around Phenix City ever really knew Jesse because he was never a resident of the area. Therefore, he felt pretty safe being there. But as fate would have it that was the least of the problems he was about to encounter.

They were having a pretty good time when Jesse got up and walked over to the bar to get them a drink. Suddenly the sounds of the music, the faces of the people and the sight of Jesse became soundless, faceless and instant shock to Elsie. She was sitting in the corner with her cousin whom had come to the H&D, just like people from miles away did who've heard that this was the happening spot. Elsie was dumbfounded and speechless.

When she saw Jesse, it took all of her strength to control the emotional anger that was exploding inside her like acid reflux. Her first thought was to go over to him, but then after seeing him go back over to the table with this woman, she decided not to say a damn word.

Elsie was so choked up by what she'd just witnessed that she immediately wanted to go home, so she told her cousin that she was leaving. But during their conversation, she changed her mind and decided it was time to face this bastard. After all, he had taken her to the cleaners and now he was here with some other woman.

They sat in the car for more than an hour waiting for Jesse and Eldora to come out of the club. Finally they came out and as they headed across the street to the parking lot, Elsie appeared out of nowhere right in front of Jesse. Elsie was holding what appeared to be a .38 revolver and Jesse could tell that the hammer was back, the gun was cocked.

"So you gonna bring your bitch up in my face motherfucker?" Elsie said. She was crying. The sight of the gun spooked the whole crowd and people started running in all directions.

Jesse's first attempt was to try and walk up on her with some sweet talk, but that shit was out of the question. As he started to move towards her, she started screaming out, "don't come up on me, you son-of-a-bitch, I'll kill you and that bitch!" she said. Elsie was hysterical and shaking. This was the first time in Jesse's life that he was looking down the barrel of a gun held by an angry woman.

Eldora screamed, "Please don't shoot me miss, I'm not from here!"

"I don't give a damn where you're from bitch, I oughta kill both of you," Elsie said.

Again Jesse tried to talk to her and make a move towards her, but to his surprise, she turned and ran across the parking lot to her car. Her cousin was running along side her trying to get the gun away from her.

Once she was in and had started the car, she backed up at a full rate of speed. As Jesse and Eldora jumped between two cars, she slammed on the brakes. She started cursing again and threatening them again, but she never pulled the gun back out.

Jesse still tried unsuccessfully to talk to her, but she was much too hype.

Eldora was freaking the hell out. She didn't know what the hell was going on, but she finally managed to ask.

"Al, who's that crazy woman, you ain't married are you?" she asked. Her words were frantic.

"No, hell no," was Jesse's response. "She's a woman I met back in Atlanta some time ago and she just won't leave me alone, but I never thought she'd be here cause she lives over

80 miles from here," Jesse said.

Elsie sped away in a tire squealing rage. Jesse and Eldora were left stunned, along with a lot of more people.

Jesse never really thought that she would shoot them, but he was nervous as hell when he saw that hammer back. They hurriedly went to the car and left the area. Jesse was much more angry than he was scared. He couldn't believe this stupid ass woman would confront him like this and with a gun!

He spent the rest of the night trying to figure out just what happened.

* * *

Doll woke Jesse up that Sunday morning telling him he had a phone call. He got up to answer it and was instantly awakened when he heard Elsie's voice.

"Hello," Jesse said.

"You still with that bitch?" were her harsh words.

"Elsie you need to get a hold of yourself before you force me to kick your ass! I don't like you drawing no fucking gun on me! What's the fuck wrong with you nigga?" Jesse asked. He really didn't have any intention of getting hostile with her, but he knew he had to get control of this situation before anything else went wrong.

She finally calmed down a little and they talked for quite a while until Jesse agreed to meet her at our mother's house in three hours.

After consoling Eldora about the situation and telling Doll a little bit about what had happened that night, Jesse decided that it might be a good idea, and to his advantage to meet and have a talk with Elsie. After all, she knew where Doll lived and could have sent the police to her house. However Jesse and Eldora spent the rest of the day at a Holiday Inn on the expressway.

He didn't think that Elsie meant to do him any harm, she was just mad at seeing him with another woman, but had he any idea that she would've been in Phenix City, never in hell would he have been there.

Jesse knew that Elsie was in love with him and all she wanted to know was that he still loved her. Now was the time for him to reaffirm that love affair.

As Jesse drove up to momma's house, he was deep in thought about what he was going to say to Elsie, and to show her that his feelings for her were still flourishing and true. He knew that if he went to her right, he could make her pay for all this excitement she'd caused the night before. But just as Jesse was driving up in momma's parking lot, he observed a detective cruiser pulling out of a side street behind him and another one pulling onto the street in front of him. Something was wrong with this picture. He started to keep on past the parking lot, but changed his mind and pulled in anyway. At that point, the cruisers sped in behind him, and before he could get out of his car, four detectives jumped out of the cars with pistols drawn.

"Put your hands on top of your head Mr. Griffin, you're under arrest!" one of the detectives said.

They proceeded to handcuff him as they read him his rights. All the neighbors stood in their doorways, on sidewalks and murmured about what was going on.

They put Jesse in the cruiser and drove off to the police station, which was less than four blocks away. As they pulled into the police station, he was even more surprised to see Elsie's car parked in a space next to where they parked.

Even though Jesse never saw her, he was sure that she identified him from somewhere, but he never saw her.

To further clarify the setup, one of the detectives made a comment that a scorned lover was still their best source of apprehension. He knew then for sure that it was Elsie.

Jesse used his phone call to contact me, hoping that I could arrange bail before they found out who he really was.

I entered the police station less than an hour later to try and bond him out, only to be informed that because there was a bench warrant on him, he would not be given a bond. Just as I was about to leave, I ran into an officer that grew up with us named Ryles.

And his first words were, "Ain't that your brother that they just brought in?" he asked inquisitively.

"No that's not my brother, that's my cousin; he used to live with us." I lied.

Even though I was certain that Ryles wasn't buying that story, I didn't give him time to ask me anything else, I walked off.

One thing I knew was that Ryles didn't know Jesse too well and couldn't really dispute my claim. But you could tell by his reaction that he knew something wasn't exactly right about this situation.

Later that afternoon, Jesse and I did get a chance to talk for about five minutes on the phone. Jesse asked me to make sure that Eldora got back to Auburndale okay and to pick up his clothes and car from Alberta's house. Eldora would know just where to go.

So Eldora and I got on the road a couple of hours later and arrived in Auburndale in the early morning.

* * *

Eldora introduced me to Alberta and her son. They were really devastated to hear all the shit that had taken place in the last 24 hours. They could hardly believe their ears, and eager to help him in any manner that they could.

I finished loading Jesse's clothes and everything else in the '78 Camaro Z-28, which Jesse had, stole from a Chevrolet dealership two years earlier.

The tag had expired. As a matter of fact, I was pretty sure that this car had never been properly registered since Jesse had it, but it was my only transportation for getting back to Phenix City, Alabama.

Later that afternoon, I hit the road in the hot Camaro and drove to Alabama with no problem, but my other brothers and I quickly stripped the car down and got rid of the body. That was the last of Jesse's freedom for a few more years.

"What is reality"

Jesse stayed in Phenix City for only three days before they transferred him back to Atlanta.

The fat ass sheriff pretended to be so furious at Jesse about the gun that he was apprehended with that. He wanted a full-scale investigation on him. That's when they decided to do a crime search and re-fingerprint him.

There were about three or four warrants that came back in Jesse's name and the whole department damn near fainted when they found out that Officer Isaiah Griffin was really escape convict Jimmy L. Ogletree. The same convict wanted in the State of Alabama for escape while serving a 45 year sentence, wanted in the State of South Carolina for alleged conspiracy and wanted even right here in the State of Georgia for armed robbery and escape.

The entire police department was so embarrassed at the fact that an escaped convict had actually come to the department and secured a job on the force for approximately nine months, that they didn't want this kind of information to make the headlines. They just let the matter die out.

* * *

Jesse served approximately ten years before he ever felt the feeling of possible freedom again. That came about when the district attorney for the State of Alabama made sure Jesse was very well punished for the crimes he'd committed. However, he along with the judge who presided over the case, had violated all of Jesse's civil rights by over sentencing him with the 45 year sentence, when the punishment really only carried a sentence of 10 to 20 years.

Jesse was tried and victimized by an all white jury that seemed to have been hand picked to put a brother away for good, or for a very long time. However, a bill had been petitioned to the House of Representatives to illegalize all white juries, and the bill was passed before Jesse was tried. Therefore a writ of habeas corpus would turn his case around.

Sometime before 1988, the D.A. (District Attorney) retired from the District Attorney's office and went into a private law practice.

Fortunately he never forgot about Jesse's case and wrote him a letter.

He informed Jesse of the fact that there could be a retrial on his behalf because of the civil rights violations. He also wrote that if he wanted to know more about his chances of at least a reduction in his sentence, that he should contact a lawyer in Birmingham, Alabama by the name of Brown. The former D.A. felt he could be a great deal of help to him.

Jesse wasted no time contacting Mr. Brown who in turn answered his letter back and explained how he was misrepresented by the State of Alabama. He explained that Jesse had a good chance of getting out of the penitentiary with proper representation. He informed Jesse that he would take the case for a mere $12,000.00.

Jesse's mind was so cluttered with thoughts for the next few days that he jumped on the phone and called me to help him put some kind of plan in operation. This was the first thought of freedom that he had entertained in the last ten years. He could even smell the fresh air.

Ruby, in Miami, had maybe $2,500.00 to $3,000.00 for him from the job years ago, however, he had contacted her on several occasions while he was on the run and got some of the money. But he was sure that there was less than $5000.00 left.

He really needed a plan, one that would net him at least $7000.00. And again he called me to visit him.

Break and Run

* * *

We had to come up with a plan that would help them make a lot of money in the shortest possible time. Jesse knew that robbery was out of the question for me, because I was absolutely out of that game.

That's when I made a comment about the quickest way to make money now a days is to get a drug bag and keep flipping the money.

That's when Jesse said, "If I could get some drugs in here, it wouldn't take me too long to get the money, cause these guys pay top dollar for a joint of marijuana."

Jesse told me to give him a little time to check out some things inside the prison.

A couple weeks later when I went back to visit Jesse, he had what he thought was a very good plan for getting him some drugs inside the prison.

During this time Jesse was confined to the St. Clair Correctional Institution in Odenville, Alabama approximately thirty miles northwest of Birmingham, Alabama.

Jesse had befriended a guy who was a trustee in the prison. He worked outside of the prison in the maintenance department. They kept the streets around the prison clean.

There was a bridge about half a mile before reaching the institution and this guy Robert Lee, walked across the bridge everyday on his way to the maintenance department.

"Do you think you can bring some marijuana out here and put it underneath the bridge right down the road?" Jesse asked me.

"Man, I know you're bullshitting to think I'm about to bring some weed out here on this prison property." I answered.

"But how else can we make this work if you don't put the weed in a place where my man can get to it?" Jesse asked.

"Well, I don't know" I said.

"Well all I'm asking you to do is to think about it," Jesse said.

"You got any ideas on how you can get something in here?" Jesse asked.

"Well the last time we talked on the phone, you wanted me to send you a Christmas box, so I was thinking of a way I could send you some stuff in the box," I said.

"I don't understand what you mean," Jesse said.

"Well, you know those Cracker Jacks you like so much that come three boxes to a container?" I asked.

"Yeah," Jesse answered.

"Well, I know how to put you about an ounce of marijuana in the middle box. I know how to open it up, put the weed in it and close it back up without anyone being able to tell that I've been inside the box." I said.

"Oh yeah, you think you can do that now?" Jesse asked.

"Hell, I can do that anytime," I responded.

"I mean, how you gone do it cause if they figure out the box has been tampered with that could really cause a lot of problems!" Jesse said unbelieving.

"Well, what you do is take a butter knife and you heat it up, then you take it and ease it underneath the top. It's sealed with some kind of wax and the heat from the knife melts the wax a loose, then I eat all the Cracker Jacks out of the box and fill it up with marijuana and then I seal it back up with Elmer's Glue," I explained.

Jesse was looking really surprised cause he always knew that I was very good with certain things, so he would never doubt me about anything I say I can do.

This was a little trick that I used to do for some of the guys back in the Tallahassee Federal Correctional, after I left the place.

Jesse agreed with me, but there would still have to be some other way, because you can only get one box per inmate. I solved that problem by telling Jesse to get some more guys that could receive boxes and give me their names.

The scheme worked just perfect, I managed to get Jesse almost a quarter pound of marijuana in the prison while they could get Christmas boxes. And Jesse made about a thousand dollars off of the staff, so it was obvious to us that the plan would work. Now all we had to do was get it in the joint. After a couple of weeks and some thought about the bridge drop that Jesse had proposed, I had somewhat decided that I probably would make a drop or two for him there. But I had to figure out how I would do it so that absolutely no one would know what I was doing.

Break and Run

* * *

The very first drop I did was on a Sunday around midday while I was going to visit Jesse. And even though everything went smooth, I didn't like the daylight move. There was too much light and too many people traveling that road, I just didn't feel good about this.

Therefore I decided that if I was going to do this, I would make my moves on Monday morning around 2:30 and 3:30 am; that's when I really felt safe. Jesse's man didn't have any problem getting the stuff in, so now everything was a go.

I made two trips to Odenville during the early hours of the morning and both of the trips were filled with nerve wrecking excitement. The first trip I made was with my brother Curtis. We were traveling on highway 280 going to Birmingham around 2:00 am. We were sipping on a bottle of Remy Martin Cognac and smoking a joint or two of weed with a half pound of weed underneath the front seat for the drop. I was very cautious of my driving, I made sure I stayed below the speed limit and thought I was driving pretty good when this car that had been behind me for about 10 miles, all of a sudden came up with police lights flashing all over the place.

Curtis had drifted off to sleep and I tried to wake him before I pulled over for the officer, but was unsuccessful. Curtis had been hitting the bottle pretty hard. I stopped the car and the officers instructed me to get out of the car and also asked for my driver's license.

"Have you been drinking Mr. Hodge?" the officer said, shining the light in my face.

I thought that the officer had probably smelled the alcohol on my breath and there was no need to tell him a lie, so I did what I thought was best.

"Yes sir officer, I had a drink before I left work about two hours ago, you see I've worked for the last thirteen hours today and we had to go to Birmingham to see our brother who's sick. I just took a drink to try and stay woke," I explained.

"Are you willing to take a sobriety test?" he asked.

"Well I'm gonna take it anyway if you insist officer, but I'm not drunk by any means," I replied.

"Well just stand straight with your feet together, lean your head back and touch your nose for me please," the officer said. He seemed as though he was enjoying what he was doing, so I complied with him. I also added in some moves of my own by stretching both arms out, raising one leg up chest level high and twisting my body almost completely around while still standing on one leg. I knew that this man was impressed with my athletic abilities and flexibility, because I did yoga almost everyday as a way of exercise and relaxation.

The officer realized that even though I had admitted to having a drink before the journey began, he knew that I was completely in control of myself. The officer shined his light in the car, aiming it straight in Curtis' face.

"Who is that?" the officer asked.

"That's my brother," I replied.

"Wake him up," the officer said.

"Curt!" I called out to him, but Curtis had drank a little too much of the alcohol to be aroused so easy. So I leaned over in the car and pinched him hard.

"Ouch!" Curtis groaned. "What the hell you doing man, get that damn light out of my face!" Curtis said. He was finally waking up and realizing that something was wrong.

Curtis sat up in the seat and looked the officer straight in the face.

"What's your name?" the officer asked.

"James Curtis Hodge," answered Curtis.

"Where are you all going?" the officer asked.

I spoke up and said, "Tell him where we're going Curt!"

"We are going to Birmingham to visit our brother," answered Curtis. His answer was the right answer.

With that answer the officer gave me my driver's license back and told me to watch my driving and be careful, and then he walked away.

When I got back in the car, I was really stunned by what I saw. The only thing I said was, "Curt, look at this!"

Curtis looked over at me staring down in the floor of the car between his legs.

For some strange reason, the marijuana had managed to slide from underneath the front seat and was very visible to anyone who just looked. With that scary situation now behind us, we both laughed out loud dapping each other. We took some more gulps of the alcohol before continuing on our journey. The rest of the trip went as planned.

* * *

It was approximately three weeks to a month before Jesse and I got back in contact with each other. We had planned things that way just in case anything went wrong, we didn't want to have to do much communicating with each other.

Jesse had done very well with the product; the money was looking pretty good for the amount. However, Jesse suggested that if he could get a pound of the stuff that would be enough to get the rest of the money. I still didn't like making the trips to Odenville, but I was willing to do whatever I could to help my brother finally get his freedom.

* * *

The day finally came when I was making what I hoped was my last run. I was pretty sure that if Jesse had done so well off of three quarters of a pound, then by my calculation this should be the last trip. It was a Tuesday night and the air was quite brisk and cool, but the sky was very bright. As I drove the long trip from Phenix City to Birmingham, I started thinking about one night when Sue and I, my childhood sweetheart, was walking under the moonlight holding hands and stealing kisses. This night reminded me of that.

I thought how different the two nights were. With Sue, my heart was at ease and melting with desire. Tonight, my heart was troubled and dreading the task at hand. I prayed that nothing would go wrong, that everything combined would total up to this being the last trip. The pressure of doing this over and over was getting to me and I couldn't continue doing this kinda thing.

After all if I ever got caught doing any of this stuff, they'd throw the book at me for one simple reason. Because I already had a record and there would be no love lost between the State and an ex-con helping a con to escape, or supplying him with drugs. Freedom for me would be a thing of the past.

I always had me a pint of Cognac whenever I got on the road. The jazz and the Cognac seemed to keep my thoughts quiet and helped me rationalize my behavior. I always felt that when you're doing wrong, you need to be relaxed. Tonight I was really thinking on the edge, because a lot of times the police have a tendency to just stop a brother and harass the hell out of him for no reason. And even more so if he was from out of town.

Even though I used to bring weed up from Miami back in the day, it wasn't like this in anyway.

Just transporting a little weed from city to city was really no problem, but transporting weed on State or Federal prison property will get your ass in a sling for a long time.

So maybe that's where the Cognac kicks in, because it always calms the mind. This kind of thing does carry a very powerful adrenalin rush though. It motivates a self-confidence that can become overwhelming. You start thinking you're invincible.

It was about 3:20 am when I turned off the main highway onto the road that leads to the prison. By now my adrenalin was beginning to flow, when all of a sudden I saw a car leaving the prison and from the illusion of lights in the background coming from the security walls, I could see the lights on top of the police car.

"Oh shit that's the police!" was my first thought. There's no reason for me to be on this property at this time of night. I knew that this was no time to panic, so I remained real calm as I started to think fast. I had to reverse the game. I needed to be lost.

As the car approached me I started to blink my lights as I stopped the car. Just as I suspected, it was the sheriff. The car came to a halt.

"Excuse me officer," I spoke. "I think I'm lost, I'm trying to go to Gadsden, Alabama. When I got directions from a man back up the road at a service station, he told me to take the next left. But this don't seem like the right kind of road," I said.

"Well, what you did was turn too quick, you need to go back to the stop sign, go left to the dead end of that road, then another left and that'll put you right on 459 Freeway. Then you'll go straight into Gadsden," the sheriff explained.

"Oh thank you very much officer, because this looks like a prison or something," I said as the officer laughed.

"That's what it is, I don't think you want to go up there," he said as he pulled off.

I was almost speechless as the car pulled away. The sweet part of the whole ordeal was that I was right there at the bridge where I was going, so I pulled over to make a turn around and jumped out and made the drop in a matter of seconds.

I made a u-turn and parked the car back on the street, so that the sheriff couldn't tell if I was standing or coming up the street. As I drove up to the stop sign at the highway, the sheriff was standing there and motioned for me to come around and go left. I waved at the officer as I pulled onto the highway.

I put Johnny "Guitar" Watson in the box as I cruised up to the speed limit. My self-ego began to grow as I thought of the way I outsmarted the law.

"Got your ass again," were my thoughts, but as I relaxed in the comforts of the seat in the Lincoln Towncar, I already knew that this was surely my last trip no matter how much more money Jesse needed.

* * *

Just as the lawyer had promised, he managed to make some kind of deal with the State parole office and they granted Jesse parole, ten years before he was eligible.

At last, my brother was legally free!!!!

"Life Turn Around"

When Jesse was released from the penitentiary, after serving more than ten years, I noticed that he was a completely different person from the Jesse I'd known all of my life. He was much quieter, more peaceful, yet more nonchalant. It was obvious that his values had changed drastically. He wanted to visit all of our family, and hug all the kids, he was a very pleasant person to be around, he spent most of his wakeful hours around our mother as though he was trying to recreate, or recapture all of the time that they'd been apart, he was like a butterfly that had sprouted new wings and wanted to just fly away!

I found this new form of character in Jesse somewhat amusing, because I to was finished with the criminal life, however I couldn't help but wonder if Jessie hadn't lost a very valuable part of himself. Had the years of incarceration finally created a form of torture that he could no longer endure? Or, had the life of constantly being on the run finally demanded a rest?

Or did God just finally say to him that, man you can't beat the system from the outside, so why not just give it up? It was clear to me that my brother was tired of the life that had caused him his life, and a change was the only answer. After being out for more than a couple of weeks, Jesse and I decided to take a ride down to Miami just to re-bond, and spend time together like we use to do before our lives became so complicated and it was probably the best time we ever spent together.

I closed the beauty salon for two weeks and we went down to Miami. I-75 offered the kind of freedom that we both had craved at one time or another, the weather was superb. The sum was invigorating, and the view simply breathe taking. We talked about our years of incarceration, the mistakes that put us there, and the nerve wrecking experiences that it took to free us from the chains of captivity. We had caused our mother so many sleepless nights, and unnecessary heart aches, it was us who were responsible for the uncountable number of grey strains of hair she had.

Was it worth it? No! Could we relieve her pain? No, but we could live the rest of our days trying to comfort and console her and that was our solemn commitment. To show her that the decision that we made was ours and our mistakes was no reflection on her motherhood. We were just bad asses in the worst way. Our first stop in Florida was Leesburg. We had to go by and see Rodgers and Marcellus, there was so many feelings and situations that has gotten crossed up, and misunderstood in the past, that we knew that now was the time to come clean and reestablish our character as men, and revive the presence of the lead that now shared our lives, Hoping to dispel the myth that we were hard people.

Rodgers and Marcellus greeted us with open arms and big smiles. I think it took a lot of pressure off of them when Jesse confirmed the fact that his criminal days was over, and he had no intentions of ever entering his old life style again.

The life of crime has a way of stealing your youth, just as a criminal steals from his victims. I realize now that if crime pays you anything, it's far below minimum wages and has no benefits. We all had a big laugh when Rodgers started telling us about the day when she went down to the police station to retrieve Jesse's belongings, and how that experience put her nerves on edge. Jesse, I was still scared three days later, Rodger said. I had you on a real high pedestal and after leaving that police station I was so mad at you that I didn't know what to do. She laughed, I just hope you have put all of that behind you now!

I have Rodgers; Jesse replied, that was a road that I don't travel anymore. After hours of fellowshipping with Rodgers and Marcellus, Jesse and I hit the road again, and this time we were headed for Auburndale Florida, it was just good to be free and with the air between us being clear now, we was all set out to have us a good time. We pulled into Auburndale around one thirty a.m. and Jesse directed me over to Alberta, and Richard Milton's house. I was busy trying to readjust myself with the streets that I had traveled some twelve years ago, but the change in time and the progress of the city's building into the future made it kind of hard for me to believe that I'd been there before.

As usual, there were only a couple of cars parked in Mrs. Milton's yard, but once we entered the house, we found a card game going on, with about eight people playing. Alberta was really baffled by the sight of Jesse's face! Oh my God, were her words, Jimmy is this really you? She asked. Baby, I've been praying, and wondering when would I see you again and here you is! She was so overjoyed, they embraced each other as Richard and I was shaking hands. This is my brother, Jesse said as he continued to hold Mrs. Milton in his arms, do you all remember him? he asked. Oh, I sure do, I remember when he came down here and brought Eldora. Baby, I often wondered if you made it home in that car, because I remember the tag had expired, did you? Oh yes ma'am, with no trouble, I responded and shook her hand also.

Everybody, Mrs. Milton said getting the players attention, however they had already pierced in on us, and I'm pretty sure it was because they could tell that we were out of Towner's. These are two of our very best friends, real gentlemen, and just as close as any of my family, and as a matter of fact they are family! She said with a big grin. This man here is amazing, I have never met anybody like him, she was talking about Jesse. This is my baby here. Jesse was just standing there grinning and eating that shit up, because he knew that Alberta was trying to talk him into the game, and she was good at what she was doing cause a lot of players don't like for new faces to get into their games especially if they look slick or clean cut. But Jesse had no intentions of playing because he didn't want to get back into that hustling life style, it has caused him to many wasted years. The entire room seemed to relax after the words Alberta had just spoken. Ya'll want something to eat, drink, or anything, she asked with her hospitality overflowing. No, no, I'm just fine, was my reply, Jesse took a glass of water. I know ya'll are tired, but Jesse you know you're at home, so just let me know what ya'll want or need. I was really astounded by her genuine friendliness, and the fineness that just seemed to be woven into the serene spirit of her warm personality.

You could easily tell that she was a real people person, and she wasn't hard on the eyes either. After a cordial between everyone, the remainder of the evening was a lot of gossip and conversation about the past, and of course, Jesse took center stage. I just sort of slipped into a relaxing mood. Later that night, Alberta tried desperately to get us to spend the night, but Jesse lied and told her that we had already gotten a room before we got there, and I was glad he did, because I've always had a problem with sleeping in a strange place with other people in the house. After getting me a good nap, and the crowd thinning out, Jesse and I finally hit the road for Miami. I was reenergized after my nap and ready to ride, so I told Jesse that we could be in Miami around daybreak, and we were. The sun was just breaking the sky, and the view of the horizon was a beautiful sight to behold.

It brought back memories of the mornings I used to jog on the Beach back in '72 when I was a recruiter on Miami Beach. There was a familiar feeling that I'll never forget, my youth was the essence of my growth during those days; life was so carefree and happy, love was misting the air everywhere, and even Marvin Gaye was trying to find out what was going on. I had driven straight over to Titus's house our cousin and for the first time I think we both finally caught Titus at home. Normally he was at work and we had to wait for him to get off, but this morning, he was home, he called out so he could spend the day with us. When I rung the door bell, it didn't take Titus but a second to open the door because he was already getting dressed for work, but we changed all of that, he was glad to see us.

Ethel got up and immediately went to the grocery store and got food items and made us breakfast that country boys like us were used to back in the days, so she really put her foot down. We had so much to talk about that the sun didn't see us until the middle part of the day. There was nothing we didn't talk about, I think we started from childhood and worked our way up, I can't remember laughing so much. Jesse wanted to go see his daughter Jessica first, so that was our first move. She wasn't home when we first got there, but Mary was so glad to see Jesse that I think she forgot about Jessica for a minute.

Then all of a sudden, the door came open, and in walked Jessica. I could hardly believe my eyes; Jessica had really grown and had an awful lot of Jesse's features. "Isn't this my daddy," she asked, looking Jesse up and down. "Yes it is," Mary said with Jesse just standing there smiling! "You've grown into a real pretty girl," Jesse said and hugged her. "I've missed most of your young life haven't I?" Jesse asked in a question.

"Yes you have," Jessica replied, "but it's still not too late for you to buy me a car!"

I think those words unlocked the door to a world of a father and daughter sharing some love, because from that moment, they spent quite a bit of time together during the rest of our stay. Jesse and Mary even went out looking for her a little car. I left Jesse with Mary and Jessica before I hit the town. My first stop was Ruby's house, but to my dismay, she wasn't home and I had no clue as to her whereabouts. So I proceeded to drive by a few of the places that I was familiar with only to find that things had really changed, and the people I remembered were very few. Eventually I headed for Titus and Ethel's house because I hadn't had much sleep or rest in the last thirty (plus) hours.

There wasn't much left to talk about once I got back to the house, so I didn't have a problem crawling into bed and drifting off to sleep, especially since I was much more relaxed here than back at Mrs. Milton's in Auburndale. Being here with Titus and Ethel was really like being at home, so I slept like a baby all night and almost half of the next day. There was no one at the house but me when I woke up, and it took a few minutes for me to get myself together, but a good hot shower did the trick. One would really have to be in Miami to actually experience the exhilarating feeling that engulfs you when you're here. The beautiful women, the tropical scenery, and sunshine so bright, it seems to illuminate from the richness of the sand. Its sort of drowns you into a world of amazement.

By now my reminiscence of the past was really kicking in now as I drove Ponce de Leon freeway. Things had changed dramatically there was construction underway, and buildings that seemed that they just sprouted up from nowhere. The city was really on the move, Cuban, Haitian, and Spanish speaking people were everywhere. I stopped to ask some brothers about some directions and what had happened to the little pool room that use to be on Third Avenue only to find out that they were Haitian and didn't speak a lick of English. I was dressed and prepared to jog a few miles on the beach, something that I used to do three or four days a week, and that's exactly what I did.

As I ran, I took in the scenery, but after a couple of miles my concentration was centered around my running, it was very invigorating and all of a sudden Ruby crept into my mind. For the last three days, I had really been looking forward to seeing her, and I had no intentions of letting this day slip away without pursuing that dream. After the run I drove over into Ft. Lauderdale where Jesse had stayed with Mary and Jessica. I thought that he might need some transportation, but to my dismay, they were gone when I got there so I then headed back to Titus and Ethel's house to get dressed. As it turned out Jesse, Jessica and Mary were there when I arrived. We talked cordially for a while before Mary and Jessica decided to leave. Jesse and I got dressed and decided to have dinner at the restaurant that we were both very familiar with when all of a sudden Jesse said, "when we finish eating, I want to go by a lady's house for a while, I need to see her." "No problem," was my response. "I use to love this city," Jesse said, "but I never really had the chance to enjoy it." "Man you was here for a few years, you mean you didn't have any fun?" I asked. "Shit most of my time here, I was running and hiding, you know. Shit it was hard to relax," Jesse said. 'Shit, I'd have to run a while and walk a while if it was me cause these ladies made a nigga stop and take note," I said. We shared a few good laughs the rest of the way to the restaurant. When we walked into the restaurant the lady sitting on the stool at the cash register was so shocked when she saw the two of us, that she almost lost her footing while jumping off the stool to come and greet us, she had a big large grin on her face as she approached us. "Oh my, what a pleasant surprise," she said. I immediately noticed the puzzled look on her face, as though she'd seen a ghost or something. She didn't know who to hug first. "I ain't seen ya'll in years," she said, "and I didn't know ya'll knew each other?" Her statement was more of a question and it was obvious that a lot of things were going thru her mind. "Oh, this is my brother," Jesse said. "Your brother?" she asked, looking and sounding bewildered. "Yes, my brother," was Jesse's reply. "I didn't know that you knew Jesse," I said.

"This is the guy that I told you that you reminded me of when you ordered that potato pie and that glass of milk, remember?" she said. "I always knew that it was something funny about ya'll," she said with a big laugh. "But I never put ya'll together like that, but I always thought about the pie and milk," she said, still laughing as she invited us to a table in the center of the dining area. The restaurant still looked pretty much the same for the most part. However, it appeared to have a new or different coat of paint, but the food had exactly the same taste, a taste of delicacy. "How long are ya'll gonna be staying this time, cause every time I think you'll be coming in, you're gone," She asked. But with all of the talking we were doing, I could still sense that she had something on her mind, and that's when she asked Jesse if he had seen Ruby since he'd been here and her question was somewhat informative, yet inquisitive.

"No, I haven't had a chance to get by there yet, how's she doing?" Jesse asked. "Well she's been doing fine, but I don't know how she'll be doing once she sees ya'll," the lady said, with a look of shock on her face. "You mean Ruby that runs the African Boutique Shop," I asked. With those words we all started looking confused. "You know Ruby?" Jesse asked me. "Yes, I know Ruby that runs the Boutique," I said. "Both of ya'll know Ruby?" The lady asked. "Ruby don't know ya'll are brothers, oh my God," she said in amazement. By now Jesse and I was looking at each other in a haze of surprise and confusion. "Oh my God, I think I've said too much already, but I'm sure she doesn't know this," she said as she walked away from the table to get our food.

Just then one of the cooks that we both knew, came out of the kitchen and greeted us, and I'm pretty sure the two ladies had spoke of the situation at hand. "How well do you know Ruby?" Jesse asked me. "I know every inch of her body with her clothes off," I replied. "How well do you know her?" I asked Jesse. He was silent for a moment before he answered, and giving me that look that I knew all too well. "I know her in a lot of ways, that's the woman that I told you had some money for me," he said. "I know her goodness, and I know her the way you know her too, Jesse said. We both just sat there kind of looking at each other bewildered. After all these years, and those miles of kidding together; we never mentioned not one word about Ruby to each other, maybe because we never really talked about our involvements with females with each other.

The understanding between Ruby and I had definite emotional feeling, but our relationship was boundless, without emotional ties. We enjoyed the presence of each other because the distance between us was so great. When we were together, we lived each day as though we'd never see each other again. Our thing was like a mellow wine we never got drunk. "Why you never said anything about her to me?" I asked. "It was the last thing on my mind. I never thought about it, I never had a clue that you would know her," Jesse replied. "I always thought of her as my sure "ace in the hole" Jesse said, because she's always been there for me." "Ah man this is some heavy shit, how are we gonna break the news to her?" I asked. "I wouldn't be surprise if she didn't already know," Jesse said with a big laugh. "Man, women are slick as hell don't ever play them short" Jesse said. "But let's go over and see the look on her face anyway, how about it?" Jesse said. "Fine with me," I agreed. We sat for about an hour and talked about various things but very little about Ruby. I think we both had our own private thought about that. Finally we left the restaurant and headed for Ruby's Boutique. By now I was eager to see the outcome of this situation, and we laughed about it before we got there. We both wanted to go easy on her. This whole thing seemed like a staged play, and we were the characters. "Hey Jesse, why don't we have a little fun with her, let's see how she'll handle this shit, what you say?" I asked. "Yeah, what cha got in mind?" Jesse asked. "Well you go in first, and get her involved in conversation for about then minutes, and then I'm goanna walk in like I want to buy something, and let's see what she'll do," I said. We was about to park the car when we saw Ruby getting out her car and going into the boutique. She would've seen us if only she'd looked to her left, but she didn't. Jesse got out the car and walked into the boutique as planned while I sat in the car and watched Jesse embrace her. I could tell that she was outraged with Joy from the sight of him and I won't lie and say that I didn't feel a slight bit of jealousy seeing them embrace like that, but what was I to say or do? Did he not have her first? Did I invade his domain? All kind of thoughts ran threw my mind before I finally got out of the car and walked into the boutique. Once I entered I immediately walked over to some artifacts sitting on a table, turning my body just enough so that Ruby couldn't get a good look at my face, but immediately I saw that look of total shock come over her face as she started walking towards me! "Piel," she called out as if not sure. "Yes," I said as I turned around! Ruby put her hands over her mouth, "oh Lord tell me this is not real," she said. "Piel, what are you doing here? Why are you all together?" she asked looking from Jesse to me. "Oh Lord my God," she said. "Well, are you goanna hug me?" I asked. "Piel, do you know Jimmy?" She asked out of confusion. "Jimmy do you know Piel?" she asked. "He's my brother," Jesse said, as Ruby face turned into a mask of tears. "I didn't know," she said between sobs, "Lord Knows, I didn't know."